Praise for Adam's

"*Despite the historical isolati___ ___ depth of losses illustrated in the stories, the people were held together by spiritual beliefs and practices that continue to protect the land and traditions for future generations.*"

– Phil Fontaine, three-term National Chief
  of the Assembly of First Nations

"*The stories and memories contained in this book are honest, gritty, harsh, and uncensored. They depict a reality that needs to be told. It is about the resilience of a People, who have lived through racism, poverty, hatred and blame - but in the end - continue to build with unwavering pride.*"

– Carol Rose GoldenEagle, author of Bearskin Diary

ADAM'S TREE

Stories

GLORIA MEHLMANN

radiant press

Copyright @ 2019 Gloria Mehlmann

Characters, places, events, and incidents are either the products of the author's imagination or used in a fictitious manner. The author has used names familiar to the actual setting in the specified time period, for purposes of historical authenticity only. Any resemblance to actual persons, living or dead, is purely coincidental.

All rights reserved. No part of this publication may be reproduced, stored in a retrieval system or transmitted, in any form or by any means without the prior written permission of the publisher or by licensed agreement with Access: The Canadian Copyright Licensing Agency (contact accesscopyright.ca).

Cover Art: Delma Stevenson (nee Wasacase)
Book and cover design: Tania Wolk, Third Wolf Studio
Printed and bound in Canada at Friesens, Altona, MB

The author gratefully acknowledges the support of the Saskatchewan Arts Board, the publisher acknowledges the support of Creative Saskatchewan.

Library and Archives Canada Cataloguing in Publication

Title: Adam's tree / Gloria Mehlmann.
Names: Mehlmann, Gloria, 1941- author.
Description: Short stories.
Identifiers: Canadiana (print) 20190090804 | Canadiana (ebook) 20190090863 | ISBN 9781989274057
(softcover) | ISBN 9781989274071 (PDF)
Classification: LCC PS8626.E3725 A73 2019 | DDC C813/.6—dc23

radiant press

Box 33128 Cathedral PO
Regina, SK S4T 7X2
info@radiantpress.ca
www.radiantpress.ca

"We think that Paradise and Calvary/
Christ's cross, and Adam's tree, stood in one place…"
- John Donne

To Jacqueline, Gabrielle, and Danielle,
my constant source of joy and inspiration

PART ONE:
While Looking Out

Beating Hearts

SIX-YEAR-OLD SOPHIE KNOWS her grandmother doesn't realize she is awake and peering out into the early dawn, into a blue-green sky. Kokum has carried a pail of water up from the creek, but instead of coming to the house, she enters the vegetable garden at the gate, trying not to spill. Inside the barbed wire fence, she sets the pail down by the lilac bush and takes a deep breath, hands on hips. Sophie inhales, too, sensing cool air in her lungs. Kokum's black tam, slanted across her forehead, makes her look like a man, Sophie thinks, but not a mean one like Mushom, who always glowers at her.

Kokum lifts the pail and splashes water onto mounds of fresh black soil that swallow down the cascades of sparkling water. Sophie believes she can smell the wet soil. She moves her knees higher onto the blanket, yelping at the cold touch of the iron bedstead.

Watching Kokum disappear back down the embankment, Sophie thinks of the time she went along to pick chokecherries in the bushes beside the creek. They came upon a doe standing out in the open, staring at them, its ears quivering. Kokum whispered that a fawn had to be close by. "That's why the mother won't run away." On the way home, Kokum told her that whenever a doe sees a man, she acts like she's walking toward him, but, at that moment, she is really walking away. "A doe hears with her eyes, too."

Sophie thinks about this as she imagines Kokum dipping her pail into the stream. The picture is so clear in her mind that she can look into the flowing water, where black and grey dappled stones shiver in a bed of green and brown grasses that fold and braid themselves into a heaving blanket on top of dark rotting matter. She worries that Kokum is like the doe, alone, with the sun not up. There could be a bear in the bulrushes. Mushom is like a bear, Sophie thinks. She is glad he is away; everyone laughs more then.

Kokum finally reappears through the poplars, and Sophie exhales. The birds begin their twittering. Off in the kitchen, the radio that Uncle Regis lent to Kokum and Aunt Mary for the days Mushom is gone away, is playing. The announcer's voice crackles like cellophane. The sound helps take Sophie's mind off a memory of Mushom slapping Aunt Mary when she confessed to listening to music on her own. Right now, the music means only that Aunt Mary is up.

Sophie slides under the covers and waits for breakfast. She studies the cracks in the whitewashed walls. This is the room that she shares with Kokum and Aunt Mary whenever she gets to stay the night. The scent of soap flakes in the sheets reminds her of the smell of rain. She studies the half-log rafters across the ceiling, and remembers the time Kokum told her, as they lay down for an afternoon nap, that an eagle is the biggest, most powerful bird in the world. "The wings can reach across this room," she said. Sophie had imagined the ceiling rafters swaying under the weight of a landing; huge wings darkened the room, and she had stifled a scream. Out of the silence and as though wide awake, Kokum had said, "An eagle could carry off that barking Delorme dog." Sophie had shut her eyes tight, not wanting to see a whole dog being carted high into the sky.

As Kokum snored that day, Sophie thought about how strong an eagle must be, but then she also remembered when a bluebird had broken its wing and had to hang onto the side of a train, the engine huffing and puffing across a harrowed field late at night outside town. Nothing but an eagle can stop a train, though maybe Mushom could too, Sophie thinks now. But she has scared herself lying here in the dim bottle-green light of dawn making its way into the bedroom. She hears Aunt Mary turn off Hank Williams. Aunt Mary sings a song as she stirs the porridge. Sophie knows it is an old song she learned by heart, she'll be driving six white horses when she comes. She sings to waken Sophie like it's a berry-picking morning.

Sophie wonders why the family doesn't like Aunt Mary. Sophie likes her because she is kind and she tells jokes and asks riddles. The aunts and the uncles call her a "cripple" and say mean things about her.

"She's simple-minded," the uncles say.

"If only she wouldn't act so silly," the aunts whisper.

Sophie's mother has always said that Aunt Mary can't help herself. "Her mind is slow. But it's a good mind, just the same."

Whenever people make fun of her, Aunt Mary leaves the table. She hobbles over to the black and white stove against the short wall of the kitchen. From there, she sticks her tongue out at the aunts and uncles and pulls faces behind their backs, her cheeks rosy. When she catches Sophie's eye, she wrinkles her nose and Sophie has to hold back the giggles. Sophie feels sad about Aunt Mary's disease; the arthritis has forced her upper body into a half-twist. Swollen hands, ankles, and knees hurt her all day.

At mealtimes, Aunt Mary tries to make friends. She calls Sophie's father "little brother," but he turns away most times. He shows dislike when the uncles and the aunts come in and sit at the table, elbowing one another and sharing little kicks. Seeing their stunts, Aunt Mary cannot help but laugh. Everyone glares at her, but this only makes it worse. The giggles get on their nerves because they are all afraid of Mushom, Sophie knows. When he comes to the table, his good eye lands on each bowed head, his hand ready at his belt. Aunt Mary ought to be careful, Sophie thinks.

Still, whenever Sophie's mom and dad are alone with Aunt Mary, they speak nicely to her. Sophie's mother, especially, likes to talk and laugh out loud when they are alone. Aunt Mary has a good memory for the things people say, whether from Kahkewistahaw where Sophie's mother used to live, or from Cowessess where Sophie's family members are. Aunt Mary is always pleased to answer all kinds of questions.

Sophie would love to be able to repeat the things she hears too. But if she does, her father slaps her so hard, lights flash in a dark dome in her head. Her eyes sting sometimes. Whatever she repeats spoils things. And the aunts stare at her as though she ought to go and wash up. The uncles, too, give her dark looks.

Aunt Mary pokes her head into the room. "Get up and come and eat, little hobo!"

Sophie sees that Aunt Mary loves the word she has just used. She is delighted to have startled Sophie with it. Not that she really has—but she has just now saved Sophie from the beginnings of a bad thought. Her mind had already begun its hunting for a place to hide. Sophie hops out of bed and throws her arms around Aunt Mary's waist, pressing her face into her tummy. Aunt Mary smells of lilacs and liniment.

Porridge bowls steam on the table. On the wooden washstand by the door, a faded green and red striped towel lies folded and waiting. Coming in, Kokum glances at Sophie and laughs at how fast she has rinsed and dried herself and shot into her chair, almost in a single bound. Kokum sits down beside Sophie, who inhales the fresh cucumber and cornstalk aromas clinging to her navy sweater.

Sophie needs to know. "Are we going picking today, Kokum?"

Sophie wants to pick raspberries. This time she will remember to pull gently on the berries so that they remain whole, their juice sacs glowing red in the sun.

But Kokum is in a hurry. "Not today. I'm going to town. Uncle Regis is coming to pick me up. I have to get ready."

"But you can wait for Mushom! He likes to go to town."

"He's down the valley at the Mission. I don't know when he'll be back. Maybe tomorrow if he catches a ride, or tonight even. We need things from town right away."

"But I want to pick!" Sophie hears that she sounds like Hank Williams.

Aunt Mary hands her the brown-sugar bowl and bursts into what the aunts call her "giddy" laugh: little accordion notes running up and down a ladder until she gets a hold of herself. Aunt Mary is sure to think that Sophie has forgotten that one and one makes two. It is not that Sophie has forgotten Aunt Mary's illness. Kokum is the only one who is able to take her picking. Aunt Mary can't walk with hurting ankles, and she can't pick raspberries with swollen fingers. But Kokum shakes her head, no.

Aunt Mary tries to cheer her up. "I'll show you how to embroider, Sophie," she says.

Kokum busies herself spreading marmalade on a piece of bread, for the road. She won't look at Sophie, even as Sophie stares at her. For Sophie, the day has begun to sour, like it so often does at home.

"Embroidery is too hard to do," Kokum scolds Aunt Mary. "All those long coloured threads and sharp needles. She's only six."

Sophie hears how Kokum forgets that Sophie is almost seven, and that she has seen the aunts embroider, even if each time that Sophie edges closer to watch, they quickly tuck their things out of sight so that Sophie won't be asking to touch things.

"I can so embroider!" she says.

After the dishes are done, Aunt Mary spreads out her embroidery threads and a needle case on the table. She asks Sophie to watch how to thread a needle and how to sew stitches so they lie flat end to end or side by side, depending. "Stay inside the blue trace lines," she says, pointing her finger at the cotton square.

Outside, in front of the house, sitting on the milking stool borrowed from the stable, Sophie puts her mind to work. She has flattened the square of white cloth across her lap, the better to see how an embroidered bluebird will look, a curve of ribbon in its beak and a pink rose at its feet. Beside her lie bright golden threads for the beak and black for the dots of eyes. Sophie is happy now. Last night, she had a warm bath in the round tin tub in the kitchen, and her laundered dress was hung outside to dry on the line. While she works, needle flicking gleams of sunlight at her, Sophie feels a mat of pigweeds, warm and feathery, brushing the soles of her bare feet. This morning feels like a bluebird sighting.

As she tacks down tiny blue stitches, she thinks how Aunt Mary is the only aunt who never looks is if she is wondering if Sophie's hands are clean. Aunt Mary doesn't flinch or scold when Sophie sits on her bed. Instead, she explains things. She tells secrets, too, mostly when everyone is off visiting and Mushom is away.

There was the time when coal oil for the lamp had run out and the evening light was too dim to work by. Aunt Mary and Sophie sat, elbows on the kitchen windowsill in the moonlight, trying to see with their ears. Out along the ravine and down the valley's slope, the coyotes howled. All that sad howling without words made Sophie's stomach quiver. It gave her goosebumps. Aunt Mary whispered, "Shh." There was a rustling in the woodpile. Skunks maybe, Aunt Mary whispered, or a bear. Sophie knew a bear could walk into a house, pushing through a barred door if it wanted. And Aunt Mary could not run.

Trying to help Sophie take her mind off bears, Aunt Mary spoke of the time when she was a little girl wishing to stay in boarding school, but could not.

"Why did they send you home?"

"I got arthritis. Oh-h, it burned like anything! The blanket was so heavy it hurt me all over, and I cried. The boarding school didn't like that."

"Why not?"

"They said I was being a baby. But then they saw my ankles and knees all red and swollen. They sent me home. I cried like anything because I wanted to learn to read and write. When the boys got home from boarding school, they said I was stupid."

"Did you tell on them?"

"No. It would only make trouble. Mushom was the worst anyway. He called me 'dumb-head' and hit me with his belt whenever I couldn't move fast enough."

Sophie knew Aunt Mary's heart was crying, mainly because her own father used his belt on her, too.

An owl hooted from the dark, throwing its calls close and far.

"Why weren't you allowed to have boyfriends?" Sophie asked.

"Who in the world told you that?"

"Mom said."

Sophie told Aunt Mary about the day her mother and her friend, Winnie, sat talking about husbands. Winnie had asked what the first visit to the in-laws was like. Sophie's mother said she had been nervous to the point of throwing up when she and her new family sat down to eat. No one spoke a word. They sat with heads bowed. The father-in-law, at the head of the table, stared meanly at her until she lowered her head, too.

"But *what* else did your Mom and Winnie say?" Aunt Mary asked.

"Mom said you could cut the silence with a knife!"

"I mean about me," Aunt Mary giggled.

"Well, Winnie said, 'Imagine not being able to get married and have your own home. Those people watch Mary with eagle eyes.'"

But now, Sophie is startled to hear Kokum call out, "I'm leaving for town!"

Sophie glances at her embroidery work with its outline of a bluebird. A whole wing is filled in. Kokum stands in the yard, waving. She hoists her twine bag to her shoulder and turns to leave up the path that joins the gravel road. She can hear Uncle Regis' truck groaning up the hill, off in the distance.

"Kokum, look!" Sophie is excited about the bluebird wing so very bright against the white cloth. She leaps to her feet, raising the embroidery high for Kokum to see. But suddenly something feels wrong. Her dress has lifted way up, too. Way up! Sophie has stitched the white cloth to her dress. It seems a bluebird is sewn onto her. She is so embarrassed and ashamed, she bursts into tears. Aunt Mary's accordion laughter sprinkles the air and then stops, like a radio turned off.

Kokum turns and hurries away.

Aunt Mary cuts the embroidered cloth from Sophie's dress with a razor blade. Sophie is unable to stop sobbing. Aunt Mary's warm hand smooths her forehead as she sings *three blind mice, see how they run,* and another of her favourites, *we will kill the old red rooster when he comes.*

Sophie wakens to the scent of Camay soap and green liniment. She has cried herself to sleep on Aunt Mary's lap.

"Let's have some tea with bread with jam." Aunt Mary takes her by the hand. "I have another white square, you know. You can start the embroidery over."

She leads Sophie into the kitchen. Sophie yawns at the table as Aunt Mary shuffles back and forth between the cupboard and the table, her face showing signs of pain. She finishes putting the tea things out. Sophie is uncertain whether she even likes embroidery anymore.

Suddenly, the Delorme dogs across the creek set up a tumult.

"Somebody's coming." Aunt Mary goes to the window beside the washstand to look out. She turns around, pale. "Put the things away. It's Mushom."

She reaches for her canvas apron on its hook by the stove. Her swollen fingers struggle to tie a knot in the belt at her middle. Sophie is about to open the door when Mushom barges in.

"What's she doing here?" His angry voice scares Sophie.

"They're all over at Johnny's, helping with the garden. We need Sophie to run over if anything goes wrong."

"Your mother?"

"She went to town. She'll be right back." Aunt Mary takes a pan down from the built-in shelf in the top part of the stove. "I'm supposed to start supper early."

"What do you mean, right back?" Mushom steps toward her, banging his Oxfords hard on the floor planks.

"She's been gone over an hour. She went for flour and sugar and twine." Aunt Mary is as white as a sheet.

"What's this?" Mushom walks to the corner to Aunt Mary and begins fingering her apron.

"My apron." Aunt Mary turns to take down the frying pan.

"I know the damn hell it is! What's this?" He jerks at her knot.

Sophie sees Aunt Mary's tears brimming.

Mushom's face is twisted. He whirls and shouts at Sophie, "Get out!"

Sophie runs, the door slamming shut behind her. She sits on the step, hoping that Aunt Mary will come out. The wind blows in Sophie's face. Leaves rustle nearby and frogs croak down along the creek. Inside the house, screaming starts. This is followed by thuds that sound like turnips and vegetable marrows falling to the floor.

Pots are screeching from the hooks, Sophie whispers to herself, *an eagle is all tangled up...*

She tries not to see the picture of the thick shoe that has kicked at Aunt Mary's legs, and that dark fork of a hand on her hair as the door shut. But Sophie's mind cannot hide. Her body is shaking. Her mind flicks to different places that say *come in* and to others that say *stay away*—places like the high steeple Catholic church at the Mission where her father warns her never to go, and like the Holy Roller meetings where people roll on the floor and make kids see a light.

Sophie runs down the dirt path. The highway looms. It recedes. Sophie can almost hear Uncle Regis's truck. But no, she cannot. She tries all the more and then gives up and sits in the hot dust of the road, away from the house, arms tight around her knees.

Finally, Aunt Mary stands in the doorway of the house, beckoning. "Don't say anything," she tells Sophie. Sophie looks her over cautiously. Aunt Mary is not all broken in pieces. A red welt shines on her cheek and another at the side of her neck.

"Mushom's asleep," she says. "Don't be afraid."

They sit on a wooden bench in the long shadow thrown by the house. Neither speaks. Sophie, her head against Aunt Mary's chest, hears deep, almost soundless sobbing, and a thudding heart.

Sophie thinks how her own father yanks her hair whenever she does something bad. Practically spitting in her face, he yells, "Do you want to be like Aunt Mary? End up a stupid cripple like her? Do you? Do you?" Sophie tries to say what he wants.

She presses her ear close to Aunt Mary's heart, and hears her own: *Yes*, it's saying ... *No*, it's saying...

All You Can Be

Hallowe'en. Sc. 1556. (Shortened from *All-Hallow-even*; see All-Hallow.) The eve of All Hallows' or All Saints': the last night of October. *Also Attrib.* In the old Celtic calendar, the last night of October was 'old year's night', the night of all the witches, which the Church transformed into the Eve of All Saints. (*The Shorter Oxford Dictionary*, Oxford University Press, 1973.)

HAD THERE BEEN A SINGLE DOLLAR! Anything for a scarecrow costume that looked like one! Sophie's mother stood before her, holding her father's jacket under her chin, stretching out a sleeve.

"I will not!" Sophie wailed.

The Hallowe'en costume competition was but a short two hours away. Ten-year-old Sophie had imagined herself dressed as Cleopatra, a white tunic over a purple shift and an asp of a paper-stuffed, stitched-together sweater sleeve under her arm. What she needed desperately now was a bedsheet, one as snowy white as the foam on the Nile and as real as the ship she imagined waiting in the harbour, outside the kitchen door.

Her mother's face dropped all signs of patience. "I said, we don't have a white sheet with no holes. Dad's jacket'll have to do!" She tossed it at Sophie.

Her older brother, Tony, going on thirteen, sat on the floor in the corner of the room, watching the goings on. It maddened Sophie to see his outfit, but he had only tittered at her. His grey sheet, a ghostly rag, edges frayed, was draped over his shoulder like a used dishrag. Their younger siblings ran bumping into things, excited. They weren't fussy, Sophie was pained to see. Nine-year-old Leta, a year and a bit younger than Sophie, looked okay in a flared yellow skirt, but without necklaces and bangles, she was no gypsy. The shawl around her shoulders was a ratty black kerchief that her mother gave up wearing long ago. Leta twirled in front of six-year-old Doco, who managed a twirl without falling.

Army medals borrowed from her father hung from Doco's plaid shirt. A black paper mask and a red play cowboy hat made up a confused Lone Ranger. *Pitch the cap gun!* Sophie's mind begged. A wave of shame heaved in her stomach. It was all make-do. None of it went together. And nothing was what it tried to be. People in town really took notice, especially of good clothes, and especially of poor Indians. Particularly, Sophie's mother said, after the war. Besides which, costumes were all about noticing.

Sophie told herself that it was the teacher's fault; he had accepted the invitation. Mr. Ready, the teacher at the reserve's one-room school, had agreed that the class would take part in a Hallowe'en costume competition proposed by a lady teacher in town he liked. It would be a joint event, she had said, a fun thing to be held in the church basement in Broadview.

"Nothing fancy!" Mr. Ready had assured the parents.

Cleopatra had leapt to mind then. Sophie had read about her in an encyclopedia from the shelf beside the teacher's desk. Cleopatra took baths in a marble tub and smoothed scented oils on her shoulders and neck. Sophie's nostrils had quivered with a scent of spice. She was pleased to think that Cleopatra's skin was the same colour as hers, and that her bangs were short and straight, too. What's more, Cleopatra had turned Marc Antony on his head. A certain realization had come to Sophie, Cleopatra smelled like a woman but thought like a man.

But now Sophie's costume had boiled down to a man's scratchy suit jacket hanging past her knees—her father's second-hand tweed, pungent with Sweet Caporal cigarettes, coal oil, carbolic salve, and Geordie Samuels's usual gifts of breath sweetener, Sen Sen.

"Everybody'll know its Dad's!" Sophie hoped her wailing would soften the firm line of her mother's mouth.

"Put it on!" Her father entered the kitchen and summed up the situation. "We don't have all day! Here, wear my pea cap."

Sophie, flabbergasted, saw that he was proud to lend it. She knew better than to refuse. His anger was easily touched off, like the explosives he hunted for in minefields overseas. But his awful grime-rimmed pea cap! Sophie gingerly placed it on her head.

Her mother, too, thought up improvements. "Leta, get me that blue polka-dot neckerchief from the box under the bed," she called, "and bring me the shoe polish!"

Stop! Sophie's mind yelled. Yet, there would be no stopping them. She was to be their idea of a scarecrow. Leta ran up, neckerchief in hand—the kind worn by Mr. Lytle, the farmer from Sintaluta who brought his combine to the reserve each harvest, in exchange for a threshing crew. Doco, as excited as a jumping bean, handed a can of black shoe polish to their mother. Sophie cringed as the lid was twanged off. Squinting, her head tilted, Sophie submitted to the smelly shoe polish being smeared over her face. Her mother, finally stepping back, admired her work. "Careful not to rub your eyes."

"Into the truck!" their father called, slipping his watch and chain into the fob pocket on his second-hand vest.

Sophie sat downwind in the back. Her brothers and sister had gotten the best spot under the cab's window, where they huddled and snickered together on the horse blanket. Wind shear sucked the acrid fumes from Sophie's cramped nostrils, the momentary relief so great she didn't fight for a better seat. Instead, she felt herself shrinking, knowing she looked silly. She wondered what the teacher would say to her when they filed into the town church.

Sophie felt less ready to go head-to-head with Mr. Ready, if she must. Most days at school, it was about ambush and counterattack, like cat and mouse. Lately she had begun to care less what he thought. Often when he spoke, a kind of barricade loomed up, something that stopped his brain and train of thought, like a Texas gate reversing cows as they tried to escape the pasture. He rarely made it to clear ground, where he might put his ideas into shape. Still, he knew a lot of things that Sophie didn't—which was not to say she hadn't called him on a few facts in class, more than once. So now he watched her. She watched him, too, square on, often realizing too late that she was doing it.

The truck purred down the gravel road. "Look at Sophie!" Leta laughed, pointing, "She looks like Geordie Samuels!"

"Yeah, all she needs is Sen Sen and a moustache!" Tony's words got sucked into gusts buffeting the truck. The motor coughed, paused, and backfired. Maybe the truck won't make it, Sophie thought. For once, she liked the idea of the motor's dying, right here in the gathering dusk. But the engine revved up again, an undefeated beast rolling on like an army tank, tossing leaping grasshoppers to the right and left of it.

As they sped along, she tried not to think of Geordie Samuels, Dad's pal, a constantly chuckling woodchuck who hung around the house as if he were waiting for something. Like it or not, he would be at the church tonight, cheering for her. She could only wonder why a twenty-two-year-old, so stupid and gawking, was not back in boarding school at the Mission—struggling, and still in grade two.

Sophie recalled how Mr. Ready sprang his "famous facts of

history" on the class. He had said something that Sophie had never heard before. She had no idea that *Indian* meant what he said. And so she had no answer for him. And it irked her. Buddy Delamere's father had marched, yelling, into the classroom that day, set to knock Mr. Ready's head off and give his arse one helluva kick. Mr. Delamere's spit flew past rotting teeth. "Nobody throws my son out of school! Come outside, if you're a man!" The class was silent and put pencils down. Mr. Delamere, short and mad as a bull, breath harsh and whistling, waited for the teacher to make the first move. But Mr. Ready, tall, thin, and trembling, refused to budge. Were it me, Sophie had vowed, I would throw the first punch, a swift upper cut, like Joe Louis. But the teacher just stood there. Finally Mr. Delamere stomped out, his shadow slicing the flagpole in two.

Later, it seemed to Sophie that poor Mr. Ready had likely just wanted to go home. But then he caught her looking at him. He blinked. Sounding mean, he said, "Close your books. I have something to say." Grades one to five closed their books. He then said, "Someday you might study from important books, that is if you ever learn to read them. You'll find out then what people think about Indians."

Classmates exchanged glances: *That's us, right?*

Sophie prepared her mind for cat and mouse. Tony lifted an eyebrow at her. She gave him a steely glance, meaning she was ready to take a stand, up periscope.

Mr. Ready cleared his throat. "Indians are the white man's burden," he said. "Want to know why?"

"No!" Objection flew out of Sophie's mouth.

The class burst into laughter and fell silent. Sophie gave Leta the sharpest *hold it* expression you ever saw. Leta might ask what a "burden" is. The little kids were nervous and they giggled.

"Is that right now, Sophie?" Clearly Mr. Ready was itching to dangle her over some cliff.

Her head hummed like a rubber band was tightening around it.

"What do the rest of you say?" he asked.

The silence swayed; then, held, held, and stayed. Sophie exhaled. The morning limped on. It irked her to think that she had missed her chance to speak up, but she wasn't sure she really knew what "burden" meant—all she could think of was a *load on an ox*.

The truck struck a bump, giving them a sharp jolt. Her brothers and sister hooted when Sophie's pea cap fell into her lap. She knew she looked bad, even to them.

Little Doco, face full of mischief, called to her, "Hey, Geordie, where is Sophie, your girlfriend?" He ducked his head, the wind nearly flipping off his cowboy hat. Leta had put him up to it, Sophie could tell.

The truck's wheels churned on chortling gravel, and water-filled ditches flew by like flickering mirrors scattering autumn's yellow, brown, and grey leaves. Dugouts further afield flashed chrome. Sophie wished to smell the sweet October air instead of the stink of her shoe-polished nose. Cleopatra would have smelled the sea, however that smelled.

It worried Sophie that she never seemed to get along with most adults. For instance, Mr. Ready said irksome things often, and sometimes on the sly. He didn't bother to explain. He was not really mean most days, but he slid around the truth every now and again. Thinking was what gave him trouble, Sophie decided.

Take the time he told the class about Hallowe'en apples. He said Hallowe'en was called "All Saints Night," way back when. He said witches flew around in the company of ghosts and cats, and that people gave out apples to ward off evil. But the Catholic church knew what to do, he had added, dreamily. "Even today, apples blessed by the church can turn witches into saints."

"How so?" Sophie had asked.

At that, a look of disdain crossed the teacher's face. Sophie tried to explain that she was just wondering if his story was like the ones about vampires—real vampires that could be turned away with garlic—or did he mean that the church had real power.

"How should I know?" Mr. Ready said, his mouth frozen. "I'm not an apple."

"I'm not either," Sophie retorted. "I just wanted to know."

That's when he sat up straight. He looked at her like he had the cat by the tail. Sophie sat tall, too, in case.

"But you *are* an apple, don't you know, red on the outside, white on the inside."

He threw his head back and snicker-laughed. The class exchanged glances. Nobody knew what he meant. And he did not explain. "You'll see—once you learn to read the big books. And that's a big *if*," he said.

Pulling her father's jacket tight around her shoulders, Sophie recalled asking her mother about what the teacher had said. Her reply was that Mr. Ready probably meant nothing at all. But she looked angry and banged the pot and kettle as she cooked that day.

The truck spluttered. Sophie held her breath, praying to the motor, *please, please, please choke and die!* But the truck picked up again. She wanted to haul off and kick its metal sides.

"Hey, Geordie, how come your nose is so black?" Tony called. He couldn't help himself; the jokes Leta whispered to him were so good. She whispered in his ear again, and he yelled, "And why are you wearing your father-in-law's old coat, Geordie?"

The truck pulled into town and ground to a halt. Sophie had succeeded in distracting herself on the way in. But now it was hope against hope.

Their father led them down the church's wide and shallow interior stairs to its lower level. Sophie wanted to throw off her hot, itchy jacket. The reek of shoe polish outstripped the Sweet Marie and Oh Henry chocolate bars and the candy set out on a long oak table near the piano. Mr. Ready and his lady teacher friend, Miss Paul, called out names while directing the parents and friends to benches along the walls. That left the costumed pupils milling about in the centre of the room, eying one another.

Miss Paul conferred with Mr. Ready. He nodded happily. She mounted the piano bench and began by speaking to the pupils. "There are more of you in costume tonight than we expected. So we'll do the judging by category. Gather yourselves up and go where Mr. Ready points. First the ghosts and witches, then the hobos and gypsies, then fruits and vegetables, and finally, the animals and ..."

Please, please just say it, wailed Sophie silently, her stomach in a painful knot. Her hope for an immediate announcement of a contest winner died.

"And, last but not least, scarecrows and—others!"

Mr. Ready led the applause. Halloween characters were hurried into their categories by the teachers. Two scarecrows joined Sophie, off to the side. Only, they were real ones, Sophie saw. Near her were a couple of 'others'—an Apache with a headband, like in the movies, and a pickle in green fabric, covered in bumps.

Mr. Ready's face beamed. "But wait! Before we let our competitors leave for the other room to await their turn," he said, "why don't we ask them to walk in a big circle, so we can all take a good look at them?"

This time, the bouncy Miss Paul led the applause. Her orange skirt and black batwing-sleeved sweater looked expensive, and so did her big silver hoop earrings.

The panel of judges was announced next, made up of Miss Paul, Mrs.Wilson from the audience, and Sophie's father. Sophie tried to smile, aware that her father might say she had failed his jacket and pea cap by acting sour. She wished she could just die and be carted out. But the general viewing was about to begin.

Mr. Ready gave finger signals. Everyone lined up. Sophie realized she had no chance of winning, even as a scarecrow. There were three scarecrows in all. One was a distant cousin, Ronny, from an estranged side of the family that had outdone itself this evening. Ronny's overalls and tall hat, hand sewn, had been cut from a piece of lovely pale blue felt, showy against his crisp, red checked shirt. Matching red patches decorated the felt hat and pants. Sophie saw how his getup exposed her family's poverty. Ronny was brandishing a shiny, new, lime green broom, its bristles turned up, the broom adding zing. Sophie's family had no such broom. Her face burned with shame.

Once in a large circle, the competitors began marching in time to Mr. Ready's count. The dreaded Geordie Samuels, spying Sophie as she went by, shouted "Hurray!" at her. In the midst of clapping parents and grandparents calling out encouragements, Mr. Ready made a circling motion in the air, signalling the end. Sophie, behind Ronny, headed to the waiting room. He turned to view her and Sophie saw that his face had been painted white! This made her black face stand out, she knew. And Ronnie's paint didn't smell. Hers stank. He flashed a big, confident, yellow smile at her.

Then it became even worse. Mr. Ready called, "Scarecrows, fall out! The rest of you, stand until I call!"

Mr. Ready, in a white shirt, black pants, and a lady's large floppy hat, made his way over to the scarecrows. Sophie's heartbeat surged in her ears.

"Okay, go stand in front of the judges' table," he said. Then, acting surprised and absolutely amazed, he turned to Sophie with a cheeky grin. "Well, now, who have we got here?"

"Cleopatra," she said.

"Quit trying to be funny, Sophie," he said. "Get in the spirit, for god's sake."

I am Cleopatra. And in the spirit, she told herself. The only difference was an absence of lotus blossoms.

Her father and Miss Paul, acting as judges supporting the primary judge, Mrs. Wilson, conferred on the other side of the table. Sophie distracted herself with facts: Cleopatra spoke seven languages, she rolled out of a carpet at the feet of Marc Antony, Emperor of Rome, and took him by the ear …

"Line up!"

Nothing could save her. All eyes turned. She believed she might stand a chance against her all-too-fancy scarecrow cousin and the second boy, who was fattened with newspaper stuffed into an ordinary plaid shirt and, obviously, his dad's overalls. The judges marked columns on long sheets of yellow paper. The room went silent.

Mrs. Wilson, in large spectacles and a tweed suit, stated her wish to be completely fair. "Just a moment here," she said looking straight at Sophie. "Isn't there a mix-up in this category? Yes, you. You in the pea cap! Shouldn't you be in 'Other'?"

Sophie was horrified. Did the judge mean with the Apache? Or did the judge think Sophie was a Negro and she should stand alone?

At this point Mr. Ready decided that a joke might be a good idea. "We could put her in with the apple!" he said. There was laughter from some of the parents. It crossed Sophie's mind but she did not say, that Mr. Ready was already more than half-stuck on a Texas gate.

Her father's voice was firm. "There is no error."

Mrs. Wilson said, "I was thinking, maybe, hobo..." She took a good look and flushed a deep red.

Sophie wanted done with it all. But there was no way out and no shield at hand. She trained her mind on Egypt.

Ronnie won first prize in his category, and he was a finalist in the overall Top Rung category. Second place went to Marjorie Lytle, a red and round velveteen apple with a knitted green stem toque. Third went to a gypsy in a black beaded vest, with silver hoop earrings, worn by "a boy of all things!" Doco received honorable mention, along with a three-year-old, green-faced little witch touting a truly sharply moulded nose of painted dough.

In the vestibule as her family got sorted out, Sophie's mother asked her father, "You don't suppose Mr. Ready meant anything when he made that apple remark, do you?"

"No, he just falls in line with what he believes is smart and funny at the time."

"To think they said the contest was just for fun! People really went overboard!"

"Well, the kids had fun." Their father turned to Sophie and her siblings like a general. "Didn't you?"

"I did!" Leta said, happy and content. "I liked the candy!"

"Me too!" Doco said. "And I won!"

"You sure did!" The general laughed as they descended the church steps outside. He turned to Tony.

"I had fun," Tony said, nodding cheerfully. "None of us ghosts won, though."

"Sophie?"

Sophie could think only that Mrs. Wilson had mistaken her father's jacket for a hobo's.

"Yes," is what she said, and when she said it, she knew she could think like a man, anytime—if she really wanted.

Loving in Code

WHEN THE MEN CAME HOME from the war, Sophie's mother and lady friends talked about them. Whenever the women visited together now, a man was the topic. The men should have stayed overseas, it seemed. They got underfoot like children. And the women had to bring them up, which is one way of seeing when you are ten and listening to what is being said.

At first the women said that the men did hard battle. But, comparing notes, they also said that many a morning now a husband might be seen picking at a toenail, distractedly, which could be a signal he was giving up.

He would have tried all kinds of things to find work. He would have chased all sources of income. But there were huge obstacles, was said. Sell gravel to road gangs near the reserve? No, said the Indian agent. This was against policy. Sell wood and pickets to people in town? No, said the Elders. The trees had already been picked over for the war effort. A survey of trees showed that dwindling numbers of birch and poplar stood as fragile saplings thinly strewn in patches across the reserve. As for deer and pickerel, Ottawa denied hunting and fishing for profit, although pelts were another matter. In the end, proposals sent to Indian Affairs, through the Indian agent's office on the reserve, became the occupation of young soldiers back from the war.

"Whichever way they turn!" the women said.

And so nothing came of nothing all the more. Ten-year-old Sophie concluded that the only thing left was love, as she listened to the stories about men in love.

Especially when Sophie's mother, Sarah, and her friend, Claudine Lazaire from the valley, took walks together, as they did some evenings, with Sophie tagging along. The two women walked in the wagon ruts that led up to a gravel road connecting Cowessess Reserve to the town of Broadview in the south, and to the Mission in the valley due north. Through a break in the bushes ahead, Sophie had caught sight of the setting sun. Wide, bell-shaped clouds on the horizon had burst into molten red, throwing orange bands of light high into bright licks of royal purple trimmed in gold. But Claudine was talking about her husband, Mattie, home almost five years now.

"He's sad all the time," Claudine said.

Sophie stole glances at her. She was a tall, thin woman with long brown hair pinned up, face gaunt and haunted in the evening light, and as wan as the faded yellow summer dress she usually wore. Sophie knew to be quiet and not call out, even if the crickets were singing loudest at this spot. And even if a night owl had just banked and landed within sight, its wings swooping over the sombre land, which, to Sophie, seemed tilted at them. Unable to read or write, there being no school on the reserve, Sophie didn't know the words to say, although words leapt like fireflies above the darkened weeds.

Claudine said, "He's afraid he'll commit suicide."

Sophie's head whirled to see what it was that came with that word, what hinted at its meaning. Her mother's sharp inhalation revealed shock, if not fear. Sophie felt a cold draft stroke her bare legs, and so she pressed closer to her mother. She grabbed her hand, asking her in undertones, "Mom, what's suicide?"

"Be quiet," her mother said, "you're too young."

I am not, Sophie wished to say, but her mother had turned to Claudine. "How bad is it?"

"He's mentioned the train tracks, his wrists, a rope; he's thought of everything, knives, hammer ... even an axe."

"An axe! That's terrible! Every day?"

"It goes away, now and again. But his nightmares aren't letting up."

"Have you tried taking him to Old Solomon?"

Claudine's voice broke. "Mattie won't go. He's ashamed, he says."

Sophie sensed how the air had grown sharp with feelings, like the aroma of earthy plants, hints that she might be able to pull together all at once. Suicide was sad, she believed, with maybe the feeling of going away on a trip alone, to a place where there would be cuts on account of an axe, or a rope, somehow, with shame and lonesomeness stuck in. She guessed suicide might be about love, a word she was working on, and so she opened her ears to that possibility.

Things being said about Mattie gave more words to think about. A glossary-in-the-making glowed in the back of Sophie's mind, setting off sparks in front of her brain. Suicide was a live coal that could burst into flame, maybe very soon.

Mattie, it was said, had snubbed people after the war. Instead of returning to the reserve, where he belonged, he had gone to live in the valley among the Métis who fished the lake near Marieval. The Mission school down there had long turned Mattie into a Catholic, but a Catholic boy who did not speak English, like French nuns. This failing got him into fist fights with Protestant boys who wished to be distinct, and who said this and that, not dis and dat like Catholics. Still, Mattie went his own way.

Sophie, all ears, hung around her mother whenever Mattie arrived at the house for the softball games played by her father and other ex-soldiers in the evenings that summer. It was said Mattie pitched a true ball, but expressed no excitement, win or lose. Claudine, having no family besides her husband, accompanied him. A sign of love, Sophie told herself.

Her walks with the women gave Sophie real things to think about—one being that men had secrets. Soldiers, having gone across the sea, had walked or driven army trucks straight into strange towns packed with girls who called them by their name, and some of whom even sent letters. The English, French, and Dutch girls had to be about love, Sophie learned. The wives had agreed on it, and then began to keep secrets from the men. Sophie could tell that the women had also begun keeping secrets from each other, lips pursed.

In fact, Sophie blamed what happened on war words. The soldiers had brought them to the reserve, and Sophie overheard her mother and friends trying them out. For instance, the men had let slip that Belle, in town, was a slut whom they had nicknamed Poutace. The women said it was evidence enough that, whenever Belle passed by their husbands leaning against the white wooden fence outside Wylie's Grocery Store in town Saturdays, they'd call Poutace out to her. But now, no matter how often Sophie's mother asked her father, he would only say, "It's European." That is, until that day his army buddies dropped by to pass a bottle of red wine around. Her father had asked, "Seen Poutace lately?" Even Sophie saw how the men laughed like boys, throwing their heads back. The laughter had grown so loud that Sophie's mother scolded the ex-soldiers for being disrespectful and for behaving no better than town drunks who talked dirty when moms and daughters hurried past the pool hall.

"I'm forced to ask your pals what Poutace means, once and for all!" Sophie's mother said, and she meant it.

Startled, her father had said, "It's French for 'whore.'"

Whore—this had to be a war word, Sophie knew. It had to be, because her father's face turned very red when her mother said to him,

"It takes two."

In Sophie's mind, it meant that there must be two kinds of Poutaces: one funny, because the men laughed; and one dirty, because the women said so. But Sophie knew better than to ask. For now, she would mind this word and the ideas and any feelings that went with it.

A secret the women kept was that the men had got the French word Poutace wrong; the real word was putain, apparently. Winnie, who lived across the creek, had run over with this fact. And Winnie was to be believed since the love of her life, a fair, blue-eyed man by the name of Julien, knew French. The women agreed it was just as well the men hadn't learned to say putain correctly, because now the wives could laugh behind their backs every time the husbands turned into silly boys who spoke no French, boys who could be accused of pronouncing both French and English Métis style. These confidences alone, Sophie noticed, made for smiles that led to merriment among wives in the company of husbands.

Sophie figured slut was a wicked word, mostly because the women used it when they got fed up. At first they had acted as if the word was but a painful tooth that, if probed with the tip of the tongue, hurt only until you pulled back. So any one of the women might work herself up just to be able to say, "That Aggie, from down the mission, could be a slut, you know." Another might rush in to help the speaker take a step back from overspill, saying, "That's right! Mind you, you can never tell." Or still another might say, "If that Cookie in Regina isn't careful, people will end up calling her a slut. And for no reason!" That last statement made the women shift in their chairs, eyeing one another.

One time they got themselves worked up over the lack of towels in their homes, not to mention the lack of soaps and bright floral sheets mixed with sharp, colourful stripes seen flapping on clotheslines in town. The result was that Sophie's mother burst out, "That Cookie in Regina is a slut and a whore!"

Winnie, from across the creek, leapt to her feet and grabbed up her headscarf. She rushed out the door, calling back over her shoulder, "You can say that again!"

On that particular day, after the women left, Sophie's mother's face flickered with worry as she cleaned house. Sophie thought it might be because her father had reported that Cookie planned to pay a visit, and very soon.

The news excited Sophie. A visiting city woman might just happen to mention the war and then accidentally bring up *whore* and *slut*— she might even tell more about three other words, counting *putain*. Sophie had seen Cookie with her husband Norman, once, when they were visiting her parents in the big room. The soft colours of her rich clothes and the scent of her perfume made Sophie's chest feel warm. She wished to see Cookie up close again, especially knowing that her mother and women friends spoke badly of her. And something strange had been said about Norman, too, about his trouble on a city crew. Norman must have done something truly awful, the women said, because his wife's family had up and said Norman was "all the worse for calling himself a human being." No wonder Cookie was staying on Cowessess with relatives this week, Sophie thought.

It was such fabulous news that it kept Winnie dashing back and forth across the creek, red hair flying, shoes in one hand, wet leaves clinging to her bare feet as she stood at the door. This time she offered to help play hostess and Sophie's mother had answered, "As if you had to ask."

Sophie sensed the excitement. However, an awkward moment fell right after Winnie's off-hand remark that Cookie was house-proud. Sophie thought that her mother now saw her own house as being poor and shabby, if not dusty and dirty, by comparison.

The next day word came that Cookie was to arrive early that afternoon. Winnie hurried over after breakfast to help smarten things up, as promised. Sophie's mother laid a keen eye on her friend now standing in the kitchen, brimming with liveliness. She informed

Winnie that Old Solomon was expected to stop by later that afternoon, to pick up a salt-lick he had asked Len, Sophie's father, to bring back from town. That had meant getting up at dawn to bake an extra two bannocks. And there was a stack of dishes to do yet. "It's either that or rake the yard, I guess."

Winnie chose dishes, saying Sophie might like to rake the yard, or beat her first in a wrestling match. Sophie, glad to escape her mother's nerves, went out into the bright sunshine and sweet summer air to pull up a patch of pigweeds in front of the house. She set to work carrying piles of these to the back, along with the raked-up twigs, dead grasses, and bits of rubbish. This done, she tried to think what looked better: wavy lines raked over the grey powdery soil from the wooden step to the edge of the grass surround, or left plain.

As she worked, she thought about words. She wished grown-ups would tell her about them. Instead, the meanings she tried to pin to words often got pulled every which way, usually by people's feelings, like two whirlwinds meeting and wrestling in the yard. She extended the rake, intent on making straight lines from the edge of the grass to the steps. The tear-streaked voice of Hank Williams singing "Your Cheatin' Heart" was pouring out the open kitchen window; it was a radio song her mother always joined in, usually at the words But sleep won't come, the whole night through. It was about love, Sophie guessed.

Her heart skipped a beat. A team of horses had entered the yard at the gate. Could it be? Two people sitting in a wagon—none other than Cookie and her father, Old Leo. A bay and roan, bridles jingling, had come to a halt on the grassy part of the yard. Horse sweat and hot harness smells tickled Sophie's nose. She knew she ought to run inside and warn her mother, but she could only stand and stare. Cookie gave instructions to the old man: "Come back when the sun is here." She lifted his arm at an angle that read 'later in the afternoon,' and then she climbed down. Old Leo, half-blind and slouching, clucked to his team. The front wheel of the wagon screeched a high grating note, in too tight a turn.

Cookie, outlined in bright sunlight, smoothed down a pale blue dress and walked to the house, her shiny black heels sinking into the ground with each step. Pink cheeks and violet lips lit her face. She passed right by Sophie, giving her but a single fleeting glance. Sniffing the air, Sophie felt disappointment in the absence of perfume. When Cookie and Norman visited her parents last fall, Cookie had worn a scent that smelled like a blend of boiled plums and faint skunk.

Now here she was again, folding a soft green sweater over a chubby arm. Coming to her senses, Sophie spun on her heel and ran inside. The kettle boiled brightly on the stove, its lid chattering. Festoons of steam danced and evaporated in the small kitchen where Sophie's mother stood, slicing an oval bannock in squares. Cookie had already climbed the step and now tapped lightly on the door frame. Sophie's mother, off guard, seemed to be trying to adjust her mind. "Oh, it's you, Cookie … come in and sit down … for goodness sake!"

The two held elbows briefly, entered the adjoining big room, and sat down at the table pushed under the windowsill. Sophie's mother glanced out the small window and up the road as she reached to turn off a radio commercial about colour-fast Burlington tablecloths.

"Of all things," she announced, "here comes Winnie! I'll just have to get us another cup, I guess."

Sophie took the opportunity to slip out of sight behind the door of the porch to wait. Soon a flash of red hair rushed past the lilac bush at the side of the house. Winnie paused at the kitchen door, fiddled with her red scarf, and then stepped into the big room. Now there were three at the table.

Sophie noticed that Winnie had taken extra care with her appearance. She had tied a red silk scarf in a bow at her neck—a gift from her husband, she loved to say. But her black Oxfords, though clean, had no shine left. Determined to hear Cookie's story, Sophie dove under the kitchen table and tucked herself in behind the water barrel, beside two large stoneware jars of speckled grey where the sugar and flour were kept. She wedged herself into the tight space to watch the women's faces.

Right off the bat, Winnie opened the conversation. "How's Norman?"

Cookie gave Winnie one devil of a nose-twisted stare. She said, "You'll have to ask him. How is it that you of all people find yourself behind in the news? Norman and I are parted!"

Winnie and Sophie's mother tried to make as if they were hearing this for the first time, each putting forward the best of their cover-ups: "How could it happen? In Regina yet! What is the world coming to? What did you and your good husband ever do to deserve that?"

Cookie studied her fingernails. She raised her cup and stared at the women in turn, dark eyes smouldering. Then she sighed.

So now, there were four, Sophie knew—Norman, invisible.

"He was so kind," Cookie began. "Forever lending a hand around the apartment. Took me shopping—Simpsons, Eaton's, Woolworth's— all the big stores. He even helped me pick out dresses. And he was good at it, polite, patient, a real gentleman."

Sophie's mother praised his thick glossy hair, his trim moustache, and his cleanly filed fingernails. Winnie recalled Norman's sharply creased trousers and that straw hat worn at an angle, his best look, she could say in all truthfulness. Sophie made a note of this, since in her recollection, Cookie outshone Norman's finer points of dress, save the hat.

"Always so tidy, eh, Winnie?" Sophie's mother tried to build a bridge between Cookie and Winnie.

But Cookie's face darkened. "If you but knew!"

"Like what?" Winnie thought to be quick. "That he was a runabout?"

"A runabout! How do you mean?"

"Well, other women. You know how some are."

31

"I only wish." Cookie took a bannock square from the blue floral plate being handed round and edged it onto her saucer. "What I mean is—a woman can always put another in her place." Cookie traced the faded blue rose design on her cup with a finger. "You know, tell her to find her own man, if she is able."

"Didn't he care for you?" Sophie's mother was direct.

"He said he did. But there were just so many things."

"Oh dear, he's a drunkard, then!" Her mother's outburst told Sophie that this was the worst a man could be.

"No! No! No!" Cookie stared at the two women as though they were the stupidest things in the world. The pair blinked. But Sophie knew, or thought she did. Her mind shouted, I know! Norman could be a slut and a whore! She wished to yell it out, but then her mother would roust her from her hiding place, where she needed to stay and learn.

"Norman never takes more than a swallow, no matter whose circle he's in! He's no drunkard." Cookie lost herself in thought for a moment. "The worst is the loneliness. He can be right there beside me in bed. It's the loneliness. I can't take it anymore."

Sophie's ears stood straight up: loneliness? Suicide, maybe!

But the three women only drew deep breaths, murmuring my, my.

"Does he have some kind of sickness, then?" Sophie's mother shifted in her chair. "You know what I mean—like, is there something wrong, down below?"

Cookie laughed. It was a town laugh, a loud, overbearing sound with meanness hidden in it. "He doesn't have the dose, if that's what you're getting at!"

Dose? The word hung in the front of Sophie's mind.

"No," Her mother said, "I mean him … his manhood."

At that, Cookie lost control. A laughing fit caught her, flinging a cry sound and choked gulps into the air. Sophie's mother stood up to pour tea for Cookie, but the cup was still full. The women waited for her to calm down. Hands trembling, Cookie smoothed her lap. She studied the tiny navy dots on her pale blue dress. She pulled her lettuce-toned sweater tight round her shoulders. Next she began breaking her bannock into little pieces, making a small pile of crumbs on the table beside her cup. She stared out the window. The hostesses cleared their throats, but respected the silence.

"Oh, all right, if you must know!" Cookie scolded, eyes sparking flame like embers suddenly stirred. "Norman is a *pünk!*"

Sophie saw her mother and Winnie flinch in their skins. Shock filled the room. But, for Sophie, what had just been said added nothing to the meaning of suicide, or to the word dose. And now, here was something else, *pünk*.

Winnie said, "And here I was, thinking maybe he lost his job!"

"Who's he *pünking* with?" Sophie's mother asked.

"Oh, you know, at work." Cookie studied a thumbnail.

"Good gracious! From his city crew?" Sophie's mother looked stunned.

"Yes, an associate. That's what Norman called him, anyway—an associate. Oh, for God's sake! It was *after* work ..."

Winnie appeared to be testing out her own mind about how to make what she just heard sit right. Sophie's mother's face also betrayed confusion and awkwardness. "*Wah-hi!*" was all the two could say.

"What will you do?" Sophie's mother's face had cleared.

Cookie pulled out a lace hankie and blew her nose. "I came here to talk about something. Norman has sent word that he misses me, that he wants me home."

There it was—love—again, mixed in with something, Sophie thought.

Misery played on Cookie's face and trembling lilac lips. "I just don't know."

"Ask yourself," Sophie's mother said. "What can you really expect of *you*, of yourself, in such a case?"

"Of me? I said it was about Norman I want to talk."

Winnie gently touched Cookie's arm at the remark. Still, she turned and asked, "How did you find out? Surely he didn't up and tell you himself!"

But Cookie ignored her. "We had it out. I told him I wanted children. He pushed that aside. Then he sidetracks me with talk about trips and clothes, and someday owning a big house with a fireplace and rugs. I blew up. I told him I knew in my heart he wasn't being honest. I deserve the truth, I said. So, he told me it. And I walked out. I never heard of such a thing as that!" She sobbed.

Squirming in her tiny space, Sophie wondered what it could all mean. Feelings were being tossed up again: "terrible" and "just so wrong." But nothing shone in her mind as being helpful.

"I know what I'd be going back to," Cookie said. Her face was pinched and mottled with the sour light bouncing off the oilcloth. "His kindness is just a game. Our going out even for a coffee was his hunting trip. Go for a drive? Why, show-off time! A stroll around the apartment? *See my new clothes*—and me, his wife, proof of what? Nothing! The worst is he goes around pretending to adore women!"

The hostesses murmured, "*Ee-a-how!*"

Sophie studied her mother's face. It seemed she might be trying to recall if Norman had ever looked at her in a sneaky way.

"He only pretends?" Winnie looked annoyed.

Cookie said, "Mind you, I never cared when Norman would finally get a woman's attention, say, across a room, and flirt with her. When she flirted back, I took it to mean that my man wasn't at the bottom of the barrel, like her man must be. But then, for Norman, it was a cover-up for something worse—his flirting with women at store counters, at gatherings, waitresses, even in our home. Norman even bragged about conquests. But it turns out he's *pünk*!"

A long silence followed, and Sophie carefully stretched her aching legs out into the still shaded part under the table.

Cookie's tears welled up. She choked out, "Same as when we're in bed. He'll pick an argument and then blame me."

"That's a dirty thing to do!" Sophie's mother was the angry one now.

"When he finally told you the truth, how did he put it?" Winnie asked. She tucked her feet under her chair, felt for her red bow, and leaned forward on her elbows.

More tea was poured, although Cookie still hadn't yet drunk hers. "He said he fell in love. His feelings were just so strong, he said, that he had to give in finally."

"Who with, exactly?" Winnie asked.

Little Sophie held her breath. But Cookie burst into sobs again. "An associate, I told you! Someone he saw every day, at work—a married man!"

Winnie slammed her cup down. The three women sat as still as mice. Sophie wished her mother would turn the radio back on. The whiny crybaby voice of Hank Williams would be better than this long, drawn-out silence. Cookie lifted her cup to her lips and took a tiny sip. She managed a weak smile.

While Cookie's tea was being warmed with a touch of more hot tea, Sophie summed up what she had learned: *pünk* meant a married man in love; what's more, there could be a *double-pünk*, counting Norman. And not to forget, *dose* might fit.

But now Cookie was saying, "It's odd to think how he dared to ask, dared to ask me to go with him, as usual on weekends, to the park. But, once there, he'd leave me sitting alone on our blanket out by the band shell. Had I known! Imagine, grown men in park bushes! On Sunday afternoons, yet! Or in the middle of the night—I'll bet you anything!" Cookie threw her hands to her face and then clenched them again. "The night before I left to come and stay here with my parents, I jumped out of bed and drove the car to the edge of the park. I screamed from the car into the dark, 'I know what you're up to!' Then I roared

35

out of there. Finally I pulled over under some trees on College Avenue and cried my guts out."

Cookie's voice made Sophie think of wagon wheels scraping on their axle. Her head ached as she tried to separate meaning from this awful mix-up of feelings. For instance, what was the harm in Norman looking for friends in the park? At least he wasn't lonesome, like Mattie. But then, again, it could be that *pünk* was a war word, and as hard to learn as *suicide*. This much she pieced together: *pünk* meant when, like Norman, you have a wife but love a man, slyly. What made it really bad was when your wife had to pretend about her love, too. Sophie was sorry Norman was a *pünk*, but she felt sorrier for Cookie. All in all, Sophie sensed she was missing a part of the puzzle, and it likely had something to do with *dose*.

Someone was at the door. Sophie's mother hurried into the kitchen so quickly that Sophie had no time to hide her feet. The sunlight had edged round, shrinking the table's shade protecting her. But it was too late to move now. Were her mother to glance down as she hurried past, she would have looked right into Sophie's face.

Sophie turned her head with greatest care. Old Solomon entered. He smiled brightly at her mother, cap to his chest. "Good day to you, my niece. Is the boss home from town with my salt? I brought a chicken for youse, a good layer. I hope youse don't mind, but I let him loose beside your coop."

"Come on in, Solomon. Len should be back any time now with your salt. Of course, I don't mind! Thank you." Sophie's mother looked relieved to see Old Solomon. She told him that he needed to eat and drink something; the trip up the hill, on horseback from the valley and in the hot sun, was too hard on an Elder. She led him into the big room, reaching for a cup in the cupboard near Sophie. Bending her head slightly, Sophie hoped to see the expression on the women's faces, but Old Solomon's backside blocked the view. She pulled her legs in, away from the sunlight flooding her feet.

The women drew Old Solomon into the circle. Sophie listened to her mother tell Cookie's story from the beginning, practically word for word. Cookie sat tearful throughout. Winnie, for once, held her tongue. Sophie listened for what she might have missed the first time around.

Old Solomon, sipping his tea, finally spoke. And the women leaned in.

"That's how it is nowadays." Solomon began. "We love in code now. All of us live that way. We have no choice. Our language pulls at our hearts still, but the words won't come. Code is everywhere. Still, we have to stick to truth and live it, no matter what. What else can we leave our young?"

Sophie, finder of words and meaning, felt like dancing. The Elder had used the word code, as though it meant something like SOS. That was what she wanted. It was the help she needed to figure out what is hidden all along, but is really there.

"How can I live the truth if my man is a liar?" Cookie's voice sounded like a child's.

"Norman was a liar," Old Solomon corrected. The women exchanged glances. "But he moved up to the truth when he told on himself. He told that he loves a city man, a married one at that. That's being truthful." Old Solomon crossed his hands over his belly as he looked up at the ceiling. "Norman has it tough. Think hard. That city man has told lies, too. And a lot of his kin have no respect for different-ness in people. Some take it out on them. Another thing, though, in this case, there are children involved. If that city associate has kids, he has to get a clear head about it. He has to face a hard decision, and truthfully—and accept that he needs to look after his children. He's a father and that comes first. Next, Norman is married, and that is where it has to stop."

Cookie fidgeted as Old Solomon measured out meaning, ignoring her side of things.

"Norman is a truth-filled man, now, a man with a clean spirit, struggling to find his way." He looked at the women, who exchanged nervous glances. But Old Solomon had not forgotten Cookie. "A few years back," he said, "there was this one pünk."

Old Solomon was beginning a story, a story that came with a lesson people might not want to hear. "There was this is one pünk who was truly lost," he began. "He went around raping men. He hated truth, that one. He took it out on his wife and kids. We all lived in fear of him because he was big and mean. At reserve meetings, or anywhere men gathered, it made our skin crawl to see his heartless eye catch on one of us, mark one of us, right then and there. That monster knew we all saw him, but he had no respect. The men were too scared to get word out to the RCMP, to call in the law. They feared being raped out of revenge later. They were also afraid no one would listen. That pünk, him, he kept a mistress, for the look of it, I guess. He put shame on others. Nothing can be as bad as that, when you think about it."

Sophie's mother asked, after a pause, "You mean there's nothing wrong with Norman? Still, you have to think that playing husband is dirty." She looked at Cookie, whose mouth was a hard line.

"You're right," Old Solomon said. "A man drawn to another man— this happens. It starts in the womb, the old people say, and mostly when a woman conceives and carries her unborn during a war. Why that is, no one can say. A man born in such times is not to blame. Ask your Elders. Long ago such a man was given his own tent in the community. He could concern himself with beautification, with sewing, or hunting, if he wished—everything. Nobody minded. People liked them. Men like that have double sight. They see and sense things far ahead. These ones never bother anybody. They're gentle, the way a good man always is."

Sophie was sure the adults had overlooked an important fact. She wished to call it out, "Men don't rape men. They rape women!" But she would have to find a way to ask about the Elder's mistake. She guessed that the next time she saw Norman again, she'd call him putain, for Cookie, because he had pretended to her and lied to her, and made her life bad.

"That city man has to leave Norman alone," Winnie said.

"Sometimes there's no choice," Old Solomon sighed.

Sophie liked the sweet ways of Old Solomon. His friendly eyes and clear forehead topped by white hair made him look like a wise old horse. When he smiled, deep furrows leapt in his cheeks; the grey-blue of his eyes twinkled like a glimpse of blue water. To sit near him was to feel the comfort of a large sun-warmed stone. And here he sat, right in the middle of the women's secrets.

"What should I do?" Cookie asked.

Solomon looked at Cookie. "Norman has asked you to come back. You might choose to abandon him, as a wife—and even as a friend. You need to talk, so the both of you can untangle that part. He loves a man he can't have; but he loves."

"What about me?" Cookie asked, her mouth looking numb.

"It depends on what you and Norman can make right. You might remain good friends and help each other out in life. You might live together, and live whatever each of you is about. That's a hard life, but it's how the Creator made each of you: to become truthful and loving."

"Hello!" It was Sophie's father calling in from the porch. Sophie swung her head around to see her father turn to speak to someone behind him. "Come in. Yes, come in."

Old Solomon called out an endearment to her father from the big room. "Hello, Nishtaw!"

Sophie wished to see who else was there. All she could make out was a man's shiny shoe and a sharp crease on a grey pant leg. Then, she spotted him as he stepped forward—straw hat at an angle, a puckish smile—Norman!

"Cookie!" Sophie's father had stopped in his tracks at the doorway to the big room. He scratched his head. Then he looked back over his shoulder at Norman, whose face had gone white.

Sophie's mother jumped to her feet. "You people are all staying for supper. It's a long ride home. If we eat by five, all of you will make it home before dark."

Old Solomon rose to shake Norman's hand. Little Sophie, trying to watch the drama, heard a team approaching out in the yard. It had to be Old Leo, Cookie's dad. And that meant Cookie's visit was coming to an end. Sophie wished it weren't so. Everyone said they had better get going, too, now, despite the chance to eat Sarah's fine cooking. Sophie, seeing her chance, crawled out from under the table and stood beside the barrel, tin cup in hand. She was thirsty, it was true. But no one would ask. Sophie wanted to examine the faces, to look for any expression that showed how adults behaved who loved in code, and knew it.

Sophie could see that Winnie was in a hurry, likely wanting to get home and tell Julien. But, as one of the hostesses, she could leave only after the others left.

Cookie looked like a bird fallen from its nest. Norman caught her eye. She stared back at him, her mouth a tiny lilac bow. And something had gotten into Norman's eyes; he rubbed at them with thumb and forefinger, smiling weakly at Cookie. "I didn't know you'd be here," he said to her.

Cookie nodded. Old Solomon was silent for a moment longer. He looked the adults over as though they were his children and that he liked every one of them. Then he spoke. It seemed to Sophie that he might be speaking about the code part. "A difficult thing is to find someone who loves you in spite of who you think you are."

He turned to leave. Sophie grew desperate. How was she to learn what words meant when people stopped talking right in the middle of everything! She could not ask her mother. Her mother would turn around and ask where Sophie had picked up the words in the first place. Old Solomon winked at Sophie like he knew she'd been sneakily listening. Her face burned.

"Can I catch a ride with you, Cookie?" Norman's smooth voice was full of gravel now.

"I suppose so ..."

Sophie ran outside to await the departure. Her father lifted the salt lick from his saddlebag and put it inside Old Solomon's gunny sack that hung from his saddle. Her mother came hurrying outside with bannock wrapped in a dishtowel and a sealer of warm tea for Old Leo. Everyone set off together, waving, until the wagon got turned around and away.

"Sophie, go to Kokum's for a while. Or go play at the stream." Sophie knew her mother wanted to tell her father everything alone.

"Come, Sophie, I'll walk with you," Winnie said. "We're going the same way."

Winnie was quiet as they walked down the thistle-lined path bordered by busy insects. It might be that Winnie was already wondering how she could make the visit seem even more exciting to Julien. Sophie liked Winnie's style of telling a story. In it, Cookie would have slapped Norman until he said, 'I'm not a pünk!' Old Leo, being half-blind, and getting it all wrong, would have leapt off the wagon and mistakenly pounded out Old Solomon. Sophie's father would have raced behind the runaway team and wagon, its wheels carving circles over the yard. Of course, Winnie would have been the one to dust the Elders off and calm everyone down—right after Old Solomon's horse kicked the salt lick that fell and killed the chicken ...

Sophie formed a question in her mind to ask Winnie before she turned off at the fork in the road. She needed help in getting at the meaning of two words, so Sophie decided on asking the question: Would you rather have a dose or a suicide?

But then, up the road, it was Claudine in her yellow dress stumbling toward them. She was scream-crying and falling to the left of her, then to the right of her, as her shrieking grew louder and louder. When Winnie and Sophie reached her, Claudine was pulling at her tumbled hair.

Hunger Pangs

IT WASN'T EXACTLY A FIGHT about food, ten-year-old Sophie told herself as she worried at home in bed that night. But it was no ordinary, short-lived squabble with the teacher either. Mr. Ready was on a mission. Another one.

That morning Sophie had tried to persuade Mr. Ready that her parents had more than enough money to buy the foods displayed on the classroom wall poster, Canada's Food Rules. Her claim was believable, she supposed, since her father, an ex-soldier, had been home from World War II five whole years now.

But things simmered to a boil when the nurse from town, Miss Hilda Ogilvy, paid the teacher a class visit. Mr. Ready sat at his desk, complaining to her that his pupils weren't getting enough sleep or something—they slouched in their seats and drowsed over their exercise books, the stuffing knocked out of them.

"It's the poor eating habits on reserves," the nurse explained, her orange-coloured curls framing a lined face that appeared, at least to Sophie, powdered with flour or chalk dust. Her sagging green sweater hid most of a white uniform. Sophie watched the nurse pull her chair up to the teacher's.

Mr. Ready ran pale fingers through his wavy blond hair. "I keep telling them to sit up. How can they think? Potato sacks—even when the superintendent walks in. It's not like I haven't said 'eat an apple a day,' for crying out loud!"

From her desk in the second row, Sophie glanced back over her shoulder. Her classmates were slouched in their seats, all right. Every boy and the girl sprawled out, chest caved in, legs stretched out under the desk in front of them, skinny arms dangling. Sophie sensed danger. She instantly sat ramrod straight, like a corporal signalling an infantry. She aimed a now-or-never stare at Tony, her twelve-year-old brother, set free by the boarding school officials finally that year, to attend the reserve's first day school. Frowning, Tony mouthed a big what?

The nurse pulled even closer to Mr. Ready. She leaned in. "Why not ask them to draw a picture of what they ate for breakfast? Your opposite number, Miss Paul, at Springside Indian Day School, got some really interesting results that way. You'd be surprised what the parents … well." She cleared her throat, fist lightly tapping her sternum.

"I'll do it!"

Mr. Ready was pleased, beaming with relief. Sophie knew he would be on patrol again, but this time with prisoners of war—though not if she could help it. The nurse smiled, hand on heart, as if she had just won at a game of Tag.

Sophie disliked the way the teacher and the nurse conspired, as if they were enemies of the kids, as if nobody else in the room counted, least of all the kid right under their nose. The two were talking about her parents, what's more. In fact, about all her classmates' parents and about what they fed their children. The meanness of it made Sophie's chest muscles tighten. It was time to call in the troops, like Dad often said to his old ex-soldier pals.

Wasting no time, she rounded up Tony and her little sister, Leta, at recess. "Listen hard," she said. They stood tense in front of her out in the schoolyard. "When we go in at bell, Mr. Ready's going to ask us to draw what we ate for breakfast. Don't go drawing pictures of flour-porridge, Klik, or hardtack. Hear? What we eat is none of Mr. Ready's business—not his, not the nurse's. Got it?"

Leta clapped her hand to her mouth. Tony giggled nervously.

Ignoring this, Sophie asked them to think of every food they ever saw pictured in Canada's Food Rules—yes, that big poster that made their stomachs growl, that one. For Sophie, the mere thought of the yellow butter and red berry jam made her mouth water for the sweet and salty flavour. She knew she had to get Tony and Leta past the tasting. Like a sergeant giving orders to his squadron, she itemized: "Here's what you draw: milk in a tumbler, two pancakes with strawberries on top on a real plate with pink roses round the edge, and Roger's Corn Syrup. Got that?" Heads nodded. "And purple grapes, and an apple, red. And, let's see, what else? Corn on the cob in a blue bowl. I guess that's it."

"What about bread?" Leta asked.

"It should be toast, shouldn't it?" Tony screwed up his face, trying to recall exactly.

Leta, doing an excited dance, flapped her hands in the air. "I know! Those big shiny buns in see-through packages at Sam Goodman's store!"

"No," Sophie said. "Make it brown bread and butter. Mr. Ready might ask if Mom has a toaster, then what?"

Tony made a suggestion. "Do both. Do bread and buns."

"I almost forgot," Sophie hollered as the teacher rang the bell, "what kind of green vegetable goes with breakfast?"

None knew. They began running for the school door.

"I know," Leta called back just in time. "Lettuce!"

"Good! Don't forget!"

At their desks, Sophie was relieved to see Leta and Tony hunched over their drawings, sweating. Craning her neck, she saw that, in spite of what she had been told, Leta had sketched a cinnamon bun so huge that she had no choice but to squeeze everything else in around it. Maddeningly, she had drawn lettuce as a border of leaves on the page. Sophie made the worst fuming field Marshall's face she could at her, but Leta would not look up.

Checking her own progress, Sophie realized that she had just drawn her glass of milk way too tall. Still, she hadn't forgotten a thing. Good enough, she thought, as she coloured in the last row of yellow and purple and black kernels on her corncob. A final glance told her that Tony had left out Roger's Corn Syrup; worse, he had drawn his corncob in a red bowl. And —could it be? A Cadbury chocolate bar from the teacher's pull-down Map of the World!

It was too late.

The teacher, drowsing at his reconnaissance centre, stirred. Sophie took a deep breath and handed in her drawing. Blue eyes drilled into hers. Mr. Ready, speaking in capital letters to the class, said, "Let us review the Stevens' Family Breakfast, shall we?"

Sophie got ready.

But the teacher, taking his time, held up Tony's drawing first. "That's a pretty big breakfast, wouldn't you say?" he said to Tony.

Tony ducked, head on desk now. The teacher had just fired a first shot. Tony peeked at Sophie from under his raised elbow. The class tittered. Not having been drilled, the class had gone to the other side, Sophie realized.

Getting to her feet, she stood at ease as best she could. "We eat like this," she began. "Our parents make us. We work hard at home on our farm." Sophie guessed it was okay to mislead the enemy on a soldier's exact location—although, in protecting her troops, she had skidded pretty close to a downright lie. The teacher glared at her without comment.

He turned to her little sister. "So now tell me, Leta, when did your mom bake all these nice big buns?"

Again the class tittered.

Leta bit her lip and then remembered. "I saw them in town at Sam Goodman's store! That's true, isn't it, Sophie?"

Sophie nodded, holding her post.

"So how is it you had two fruits for breakfast?" The teacher directed his remark again at Tony, who had lifted his head out of the trenches too soon. Stumped was written all over his face. Worse, he appeared on the point of confessing everything.

"Mr. Ready," Sophie said, her heart beating hard, "you'll have to ask our mother. Because our father will wonder why you're asking us private questions."

Mr. Ready opened his mouth, then shut it, and then glared.

Sophie took her seat. The teacher, agitated, sifted through the class drawings. He sniffed loudly and pawed into other stacks of paper on his desk before he settled down. Sophie took another deep breath. Mr. Ready had retreated, leaving her alone. For now.

She'd have to be ready at first bugle call, any day of the week now. For starters, at noon today she'd eat her greasy Klik sandwich out of sight behind the school, well after the enemy had hurried back to the teacherage and disappeared into his mess hall. As for the army-issue dog biscuit in her lunch sack, she'd roll the tasteless, rock-hard thing, first chance she got, straight across the classroom floor in arithmetic period—hardtack ticking and clacking on its axis right up to Mr. Ready's desk, like a decoy, maybe—white flag under her pillow at home.

Truth Is a Patient Nurse

WHEN SOPHIE WAS ELEVEN, she got so sick she could not say what was real, what ought to be true, and what couldn't be true—but was. She had been taught to tell the truth, and sometimes failed, or thought she did, and might still.

She sank in and out of a high fever, four days in a row. Dreams and nightmares became one. Her mind was a sieve wherein strange images rose and departed. Her father blew cooling breaths across her forehead. Her mother pressed damp cloths to her temples. Still, the fever burned on. Night was day. Day was night. On the fifth morning they brought her to the hospital.

It came to her that she had been taken into town. And that her parents had already left, likely trying to beat the dark home. Women attended to her: a receptionist, two nurses, and nuns. She had always been around women and felt comfort in their presence. Sitting in the nurse's office, she forced her mind to align with what she saw: white enamel trays, a white-painted cupboard with a glass front, and glass bottles filled with liquids of red, yellow, green, and clear. But all she could think was that liniment is green. And that her grandmother's arthritis bottle on the windowsill at home was green.

Seated in a chair across from the nurse, Sophie tried her best to watch and listen. She tried to still a wavering picture, because her grandmother always said that truth came with care and exact remembering. Sophie told herself that she had been awake the whole time, but maybe a dream had interfered.

Whispering rustled in the nurse's uniform as she sat writing. A car swept by the window. Female voices echoed in the hall. Instruments clattered on trays and trolleys going by. Sophie struggled to name the scents, the depths of smells in her nostrils: freshness, sharpness, coolness. The nurse spoke. "How old are you?" Her voice rang, a tinkling bell.

Sophie's mind processed each word, and finally she could answer. "Eleven."

The nurse smiled. "What grade are you?"

Sophie wished the nurse had not asked. "Grade two."

Surprise lit grey-green eyes. "That's good," the nurse said.

But Sophie's mind swirled. There were two stories to tell, one simple, one not. Just telling one wasn't telling the truth. Yet the nurse had not asked for the second one. Sophie drew a breath and said, "I started school only when I was ten. There were no schools on the reserve. I wanted to go when I was five though."

The nurse stuck a cold thermometer in Sophie's mouth, withdrew it, and studied its markings against the light. She smiled. "At least you're in school now."

Sophie did not want the nurse to think how tall age eleven is compared with grade two kids. Grade twos struggled with tying shoelaces. The very thought made her face hotter. It was as if a square of Thermogene, cut from a bolt at the Indian agent's office, lay against her face, like the ones the Indian agent insisted her mother place flat on the chest whenever there was a fever. Sophie struggled to steady herself. The room began a slow turn. She tightened her grip on the chair. Everything swayed in a half-turn, then stopped. The walls straightened but the floor underfoot felt slanted.

Sounds and pictures roamed her mind: the little ones at home have the croup. An odd catch-less cough convulses the baby's body. A breath-robbing whoop turns him blue, then purple. Sophie's mother, frantic, walks him around and around, holding his squirming body up to the air. She screams at Dad, "Get something!" And he rides off, full-gallop, to the agency. With the horse flipping froth, he returns—with Thermogene. "But it burns their skin!" Mom cries.

"Are you all right?" The nurse stared at Sophie, who tried to anchor her gyrating brain by focusing her mind on a short, round-faced clock ticking on the small, white, wooden table beside her, its ticks echoing from inside the wood. A wave of nausea swept over her. The nurse said it was time to go to her room. As Sophie tried to stand, the office spun, lifting itself into a spiral. She fought to make it stay right-side up.

Grey-green eyes peered into hers. "Can you walk? Shall we get someone to help us?"

"I can walk," Sophie whispered.

"Okay. Here we go."

They made their way down a pale, wide hall. When they arrived Sophie turned to look over her shoulder. She wondered what had taken so long. The nurses' station was only a few steps away. Sophie blinked into the dimly lit room. It held two beds. The nurse pointed Sophie to the one nearest the door, its iron feet wavering in a watery reflection on polished grey and black linoleum squares. Everything about the room was white: the bedstead; the bedding; the chairs; a single, tall, window frame; and a white pull-around curtain for the bed.

"Take your things off and pop into this." Pale hands slid a hospital gown out of the corner cupboard and onto the bed. The nurse showed how the strings tied in the back. "Climb up and get in. I'll put your clothes away." The nurse zipped shut the curtain on metal disks that zinged round the ceiling's curved metal track. "When you need me, pull this cord."

Sophie struggled to undress. Weakness undid her knees and hands. Finally she lay her head down on the pillow. It seemed that at some point the nurse had pulled a layer of sheets and a blanket over her.

A kind of sleep pulls her under now in a rumble of sound; the wheels of the wagon roll into town, clattering in her ears: horses snuffle and snort, hooves pounding and pouncing on the gravel road threading through the reserve.

There is a voice by her head. "You okay?"

Sophie tries to reply, but the room is swallowed up in a vortex of opaque light spewing back dim pulsations at the window. Her parents' voices echo from the depths of a rain barrel. Sophie fights to sit up. She believes she knows what they are saying—their words of delight, distress—so that she keeps trying to call. They worry. They quarrel. They scold the horses bitterly as they bump and shudder through a funnelling road ... there onto her hospital bed ... and on the road, the wind roars up, and she cannot stand it anymore. It is dusty on the road into town and the dust hurls hard. The roofs of town spring up, and it is easier by the buildings, down along the street. The Cree people huddle outside the stores ... chaskwa! mahka mina ... where dust keeps its place. The hospital stands white and strong as black crows weave through the trees, wind in their feathers. It is a dirt road and the wind had leapt out of nowhere ...

Sophie's eyes fly open. A face hovered over her. She could only stare. Something in that gleaming fall of auburn hair and those friendly grey-green eyes steadied Sophie's way to the top. That, and the nurse's warming smile.

"You fell asleep the second you lay down. Would you like a drink?"

"I have to go to the toilet."

"Here, I'll take you. We'll walk together."

"I can go alone."

"Wait until you stand, then you'll see."

The nurse said she would wait around the corner. She warned, "Pull the cord before taking a step." Sophie eased herself onto the floor, bare feet cleaving to cold. She struggled with finding a standing position that felt like one. As she reached for the cord, her eye caught on a patch of dark markings on her pillow, a fuzzy checkerboard pattern, oval in shape. She peered more closely and recoiled. It was an indentation of her head! Road dust and grit had found its way out of her hair and formed little piles on her pillow as she lay drifting. She didn't want to be thought dirty by the nurse. She quickly turned the pillow over; the dust didn't pounce out from under. Still Sophie panicked. Her mother had scrubbed and rinsed until her scalp hurt. Would the nurse believe she had ever been clean? Her hand was on the pull cord, but Sophie's mouth filled with the bitter flavour of a lie. Her grandmother had always said that truth is "always alive somewhere." Truth-hiding, like now, made Sophie want to vomit.

Her mind switched to the time her father tried to force her, her brother, and her little sister to believe that the young priest was bad. Their father had to be mistaken, but he had chased the priest away, not asking first.

The priest had only wished to be friends. Sophie liked the sound of his laughter. She liked his robin's-egg blue eyes. He would come to the reserve from the Mission in his Model T, roaring around the bend in the road where a bush hid the rest of the route that her father took when he left for town. Sophie and her siblings, Tony and Leta, tumbled out of the house that day, calling to their mother, "The priest!"

As usual, breathless, they ran to the vibrating car. And there he sat, smiling in his long, black coat-dress, blond shock of hair standing on end like a stook. Sophie hoped his grin meant a surprise of candy. "Get in." He would say this as if throwing open the whole world on all sides. This visit had begun that way. Into the car they piled, Sophie startled by her lack of manners. The sheer joy of being near the smells of leather, gasoline, and hot oil off a humming motor egged her on.

She fought to sit in the front seat where she would be right in the centre of the priest's bright gaze, in the centre of his wild sense of fun and mischief. Like always, the priest's fingers, long and electric, grew quicker with little tricks that slipped a leaf into her hair, a small twig down her blouse, a smooth little pebble in her shoe. "I'm faster than a magician!" he bragged. It was hard to catch him. He fake-grabbed sleeves and collars, and squeezed the top of Sophie's knee, making her scream with laughter—and he had already popped a peppermint into Tony's pant pocket. The priest laughed all the more as they hunted all over him for a jawbreaker that each wanted in deadly earnest, their minds lost in a furnace of competition. "A hundred little fingers and all brown!" he had called out, jubilant. Sophie wanted to make it two hundred. She wanted that pink jawbreaker with its dark centre. If you found it, it meant you had won a trip to Chicago, a shiny faraway place. So then, it was all their little fingers in his shirt, his long coat-dress, his stook, what with Leta pushing hard against Sophie and Tony pulling her hair with all his might.

"What the hell's going on?" It was their father's face darkening the car window.

They sat as still as mice. Sophie realized that she had somehow managed to stay in the front seat. The afternoon sun shone through a dusty lace of tiny flies swaying in the air across the windshield.

"Get in the house!" The thud of little feet, muffled grunts, the groan of the car door opening, the squeaks of bums and hands rubbing across the leather seats, Sophie and her siblings fled with their hearts pounding. Chicago closed down. And sickening untruth unstrung. Sophie's father told the priest that the RCMP would be called in if he ever showed his face again. Later her parents told Sophie she ought to be ashamed. She shouldn't have sat up in the front, looking like that. Like what? The unexplained darkness of the remark made Sophie throw up.

Nurses stood laughing outside her door. Sophie left the pillow with its bad secret where it lay. She pulled the cord.

The nurse and she began their walk. One step, two steps, three, and four … and Sophie felt herself falling.

"Oh, oh! Good thing we were ready!" the nurse laughed. "Come on, I'll carry you."

"No, thank you, I'm heavy." Sophie's words were whispers, though she tried to speak louder. Sophie believed herself much heavier than the actual lightness of her frame. She saw that her nurse was young. The thought of being carried embarrassed Sophie, even though the nurse was the taller by almost half.

She ignored Sophie's protests. "You're weak with fever. It's you we have to worry about. Now, be a pal and lift your arms. Grab onto my shoulder. Hang on with all your might! Ready? You have to help me now—one, two, and three!"

The nurse turned the journey into a kind of game, a friendly competition with obstacles. She and Sophie were a team of ponies straining and staggering down the hall. Sophie clung on. The nurse pushed open a big, heavy, dark brown door and they lurched into the washroom. Sophie looked at a room with its two stalls. Its white basins and silvery taps. White tiles. The nurse was about to let Sophie slide to the floor when she, herself, lost her footing. She staggered and banged hard against the wall. Sophie somehow found herself seated inside a stall. The nurse leaned against the wall by the open door, her eyes tearing.

On the way back, the hall banked toward them in a harsh glare. Pain jabbed at Sophie's eyeballs. She clung to the nurse's shoulder. An unfamiliar voice grated in her ears as she tried to see through shattering light. A new nurse, older and taller, stood outside the door to the room. She said to Sophie's nurse, "We're putting the baby in here until space comes free."

Sophie looked into the room. A baby lay sleeping in a crib by the window; the second adult cot was gone. The older nurse turned to leave.

The young nurse smiled at Sophie. "Wow, you have company!"

But Sophie felt too ill to care about a baby. Sleep loomed in waves, threatening to drain everything away that was, and everything Sophie struggled to keep in view.

Unaware that she had slept the day away, Sophie awoke in the middle of the night to a thick silence. She sat up and peered at the baby across the room. It made no sound. It was a tiny, inert form with no covers whatsoever. The stark, tight-fitted sheet made Sophie think of starlit snow. Maybe the baby was dead. Light slanted into the room, barely enough to see—and Sophie sensed that somewhere a fence was down … Her head spun tightly and she fell back onto the pillow. Her mouth tasted ashes. She thought to reach for the water pitcher on the night stand. Instead, she lay in the dark feeling awful about not having learned enough about the Red Cross. A window had to be quickly shut on Mrs. Pell, she knew, the teacher's wife, who wanted a baby very badly and had adopted one. Sophie tried to block the memory of the Pell's adopted girl, the same size as the baby in the room. A baby asleep was what Mrs. Pell wanted, and in the worst way. It was all so true, Sophie had to admit, or risk puking on the hospital bed.

She stared at the shadows on the ceiling. Phantom sand in the back of her head and in her ears hissed and whispered. Mrs. Pell, that day, had given her long blonde hair a flip over her shoulder, smiling as she walked into the room. The teacher had invited three of his pupils to come to the teacherage over the noon hour to learn about forming a Red Cross Club. Mrs. Pell came in to show off baby Delaney. The baby girl was wrapped tightly, arms inside a diaper wound to the neck. The baby looked hot. The glaring sun shone through the window onto the small head of black hair. Black button eyes glimmered in a tiny roasting face. Mrs. Pell swung back into the bedroom, saying, "Okay, time for a nap."

The teacher had just begun to tell us about the Red Cross when

Delaney started fussing. Mrs. Pell hummed a short lullaby and said, "Shush."

Sophie sat up in her hospital bed, head a swirl of rising nausea. She wanted the relief that only facing truth can bring. It was true—the word Mrs. Pell said was, "Shush!"

The teacher had twisted in his chair as if someone ought to throw open a window. He kept talking, but only mumbled the words, eyes downcast. Whap! He stopped mid-sentence. Whap! Whap! Whap! came from the bedroom, followed by baby screams. More whaps and tiny Delaney's breath dragged on and on, far away in a cry without end, like the croup. Mrs. Pell walked back into the room, flipping her hair. A scream from air-starved Delaney filled our ears. Then, there was silence. "Oh," Mrs. Pell said, smiling, "a smack or two is all it takes, every time!"

That year little Delaney died from a hole in her heart. Sophie told herself that was true; it had to be, because it came with remembering about the Red Cross and the teacher at school, tears in his eyes, saying, "Our little Delaney died." But then she knew very little about it, if anything—very, very little. She turned away from the light coming in under the hospital door. The room had spun into frightening darkness.

Sophie awoke next morning to an empty room. The baby's cot was made up, covered in a flat white sheet. Sophie thought the baby might have been taken away by the parents. Light washed the walls and the smell of menthol and mothballs filled the wintry air. Sophie felt her mind clearing. She knew she was getting better and that her parents would come for her.

At four o'clock that day, the nurses emptied the hallway of patients. Vespers were to begin. Prayers echoed in halls that seemed wide, high, and fresh with the sound. Sophie waited by the door of her room. The young nurse came by and whispered that to stare at the nuns would not be polite. Sophie, stepping back a bit, listened to the chants drifting toward her. Her heart pounded as the nuns came into view. Four passed right in front of her. At the end of the hall, they turned and came back, their voices soaring and fluttering in repeat patterns, ascending higher than the height of the building, "Blessed Art Thou among ..."

Sophie stared at the crisp triangular forms. The chanting made her think of bluebells against a sky of fine rain. She clasped her hands at the sight of bright white wimples catching the sunlight. Rimmed in light, the nuns looked like shining paper dolls, cut sharp and clear.

"Why do they do this?" Sophie asked the nurse.

"It's Vespers, to keep us safe from harm."

"Does it work?"

The nurse laughed. "Hey, someone's feeling better! Yes, it works. If you're Catholic, especially, I suppose. It probably helps." The nurse laughed again.

Sophie wished to be Catholic. She wished her father was wrong about them.

The days passed. Sophie felt her illness lifting, more and more.

One morning, an event reawakened in Sophie the thrill of Chicago. A new nurse arrived and came in to tell Sophie that a patient in the room across the hall, kitty-corner from hers, had taken notice. Sophie had indeed seen the woman looking at her. Whenever Sophie raised her eyes to gaze out the door, there she was. The woman's curiosity warned of invasion, and Sophie's eyes fluttered like a moth searching for softer light.

The haggard nurse, big and bossy, stood at the door. "See that lady over there? Well, she's good enough to invite you. That is, if you're clean head to toe, and polite. You have the privilege of staying when her folks arrive today. I told her you're not dying of scarlet fever." The nurse laughed at her own joke.

Sophie attuned her ear to the nurse's raspy voice; up close, her long, liver-spotted hands, wide shoulders, and square jaw made Sophie feel her own body had shrunk. The nurse's hard glance called to mind a kind of blue that is cast by January snowdrifts. A white nurse's cap sat upon the grey-brown hair pinned up in a roll today. A hand reached out and tilted Sophie's head back. "Say ah." The hand was cold. "Anybody from the reserve visit you these past four days?" Her voice boomed almost as if Sophie might be in the far corner of the room. Yet here she was, freshly washed and combed, sitting in the bed close to the door where the nurse stood.

"No. Not yet." Sophie wished to, but knew she couldn't count the young nurse as a visitor. Anyway, lately, the young nurse rarely had a minute.

The stout nurse tilted her head toward the other room. "Okay. Good then. Get up and let's go!"

Did she mean now? Sophie found herself crossing the hall, following the nurse. Her thin hospital gown told Sophie that she needed panties at least, and Oxfords to cover her feet. But before she could say anything, she was sitting in a chair at the foot of the bed of the woman across the hall. The woman asked, "Why is she alone so much?"

"Tell me and we'll both know." The old nurse leaned tiredly against the door jamb.

"No family?" The woman in bed checked little glass buttons on her bed jacket of brightly embroidered pink flowers and blue hearts trimmed in lace. Then she looked Sophie over.

"She has family, all right, but the minute they dropped her off— neither hide nor hair."

Sophie studied her hands. She wished she had curls in her hair at least. But all the days she'd been at the hospital, she could not bring herself to ask the young nurse to lend her some curl rags.

"What a shame!" The woman stared at Sophie. "She looks lonely."

"Oh, I don't know," the nurse sighed. "That's a capability, isn't it?"

"How old is she? Why is she so thin?"

"You heard the lady! How old are you? Wouldn't your parents

want you to speak up when spoken to?"

Sophie realized they were talking to her.

But Sophie's guts were tied in a knot now, because her mother and father were being talked about. Her parents weren't here to witness a flash too sharp for eyes, like snow lying flat where the sun hits it square. Sophie wished to explain that her baby brother might be sick, or that the Indian agent might want even more papers filled out. Or that maybe her mother's nosebleeds had started again. There was no telephone at home either. However, butting in would be rude, especially with adults speaking.

Still, Sophie was about to ask what the question was again, please, when people appeared in the doorway. The nurse quickly stepped aside. She held herself very tall and tidy now as she waited, hands clasped, beaming.

There were swift hugs for the woman on the bed. Her husband and a thin elderly lady stepped in and around each other as they bent down for kisses. The dead air of the room traded places with the fresh air brought in from outside. The man, heavy-set and red-faced, nodded at Sophie without looking at her. The old lady studied her steadily through bifocals.

Sophie got up to leave, glad to get away, but the woman in the bed whispered stay, and so Sophie quickly sat back down. The woman made introductions. "This is Nurse McElroy. You won't find a better one, no sir."

Staring at Sophie, the visitors at first were very polite about her malady. The husband asked what she had done to get it. Nurse McElroy held Sophie's arms up to the light to prove that they weren't riddled with spots and not full of blisters and sores but, instead, with the tan removed, might mistakenly be thought contagious—because the girl had been alone so long, and was not from here.

"See?" Nurse McElroy dropped Sophie's arm.

After that, the smiles flowed politely toward Sophie, as though she belonged now. Her illness was no threat, but Sophie was not really one of them, even after they learned of her situation, because it was different with them, and their patient had done very different things to get her illness. Whereas, Sophie had done nothing she could think of.

Still, Nurse McElroy wanted Sophie squared around. "Native. Straight off the reserve—came in with one devil of a fever. She's over it now and can leave. But the parents keep on forgetting, or something, to come and get her. They haven't been seen. Nope, not once. Your good wife here took pity."

Sophie felt a wave of numbness sweep over her. But Nurse McElroy had grown suddenly delighted, and so the people in the room were glad she was so happy and they wanted to spread joy. "Poor thing! No visitors!" they said.

It was then Nurse McElroy told about the clothes. Sophie knew the nurse meant her. Because the nurse had looked right at her and spoke loudly, again as if Sophie stood in a far corner of a room where only a finely tuned message might reach and where no living person might mistake what was being said. "When your parents come to get you, tell them to come by my house and knock on the back door. There'll be boxes of clothes waiting there for you."

Everyone looked really happy now, and the visiting went on merrier than before. For Sophie, the feeling of Chicago had sprung up—store-bought clothes! In her size! Sophie had always wanted real clothes. Finally, she might chuck the hand-me-downs her mother had altered: baggy slacks, limp jackets, sagging blouses, year after year, cut down from her aunts giveaways. Sophie all but held to her face an imaginary soft grey sweater with the smoothest buttons ever. She might even get a chance to wear it for the young nurse someday. Sophie's nose recalled the smells of coffee, tar, and gasoline that followed her down a street in Chicago—just like the priest had said.

"My daughter is getting rid of a number of things," Nurse McElroy explained to the hospital visitors in whose admiring light she stood.

Heading back to her room, Sophie felt over-excited, yet drained. The nurse clucked, saying she was pale and that her eyes were glassy. She told Sophie to lie down and rest. But Sophie hoped to see the young nurse and tell her about the clothes, and Chicago. She would ask the young nurse if she liked priests, and if she were friends with them. But at rounds that evening, it was the bossy nurse again, pushing in a trolley of glass tumblers half filled with blue liquid in which glass thermometers tinkled and gleamed.

On her last day, Sophie was glad to be leaving. But she was sad, too, since she could not find and speak to the young nurse one more time. She needed to tell her the truth—that it was grit in her hair dirtying the pillow that time. But the halls and grounds showed no sign of her.

Starting out on the ride home that afternoon, Sophie told her father how she had been asked by Nurse McElroy to stop by her house for the boxes of clothes.

"We're not a bunch of beggars!" he exploded.

Sophie's mother scolded him, reminding him that life overseas had spoiled his thinking. His manner had worsened, she said, and he wore his pride like a war medal now. Finally he gave in. Sophie, trembling, asked her mother, "Will there be a satin blouse and a green velvet skirt?"

"How should I know? There could be."

But Sophie recognized delight in her mother's voice, even if her face gave nothing away. Her father's ear caught the happiness, too, and so he pulled up to the edge of Nurse McElroy's backyard, beside a black Ford. Happily, Sophie was chosen to go in.

"What'll you say if she asks if we're hungry?" Her father spoke in a gruff voice.

"I'll say no, thank you."

Nurse McElroy's home was yellow stucco with a single elm leaning tiredly away from it. The yard's barbed wire fence was down in places. The gate, covered in peeling grey paint, was shut. Sophie wanted to call out, "I'm here!" She wished to break into a run through the tall grass up ahead, where goldenrod and thistles fidgeted in the breeze.

"You speak up, now." She heard her father call.

"I know."

Sophie did know. She was impatient. She had hundreds of things to keep in mind, like where to step when blue-flowering thistles sprang up with their hidden spikes, like what her first words would be to Nurse McElroy, like if there was a pearl button blouse—and remembering to say no when asked if she wanted a drink, even if her mouth was as dry as dry can be. As Sophie approached the house, tall weeds in every shade of green and grey danced at her. A patch of black soil in a half moon spread out, advancing from the house as though coming to greet her. The dry soil was powdery underfoot, small dust clouds puffing out with each step. Finally she arrived at the entrance to the back porch.

The door hung open, so she knocked on its wooden frame, loose boards muting her taps. Clothes lay in piles on the floor of the porch. Wet garments hung over the backs of a couple of scarred chairs and on the dented washing machine. Garden tools and shovels, inflated rubber tubes, and kids' toys lay scattered about. It smelled like the middle of washday at home. Sophie tapped louder. A woman's gravelly voice answered. Sophie crossed the porch, stepping over objects. She arrived at the door, ajar to the kitchen.

People sat eating. Nurse McElroy's chair was opposite the door, at the head of the table. Sophie could not believe she was actually looking at her. Nurse McElroy stood up and came over to her, blocking the view of the people at the table. All white-haired. Nurse McElroy looked tired. Her floral dress hung limp, nothing like her usual smart uniform. Her hair, steamed out, hung loose. The air smelled of boiled potatoes. The last thing Sophie saw was the nurse's impatience.

"Yes?"

"Hello, Nurse McElroy. It's me."

"Yes?"

"It's me—from in the hospital."

"And?"

"I've come to ask about the clothes."

Nurse McElroy raked eyes over Sophie. "Clothes? What are you talking about? We don't have clothes, if that's what you want." She said this as though Sophie were a crowd, and a lot farther from the house than where she stood, directly under the nurse's nose.

"Nurse McElroy, you said I could come for a box of clothes, clothes your daughter is getting rid of—things that might fit me."

Perhaps Nurse McElroy had only momentarily forgotten. Sophie's mouth tasted of ashes with the idea of her parents' thinking she had lied.

Sophie made a last desperate attempt. "My father fought in World War II. He's an Esquire now, and I'm his daughter." Surely Nurse McElroy had heard? After all, the whole town had come to the skating rink where the hockey team, on skates, carved out his title, Esquire, on the ice, and gave him medals from the queen, the king's daughter.

A man's voice called from inside, "What the hell is it now?"

"Some kid from the reserve, begging!"

Nurse McElroy raised her voice. "Sorry, I don't have anything!" She looked at Sophie as though she wished to say more. But she turned away. "And not tomorrow, neither. Go home!" Sophie was a crowd, again.

She pulled herself away and ran off into the field. Crossing, she cared less that thistles and spear grass jabbed at her feet. It was a pearl button blouse and a green velvet skirt and red sandals, now gone up in flames. Vespers and Chicago, in cinders—flown! Where the red sandals came from, she didn't know. But she hated how fast they burned.

A Dog's Life

SOPHIE UNTIED THE TETHER from the base of the tree and dragged Small Boy's body to the lip of the hill where the ground dropped away. The weight of the lifeless carcass felt too heavy to be him. Sophie looked over her shoulder at his blond remains wave-rippling in the grass behind her. Only moments before, Small Boy had been quivering at her side. She unwound the rope from a lifeless neck and walked back to the tree at the edge of the ravine.

Now Lady.

But first Sophie had to catch her. Lady, always quick, yipped and howled and raced off onto a stretch of black fallow. Sophie called, coaxing. The dog obeyed, hind end in a half turn, thin body trembling as she made her way over. Sophie slipped the rope around her neck. Then, pulling on live resistance, she set things up once more. Stepping back from the angle of the tree, off which a bullet might ricochet, like her father said, Sophie took aim, but couldn't pull the trigger, couldn't get past numbness in her brain, couldn't shuck the frozen grip of her hands. There was no way in, no way out, and no way back—the sky had pounded the life out of its day.

Earlier that morning Sophie's father arose from bed in one of the worst rages of his recent bingeing. He had gripped thirteen-year-old Sophie's arm in a painful knot and barked in her ear. "The dogs better be dead by the time I get home!" Her head reeled against a suddenly swirling ground and, staggering, she fought down a wave of nausea.

Last night, Small Boy and Lady had broken into the chicken coop and killed the family's last hen. Feathers lay scattered in the yard near the barn, like a pillow had burst open. When Sophie's father saw it, he flew into a rage, yelling that the family would die of hunger, all five of them—and how long the dying would take, he sure as hell didn't know. Make no mistake, he said, somebody would pay. So that day bleak winter's dread entered the heart of summer.

Sophie's parents were off to town for the day, to buy baloney on credit, if things went right. Sophie's father had turned to her, and, pointing to a spot on the ground, said he wanted to see the dogs' carcasses laid out when he got home. "And don't get any ideas."

The one idea Sophie had in her head was how to avoid another beating. The whippings had been several days in a row now. Her brother and sister were in the same boat, each of them fingering trails of welts and bruises that crossed arms, legs, and shoulders. Their father had said, more than once when drunk, that he was going to kill someone. Sophie worried that he might just do it one day. She mistrusted him for another reason. She had once overheard him say, although possibly he was only joking and probably just to frighten her, that she had until Christmas to make up her mind to marry Geordie Samuels, a twenty-five-year-old man to her thirteen years.

Today, she called fifteen-year-old Tony and twelve-year-old Leta to her. It amazed her to see how they seemed so much younger than their age, often fretting and fidgeting like frightened six-year-olds. They looked young, and cried too. Out in the middle of the yard was where they sat together when their father was home, so as to "stay in sight" as ordered—and as a hedge against being overheard. Today they sat there by habit. "Can we at least draw straws to see who'll pull the trigger?" Sophie asked. After all, she had already killed Small Boy, dead now, lying by the hill.

Nope, was their reply. All of it was Sophie's job, they said. "Dad grabbed you when he said it." Again, before her eyes, Sophie's siblings let fear turn them into babies.

But Sophie told them she just could not make herself do it. "Lady's a good dog. She was Kokum's best. Lady always helped Small Boy round up the cows. She's quick, too." Again Sophie felt like vomiting. The three tried to guess how long killing the dog could wait. Lady might get too full of terror, if it was put off too long. Tony said a dog smelled fear only when left on its own, or when it thought no one was coming to take it home. Sophie knew differently; animals sensed their end. Even chickens ran and hid, every time.

"Kokum said Lady's owner beat her when she was a puppy. And that's why she belly-crawls," Sophie said. "Lady is always scared."

The three studied the faithful collie lying in the grass in the sunlight, one ear cocked.

Off in the ravine, a bobolink's watery trills joined the drumming of a partridge echoing in the hills. The sound reminded Sophie of gunfire. Her eyes were drawn to the line of poplar matching wits with a shield of brush and shrubs. Without warning, the leaves parted. Geordie Samuels, in a flash of a bright red and white leather jacket, came swaggering up, likely, in his mind, followed by a rodeo-full of applauding people. He had ogled Sophie for months as he did the chores and odd jobs, flattering her father and making himself indispensable. "Need help hauling wood? Want those fence posts sharpened?" It sickened Sophie to think that a sneak held such a strong place in her family.

With Geordie hanging around so much, Sophie's parents began looking oddly at her. Nudges and whispers assaulted her, especially when her mother tried to corner her and talk about sex. Sophie refused to be told any of it. Farm animals did all of it in plain sight. Sophie knew animals mated, mainly dogs. She'd seen their dazed, mindless activity. It wasn't as if she didn't know what her parents hinted at when they teased her about being old enough to marry, and how they cleverly threw in that Geordie would make a great son-in-law. It made Sophie's guts boil.

As Geordie drew near, jacket ablaze, Tony poked her. "Couldn't Geordie kill Lady?" he asked in undertones.

Sophie's spit caught in her throat. She choked on a cough. This was not the worst idea she had ever heard.

"Hello there!" Geordie called, practically upon them. Wearing his leather jacket like a pledge now, he smiled a pitiable smile, like a hound making friends. But then, even Lady hadn't bothered to look up.

"Hey, Geordie!" Sophie's voice rang so clear and full of cheer it surprised even her. "How are you?" This was the first full sentence she'd ever directed at him, and so now he stood still, blinking. Her ringing tone had carried a trace of artillery against Geordie's possible enthusiasms, but she had left a tiny trace of hope blooming in the air.

He stopped smiling and blinked all the more. "Fine, I'm fine, real fine." Nervousness played against his attempt at a casual S in his posture.

"Can I ask a favour, Geordie?" Sophie smiled squarely at him for the first time in his entire life.

"Yes, anything!" He stood straight, a slavering hound.

"You sure?"

"Yup, just say the word, Sophie!"

"Kill our dog."

"What?"

Sophie's gaze cut him no retreat and he realized too late that he had already slammed a door on himself. He staggered as though knocked on the head from behind. Sophie knew to push hard now. "You heard me. Or shall I say it again?"

"No, no. I mean … how?' His voice had grown small.

"With my 22." Sophie pointed to the gun lying on the ground, its black metal barrel and action-works glinting on the grass, less than a stride away.

Geordie had the presence of mind to try to buy himself time. "I could. But I need to have a little rest. I'm kind of dying of thirst."

Tony slid Sophie a look: halfway there …

Sophie decided on a show of kindness to move things along. Besides, Geordie's hairline was pouring sweat, and she knew that leather held in the sun's heat. She motioned Tony to take him inside and whispered to Leta to give him water.

Sophie thought she'd best wait at the edge of the hill near that tree. This way Geordie would be forced to walk over, and then he'd be right in the middle of it. She sat with her back to the dead dog, gun beside her, feeling numb. She realized she'd have to speak to Geordie after the killing, when he was apt to think their friendship sealed. "Over his dead body," Sophie said, complying with her worst side.

As the older sister by almost two years, Sophie knew she had to set an example for Leta. Yet, Sophie reckoned, she had failed. Glancing fondly at Leta, her mother would say how magazines in town featured movie stars that looked like her. Sophie battled mixed feelings. It was said that Leta's lips were straight and thin, meaning Sophie's were fat. Leta's eyebrows were arched like pencil lines, meaning Sophie's were thick. But it was true that only Leta had the dimples. Though she felt she was lacking in beauty, Sophie knew she was strong. She compared well with boys. Whenever boys came over, usually with an eye for Leta, they split the wood and filled the reservoir in the kitchen; they raked the yard and hoed weeds in the garden. Sophie could do this work, too. In fact, she knew she bested boys in pretty damn near anything. Her father, though, was another matter. The army had made a man of him, he'd say. But Sophie saw how booze had turned him into some kind of dumb kicking mule.

Strong or not, Sophie never felt at ease. Helping her father around the farm usually threw her into Geordie's company. She walked on eggs whenever Geordie came by. One day, her father said, "Think of all the hot water you're in, Geordie, with those Holomny women—on account of not speaking with Rena-Louise in town that time. Better tie a knot in it, pal!" At that moment Geordie had dared to look at Sophie, and that enraged her.

Still no sight of the sneak! What was taking him so long? All he needed to do was come outside and take hold of the gun. After all, she didn't have all day. Her parents might pull into the yard any minute. Sophie felt dread rush through her limbs. Geordie hadn't as much as poked his head outside. He was taking his sweet time while Lady, beside the step, waited with ears cocked. Sophie got to her feet. She would give Geordie five minutes more, count to ten, and then go inside and ask him what the hell he thought he was doing. Go in too soon, and he might bolt.

Sophie distracted her raging self by thinking about cowards and their cowardly acts. Like Geordie and those pushy Holomny sisters.

Take the day he came to help with the stooking. Sophie and her mother had arrived at the field with lunch. They carried between them a towel-lined cardboard box packed with canned salmon sandwiches, hard-boiled eggs, and rhubarb pie, plus two large jars of cold tea, plates, and utensils. Sophie caught movement out of the corner of her eye. Someone sat, a dark blob in the distance, out in the field. Sophie's father said that a woman had arrived and spent the entire morning there. She had not come over to say hello. Sophie squinted across the shimmering stubble. A breeze, shivering in the sheaves nearby, came stroking past Sophie, who shielded her eyes from light flashing off a spinning veil of grain dust lifting off the field.

The men joined Sophie and her mother waiting by the truck parked in a grassy spot under a shady poplar. Geordie collapsed onto a corner of the blanket on the ground. Her father teased him, "Better watch it,

Geordie. Rena-Louise out there, one who never forgets a wrong, like they say —don't ask how I know it's her—might come for you one night with that Methuselah of a big sister of hers, and her other six-foot twin. Don't say I didn't warn you."

Geordie laughed, but Sophie caught a spark of fear in his sharp glance. His expression told her that a Holomny woman did, indeed, sit in the field. Sophie guessed that Geordie was a chicken when it came to the Holomny sisters. She knew that in his scaredy-cat mind, a shadow had loomed big—much bigger than needed. Sophie knew this, as she had proof of his cowardice from before.

She had seen the Holomny sisters once. They had arrived uninvited to a reserve dance that summer past. People had pooled their money to hire a Métis fiddler and two guitar players. Kokum let her house stand for it. Word was that the Holomny girls were on a hunt and might come by. As city women living on their own now, they wanted men and music, was said. Couples had already arrived, feet flying under the hanging kerosene lanterns when the band played a Scottish jig, followed by cowboy music. At eleven-thirty sharp, the door crashed open and the three strode in.

To Sophie's eye, the sisters looked like men playing dress-up. They stood with feet apart, hands on hips. Rena-Louise, her profile but a cork of nose plugged into a quarter-moon, roamed button eyes over the dancers. Big Norma, tallest, broad of face and impatient in manner, managed a loose, lopsided grin. Sophie, though, stared at the one called Dora. She looked the most mannish as she flicked thick eyebrows at the men. The three wore plaster-thick white powder that made their lipstick a bright red and their black hair shine chrome. Tight-fitting white blouses, collars turned up Dick Tracy style, showed three sets of brassieres as sharp as highway cones, jutting out over black leather skirts. As the sisters stepped forward, the dancers stepped back.

Rena-Louise, reaching into the crowd, grabbed the man closest to her. She yanked the startled Jimmy Kay, slight of build, tight against her cones and polka dotted him across the floor. The other sisters each seized a man, their laughter ringing like gravel in a pail. With the beat of six spiked heels tightening the band's rhythm, Sophie felt the room begin to shake. Dust rose from the floorboards into the air.

"They sure sized us up good and proper," Sophie heard her mother saying.

"I'd hate like hell to be the one they want," her father replied.

Geordie Samuels chose this moment to run off into the dark night.

The afternoon sun burned into the side of Sophie's neck and arm as she stared at the house. Leta came leaping down the step, not a care in the world. "Hey!" Sophie called to her. "What's Geordie doing in there so long?"

"Talking."

"About what?"

"Don't know."

"Go tell Tony I want to see him."

"No." Leta ambled off.

Sophie knew what might be happening. Geordie, stringing a line, had captured Tony, and would be right in the middle of one of those long-winded, artless tales of his. But Leta was not about to say. Instead she lazily picked up a length of rope lying in the yard and began whipping it up and down and around. Next she swatted the ground with it and flipped it high in the air. On the way down, it looked alive.

It recalled to Sophie the actions of people Geordie once described when he was talking about how he had gotten saved by religion. He told Tony how he had joined people who howled and rolled on the floor in the town church. Tony had asked, "What do people want to get saved from?"

"Sin," had been Geordie's inadequate reply.

Okay, this is it, thought Sophie. From the ravine's embankment, she shouted at the top of her lungs. "Geordie, it's time!"

He emerged from the house and descended the steps. He slouched toward her, his feet dragging. He stood looking at her, face drawn and mournful. "I'm not gonna."

"You're not gonna what?"

"When I think of Lady, I can't. What sin did she ever do?" He stood as if glued to the spot, an entire Holy Bible in his hand open to earth and sky.

Sophie's heart hammered in her chest. "But you said!"

"I'll do anything else." He held his palms out like a beggar. Then he turned and trudged back to the house. Leta followed behind. She snickered over her shoulder at Sophie.

Tears of rage burned Sophie's eyes. She stomped up to the house in time to watch Leta go inside and then come out carrying a bowlful of green garden peas. She handed the bowl to Geordie, saying, "Here, shell these."

Sophie stared in disbelief. Leta had just let Geordie off the hook! Geordie, relief dancing in his face, grabbed the bowl, sat down on the steps, and began shelling peas.

Sophie retraced her steps to the lip of the ravine, trying to quell her fury. She had to take charge she knew. She realized that she had unthinkingly scooped up the piece of rope Leta had been playing with. Sophie dangled the rope as if it were a snake. Flipping serpentine loops, she knew what to do. She began screaming like a frightened girl as she raced toward Geordie on the steps. He spotted Sophie— and came undone. Leaping to his feet, he whirled and crashed down the hillside. Sophie chased him, surge of power springing in her feet. Down the slope she charged, flying over prickly brushes, pedalling her legs madly through swishing stands of grass and willow. Now it was poplars and saplings, and she was closing in on her prey. The twenty-five-year-old stopped suddenly, white as a ghost, struggling to catch his breath. He offered no defence; he was unable to flee. Sophie, shocked, realized that if cornered, a coward did nothing to save his life.

She had never seen such raw fear in a grown-up before. His eyes swam. His frame trembled. She never imagined that so lifeless and small a thing as a piece of rope could extract such an extraordinary reaction. She thought to take pity, but Geordie had cast aside his promise, like it was nothing. And there was a killing to be done.

"Come on, Geordie," Sophie said. "There's nothing to be afraid of." She wriggled the rope and took a step toward him, not caring about the poison ivy, thistles, and burrs. Sophie felt a rare, keen-edged sense of triumph at having absolute power and control over another human being. She felt the way a man must feel, gun in hand—until, of all things, Geordie began to cry huge choking sobs.

"Please, don't," he begged. "I'll do anything! For God's sake! Really! Let me go!"

She stared. She dropped the rope to her side, shocked at what was happening. In that instant, uttering no sound or word, Geordie turned and bounded diagonally up the side of the hill. He loped across the yard over the meeting spot and then splashed through the green bushes that swallowed him whole.

Shaking, Sophie returned to the house. Leta screamed at her that Geordie had pitched the peas all over the ground and that it was her fault and she'd better help pick them up, or she'd tell.

"Good!" Sophie shouted. She didn't give a damn. She knew Leta would tell anyway, and a belting was in store with likely a few punches. It didn't matter now. It was time to put her feelings on hold. She had a job to do, same as any marksman.

It had been a bad beating Sophie endured on account of the peas.

But, days later, it was a different brand of sorrow that settled, after a freak snowfall that had followed a sudden, rogue cold snap. A howling wind jammed against the house and roared along the hardened ground of green whipped-off leaves.

That strange ice-bitten Friday night, Sophie's father, on his way home from town, found Geordie hung from a tree, just off the side of the road. Men in town had answered the call to help bring the body down and transport it to the hospital. The body might have been missed altogether, Sophie's father said, but for the sudden appearance of the moon. Geordie had taken a rope and hanged himself. But no one could say how. Except this, Sophie's father had said, a religious man would not just up and kill himself. Besides, Geordie loved life, he said, and had many women on the go.

Sophie thought it did not help to know if Geordie had howled like Small Boy, or like Lady—or if he had even cried and begged for his life. But what stunned her was her father's final statement: "The way he was tied, it'd take three to hang him."

Blue Baby

MAGPIES HAD EATEN THE EYES of the baby and mother. The two of them lay in the snow. Sophie tried to erase the picture from her mind. She lay awake, waiting for dawn, trying to recall how she had come to know. On Tuesday morning the search party found them, faces and necks bare to the sky, lying side by side by the haystack, eye sockets filled with rime. Sophie's father had brought word. He said the end likely came soon after Brady held a drinking party at his shack in the bush off the main road. That night Adeline had tried to escape in a blizzard, the baby on her arm.

Sophie tried not to think of the baby, and of Brady and Adeline. People used to call the couple "the newlyweds." The baby's name was Rosie, short for Mary Rose.

As Sophie waited for the day to begin, she tried not to think about the funeral that would take place later that afternoon. In a few hours, chores would be done, the family would be dressed in layers, and they would leave for the winter drive to the whitewashed church on Kahkewistahaw. Sophie dreaded being near knots of grieving people; their adult sobs always broke down her sense of safety. Worse, their crying might distract her from her intention to look at Brady.

Sophie had acquired a secret liking for Brady.

She watched him when he showed up at Kokum's house to join the other young men from the reserve who, like him, had nothing better to do. They'd sit and talk and match wits. Sophie's aunts liked Brady well enough. But, they said, he thought a lot of himself. His one great joy, they laughed, was to look in a mirror. Their laughter rang harsh and irritating to Sophie's ear. Her grandmother, being wise, had only ever said that Brady's one flaw was his need to show power. Still, Sophie was drawn to him. She admired everything about him. She liked how his teeth flashed white as he talked, and how he chewed twigs to keep his breath as fresh as a willow. Sophie liked it when his grin ignited a tiny interplay of muscles at the corners of his mouth. She knew Brady liked her to notice him. He called her Bright Eyes, under his breath.

Sophie knew very little about Adeline, his wife. She had remained almost a stranger, so rarely did she accompany Brady. The aunts said that he simply could not share the spotlight with such a pretty wife, so he left her at home. His disregard of Adeline distressed them. Cut off from her family, her home reserve being two days away by team, the young bride was left alone a lot. Loneliness kills, the aunts said. But then, whenever Adeline did come, she preferred to sit by the kitchen window, eyes only for her baby. The first time she visited, and only after prompting, she told them the baby's name. Thereafter, to all questions and comments, it was yes, no, or thank you.

Once, Sophie sat studying Adeline's auburn hair, thinking how a yellow ribbon tied in the back might look better than that thin grey parcel string. But then she had found herself locked in a spontaneous staring match with the woman. Adeline dropped her gaze before Sophie could even think to stop. After that, Sophie suffered torments of shame concerning a sudden and unwanted sense of forced equality with an adult, let alone one so close to Brady.

She had suffered anxiety earlier that fall, too, when she overheard the aunts talking in her grandmother's kitchen. Sophie knew something was up because they sent her away. "You'll be wanting to run along then, Sophie," said one of them. Only Sophie did not. She stood outside by the open kitchen window instead, eavesdropping.

Aunt Merceline started. "Anyone notice how Brady acts around Sophie?"

There was an audible intake of breaths. That meant two or more of the aunts knew.

Sophie's heart pounded. It practically stopped altogether when Aunt Ida said, "He knows very well it confuses Sophie. Can you blame her, a thirteen-year-old?"

"He knows her age. He'd better set his mind right. Use his man's sense about children. Or there'll be trouble."

Sophie, dizzy with the pounding in her ears, realized her aunts suspected. She could think only how Brady had made her blush. He had lowered his voice and told Sophie once that she gave him the feeling he was as tall as the sky and as light as a sparkling feather. Sophie's gaze had darted away when he looked at her full on. Bewildered and thrilled, she was on the point of running off somewhere. But she hung around long enough to overhear him ask the men if they knew that story of "a small slip of a spring bird untried by fall's most piercing weather." The men had laughed so loud that the aunts, scowling, came in early with the sandwiches and tea.

Sophie had wanted to ask her mother what was funny. But she knew better. Her mother and the aunts were forever on the lookout for oddities in men raised at boarding school. Anyway, her mother didn't much like Brady. She said he lacked courtesy. The aunts had nodded their approval when her mother said that Brady was living proof that it was hard to have manners when you lived in town and wore top clothes. Sophie was put out by the sarcasm. Her mother's opinions drove a wedge between them.

Sophie decided to keep things secret. In fact, she began to notice all the more how Brady leaned in doorways. His poses easily read come here. Then, satisfied at having set Sophie's cheeks ablaze, Brady would rejoin his buddies at the table. He bragged for her benefit, it seemed. He talked loudly about his life out in the world, describing exploits that were meant also to amuse the aunts, busy at their tasks. Sophie, curious about what people did out in the world, listened hard. She heard him say, for instance, that when he was a temporary farmhand, he had once over greased a farmer's tractor to the point that it "blubbed black tears as it went chug-a-lugging across the fields coughing and spitting like a souse." Or take another time when, as an elevator operator, he jerk-stopped a department store lift to see old ladies and fatties bob like corks in water. According to Brady, his funniest time had to be as an orderly, when he upset other hospital workers by causing little accidents to happen around them—like their reaching for a puking pan and, instead, grabbing a substituted bedpan.

As Brady talked on, Sophie and of course the aunts who spoke of it, noticed that sometimes, in mid-sentence, Brady's face would drain of colour. He would sit there, a stalled car, staring fixedly, waiting for someone to fill him up. Poor Adeline, whenever he turned her way, would grow anxious, her hands fluttering like birds. Her gaze rose and fell. It generally began to seem at the moment, that Adeline was the problem. This calmed Brady. Then, with his liveliness won back at her expense, he'd supply his pals with a new round of remarks that sent them into spasms. Sophie loved the sound of Brady's laugh. But the aunts, not in the least like-minded, said that as soon as he took a pull on the bottle, he didn't need Adeline anymore—or anyone else, for that matter.

Sophie hated to think that Brady might be too upset to notice her at the graveyard. Lying in bed in the strangeness of the morning, the image of Adeline's final hour seemed lodged in her head. The pale wintry light held Sophie captive to the twists and turns of thoughts and feelings about Adeline and the baby. If only Brady might shine there forever instead.

It was still too early to rise. Sophie went over another part of the terrible event. Her father had come in from putting the team away. He said that the search for mother and child had turned into a nightmare. The radiator in Sam Laval's truck had frozen solid, so the motor would not turn over. The men trudged on foot to the nearest farm to borrow a team. The horses, harnessed and hitched to a sleigh, struggled to breathe in the searing air. Icicles clinked from their muzzles. "It had to be forty below. And Brady! Drunk, when we got to him. He said Adeline took off in the dark in her summer dress and light coat. He said he thought the baby was wrapped up good and tight, though, but couldn't say for sure."

"He kicked her out?"

Sophie flinched at her mother's ill-founded notion.

Her father flicked a live cigarette butt into the stove. "Brady said Adeline got all upset over nothing. Said she had complained about his buddies keeping the baby awake. Said she ran up the road in a blizzard in the dark, and wouldn't stop when he called to her. Said he didn't chase after her—what with his buddies waiting. Said he thought the wind and cold would force Adeline back. But now, he goes and passes out and doesn't miss her till morning. Oh yes, people say he kicked her around, all right. She ended up black and blue many a time. So they say."

Sophie wanted to ask who they were. People always made things up. They lied to make things worse. But her father, impatient at the best of times, would more than oppose anything that might sound like a defence of Brady. At breakfast she held her silence as her parents discussed funeral arrangements. Then, without any warning, Sophie's mother asked the worst possible question anyone could possibly ask. "What did they look like when they were found?"

Sophie tried to plug her ears. Her father pushed his bannock away.

"Sam was the first to spot the haystack. The magpies were dipping down, again and again, so we kind of knew. We readied ourselves—but you can't, not really. The birds ate the eyes out. The sockets were snowed in, like they were blind. They looked like that Madonna statue down at the Mission. Stone cold."

Sophie froze. She pressed her fingers to her eyelids to feel more than empty holes.

"We figured how it went," her father said. "Adeline tried to dig a small cave in the side of the stack. But then the hay was cased in ice from the melt and the sudden freeze the day before. It'd be impossible to dig there with bare hands. She tried setting fire to the hay. But her matches, only four, ran out. A kind of dug-out space in the haystack was charred at one end. Burnt matchsticks lay in there."

Sophie watched her father struggle to drink his tea.

"And the baby?" Sophie's mother leaned back in her chair, hands to her chest.

"The baby was tucked inside her mom's coat, face out. Christ Almighty!"

Tears slid down Sophie's mother's face. "At Christmas time!"

"Sam's going to take Brady to town to make a report for the RCMP. I said I'd go along to help with the arrangements."

Sophie's heart did a flip at the mention of Brady's name, despite everything. Brady in the vicinity! The image of his soft gaze shone in her mind.

"One more baby lost," her mother said, standing to clear the table.

Now, sitting in bed, Sophie peered into the dawn. Falling snow crystals had feathered the barn's roof and covered the poplars across the yard in a white furry mantle, edged with a soft trim of light. It was going to be a grey day, the kind that calmed. She heard her parents stir. Her father was starting the fire in the kitchen and in the big room. The scent of burning wood began filling the air. A clatter of kettle and pot lids grew as her mother began the porridge and tea. Sophie felt sad.

She felt robbed, too. Nothing, aside from the crackling fire in the stove, hinted at Christmas. Yet this was to be the best one. All of Kokum's Steven's family would be together this year, soldier-sons back from overseas and the little kids home from boarding school. It pained Sophie to think how a funeral stopped everything. She'd miss that sparkling feeling that came with wreaths of steam rising off newly scrubbed floors and the unmistakable lye soap and Javex scent. The feeling came also in a last scrub, soapsuds sliding down arms and hands before visitors arrived. She looked forward to hearing her mother join Gene Autry in singing "Here Comes Santa Claus" on the radio, while rolling out the cinnamon dough. Not to mention the two little boys certain to come to the door, boots squeaking on the doorstep, noses red, to borrow "sugar and lard until next week."

Sighing, she looked across the yard at the wash on the clothesline. There wouldn't be time to haul in the shirts and long johns, frozen stiff overnight. She liked to stand them on end like boards on the kitchen table to watch their comical collapse.

"Sophie, hurry and help get ready!"

Sophie jumped at her mother's impatient tone. As she pulled on her clothes, her mind fell to thoughts of Brady. Before the bad news she had daydreamed of the possibility of his coming to visit on Christmas Eve and maybe even sleeping over, should the weather turn bad. Of course, he would be joining relatives from Sakimay who usually brought raisin pies, and the family friends from Ochapowace, who would be bringing their marble and spice cakes. Brady would like that. But now her hopes were dashed. The day ahead looked dull and gloomy. Even the canned beets and mixed pickles in mustard in sealers on the kitchen windowsill held back.

Sophie yanked on hated woolen stockings and pulled on her one good plaid blue dress over her head. She then set to work making the beds.

Breakfast over, her father zipped up his parka and went outside to check over the truck and to split billets for the night's firewood. He said that if the weather held and roads didn't blow in, the funeral could be over by four o'clock. He said it was good how people agreed that it would show disrespect to put the burial off until Boxing Day. The minister from town planned to come for service on Christmas Eve. They could not ask him to leave his family twice. When her father shut the door behind him, an icy gust shunted into the kitchen.

"For heaven's sake, Sophie! Why are you in a dress? Put on your slacks. You'll freeze to death waiting outside for who knows how long!" But Sophie didn't mind suffering for Brady. "I'll change later," she fibbed, knowing adult minds would be occupied. Besides, "later" didn't have to mean today, should her mother see that she hadn't worn slacks, as told. Anyway, Sophie didn't care if she got caught and was belted for deceitfulness. She would take it without complaint—a painful belting or not, anything for Brady.

After chores Sophie's father came in to warm up. He blew on his hands and stamped his feet. "Sam will be on his way back from town by now. He might be at the agency already. They're trying to get word to Brady that the funeral is today. Bastard took off. Left for the city. That leaves Sam and me to look after the whole thing."

Sophie wished to hurl a question or two at her surly father. Why couldn't Brady leave, if he wanted? He was the one suffering! Anyway, people always left big decisions to Sam Laval because he was old. Besides, Sam and her father usually solved the big problems together. So why take it out on Brady?

Her father moved closer to the stove. "Nobody came from town to help dig the grave. Brady's friends can't be found anywhere. Ended up some of our boys took turns last night, with our one good shovel and a couple of lanterns. It's ready."

"Whose boys?"

"The Crowes, mainly—Ronnie, Jimmy, and Brady's cousin, Goody. And the young Smoker kid."

"Whereabouts?"

"Just behind the church, the far corner facing the road. We'll bury them together there."

"Does the minister know he'll need to stay longer?" Sophie's mother poured tea. Her father placed his boots almost touching the stove. The sight of steam rising off them made Sophie shiver. Her father said, "We asked the Indian agent to get word to the reverend. He said not to hold out hope because people are trying to have a Christmas, and the weather is another thing."

"Oh dear! I hope not!"

"I know."

It turned out to be true. Sophie's family got to the church at one o'clock. Those arriving early said they had found the door locked and no minister. Sophie was disheartened. She wanted to hear the hymns and the carols. The minister always told people that he heard no finer voices than former boarding school singers like her parents. It was approaching two o'clock. People began gathering in the yard behind the church. Sophie eyed the mound of mud and snow lying close to the fence. A grave, she knew, had been dug there.

Adeline's relatives stood near it. They looked drained of life. Adeline's aunt, Eva Moose, a wide-hipped woman with long shiny hair, told Sophie's mother that they'd started out the day before, early, and travelled late through the night. "Anybody seen Brady?" She scanned the yard full of people. Sophie's mother shook her head. "Oh my," said Eva Moose, holding a hand to her heart, "he sent word, you know. Said he was going to bring her and the baby home for Christmas. 'Tell them not to worry' is what they said he said."

Sophie noticed that her mother spoke not a single word on Brady's behalf. Sophie was livid. That was unfair! How was Adeline's aunt to learn the truth about how Brady's friends got him drunk, for instance? Why hold this part back? Sophie's eyes probed sleighs and trucks stationed along the barbed wire fence in front of the church. Brady was nowhere in them.

Out in the cold wind whipping past the church, Sophie's father and Sam Laval conferred. They had waited, but now it was time. It was plain the minister wasn't going to make it and, by the look of it, neither was Brady. Sophie's father, face drawn, went to stand on the tamped-down part of the mound beside the grave. He announced service would commence. He asked that all present join in the Lord's Prayer. He said that Sam Laval would be the one to commend the souls of the deceased to God in heaven. The service would close with everybody singing the hymn "Abide with Me."

"As we sing, we'll lower the coffin and pay our respects."

People began to cry aloud. Those who found their speaking voice joined in the Lord's Prayer. Sophie looked out toward the snowy road. Her eyes followed a grey horizon dimly backlighting a cross-hatch of bare trees welded to a frozen ground and leaden sky. Sophie didn't want there to be magpies. She blinked hard. She shivered.

Sam Laval, in a red and navy checked mackinaw, stepped forward so that all might see him. He removed his flap-eared cap, the wind ruffling his white hair. He made a short speech, saying that life was beautiful, as beautiful as the life of a young mother and her baby. "These are gifts to us," he said. "May memory of them keep well our heart."

Sophie scanned the road once more. Her father had begun the singing of the hymn, voice quavering. She could not sing, so only moved her lips. Reserve boys, pallbearers now, approached the coffin, raised it, and carried it to the edge of the grave. The moment they began these motions, mourners' voices rose up in singing the hymn— help of the helpless, Lord, abide ... At that brief interval, as Sophie's eyes fell between eternal light and death's darkness, Brady pulled into the yard. Her heart leapt like a startled bird. Brady stumbled across the snow-filled graveyard in a suit and tie and no overcoat.

Sobbing brokenly, he called, "No, no!" He waved his arms. The pallbearers, uncertain, stopped the lowering of the coffin. But Old Sam nodded to continue. As they let the coffin down, Brady fell near to full collapse at the edge of the grave. Eva Moose and family struggled to get him to his feet, to hold him upright, his terrible sobs ringing out, dark suit jacket pulled off to one side. Brady's agonized cries joined a font of voices finishing the hymn.

Sophie wanted the real Brady—not this crazed person who slumped like a pair of long johns thawed right off the line. She grew frantic with the feeling she might hate him. She wanted, instead, to be mad at him and to not feel this awful tearing in her chest. She knew she ought to cry, to join the others in grief, but she didn't know how to start. And there was the baby to bury.

A Sudden Fall

FIFTEEN-YEAR-OLD SOPHIE ran up the steps of the bus, anxious for home. Spotting a row of empty seats, she dove into the one nearest the window. Now for that final goodbye to Mr. Garwin. Head of the host family, he had forgiven her, it seemed, for locking him in the chicken coop. The thought made her feel less weighed down.

It had been a granite-stone of guilt she had shouldered—this for having worn too bright a red lipstick on the night of the year-end high school dance. The brightness was what did it, what made Mr. Garwin forget himself. She had arrived back at her boarding home, close to midnight. He had waited up while the rest of the family had gone to bed, and when she passed by on her way upstairs, he stepped out of the shadows and grabbed her around the waist. Without warning, he slammed a scrub brush of a mouth onto hers. He had leapt out of the shadows at the base of the stair, pulling her tight against him. At the same time he rubbed a sausage link against her thigh.

She yelled, "Quit!" An image of a bull flashed across her mind. Mr. Garwin had reeled backwards, whisper-calling, "Sophie!" as she fled up the stairs, her heart pounding.

Next morning at breakfast, he sent soft gazes across the table at her until she didn't know where to look. Then, with a self-satisfied slurp of coffee, he announced that he needed help cleaning the chicken coop right after breakfast. And before Sophie could beat a retreat, Mrs. Garwin smiled over her cup of coffee, saying, "How thoughtful of you, Sophie."

We'll see rang in Sophie's head.

Sure enough, out in the yard, in the bright sunlight ahead of her, strode Mr. Garwin, confident that she would follow him. Sophie knew she had no choice. She was alone, a boarder, a Native girl, and far from anywhere. He was the head of his family and got away with things.

Without realizing it at first, an idea for his punishment formed in Sophie's mind. Mr. Garwin had yet to say a word to her. He acted instead as if he had just kicked an obedient but deserving dog. Straight up to the dimly lit chicken coop he tramped—not once turning around to explain or to apologize. The second he stepped into the coop, Sophie banged the door shut behind him and slid the bolt into the lock. The screech and clunk of metal on metal thrilled her. Captive in his henhouse, with only a small grimy window to see out of and, unavoidably, up to his nostrils in a funk of feathers drowning in a ripe soup of rooster skitter, he cried out like a child, "Please, let me out! Oh, please! Please open the door, Sophie!"

And so, after a minute or more—if anyone was counting—she undid the lock and walked back to the house.

After a day of confused silence upstairs in her room, a question rolled in her head: Is this a good man playing bad or a bad man playing good? It was nearing suppertime, but nausea kept jerking at her gut. A half-hour later, someone tapped at the door. In came Mr. Garwin. He sat on the edge of the bed where Sophie lay curled up, her jacket pulled over her head—the family downstairs at supper. He said he had been stupid and that he was sorry, and that he would never do such a thing again. Sophie finally peeked out from under her jacket to see if he meant it, and he did, and so that was that.

But the rest of June felt as if she carried a different kind of heaviness. The naughty-but-innocent playfulness that Mrs. Garwin and the church ladies and daughters usually pretended around men could only get worse, Sophie knew. And were she to say anything, it would be her word against his, a man behind a curtain of floral dresses turned mean. There was no one to tell—although, she thought, maybe Kokum.

So now, there he stood, at the side of the bus that bright end-of-June day, face scrape-shaved to beet red. He waved up at her, a dried-out stook in a hot wind. She thought him pitiful, and pitiless. But she breathed deeply now.

The motor thrummed through her sandals, massaging the soles of her feet. Leaning back, she nestled her shoulders into the warmth. At this very moment, she was engulfed in an old feeling of lonesomeness. Or was it just aloneness? For certain, it was goodbye to the farm and the barnyard: to the life of cows ruminating like contented old aunts, of squealing piglets shouldering one another in a fast race to the trough, and of the comically muttering chickens. As for school, it was the end of drama, plays, and festivals, and of ball games, with pals packed into idling cars acting as if in a movie, the sounds and motion roomy in the mind. There would be no more fowl suppers of turkey, gravy, and cranberry sauce, and no more singing in the church and school choirs. Here was the end of the Bible study group, when people talked awkwardly and didn't look at one another straight on. She would miss the family's Sunday dinners, too, when the teacher or the minister sat and discussed people whose oddities might curl your hair. Not to forget the times she secretly listened in on the community telephone line when adults, even if married, planned dates with one another. And there was the incredible view of long grain fields and tall trees bathed in light, where the girls went on picnics along the banks of the Saskatchewan River. One time, walking along the sandbars before heading home, the four girls had stopped to inspect a naked female figure with sand-moulded long legs, bare crotch, and huge pointy breasts. No, this hadn't been done by teenagers, the older girls insisted, but by a man. Then, another time, one of the girls and Sophie, on a dare, had stopped on the way home to tease a bull, only to find themselves tripping, screeching, and fleeing its charging bulk, knees all wobbly, bodies shaking, finally falling into the car full of screaming companions.

Sophie wondered where all this was to go now.

A letter arrived from her mother, she insisted it was time for Sophie to come home. With her mother sick, Sophie had to help look after the kids. Tony, her older brother, had joined the Air Force and was off for training in Coldwater, Alberta, and so now her father needed help around the barn. Guilt and desolation descended like a long, dark, heavy rain. Her stomach had practically turned over. The return of the all-but-forgotten ashes-in-the-mouth taste signalled captivity. She reached into the shoulder bag on her lap, thinking to put the letter back into its envelope. Instead her fingers touched the cool edge of a small white plastic purse. It was a gift from Mrs. Garwin, who had said, "You'll find use for it, I'm sure."

When she held the purse against the light of the bus's windowpane, it practically shone. Sprinkled with rubies and other gems—not for real, she knew, but still—the purse looked very rich with its sparkling rose and green curved vine. What's more, only as long as the length of her hand, the purse held twelve whole dollars, earned and saved. Sophie tugged at the thick zipper and recounted the money. She would hand over each and every dollar to her father as a gift, while her mother, standing to the side, beamed.

But damp palms rubbing against her slacks signalled mounting dread. Nothing could budge the sick feeling. Having been ten months away from home could mean that her family's opinion of her had improved. Besides, she had things to tell now, it pleased her to think.

What about the principal's having praised her grades? Would her mother's face light up at seeing her? Perhaps her little brothers and sister would spill out of the house, happy as little ponies. Or might they stand in a tight knot, refusing to run up and greet her? Would her father's angry outbursts have stopped?

Her mind drifted to beginnings and endings that dogged the story of who she was, and who she would rather be. Still, a protective dome often came down over her, a place wherein she could ignore all kinds of sad evidence, like the steady motion of the bus carrying her non-stop to its destination.

Away from home and on her own, she often felt shunted onto a stage under harsh lights, like an actor having been given the wrong lines and forced to speak through a loudspeaker to an audience that never warmed to her. Yet, of the characters she portrayed—whether school girl, farm girl, smart girl, or even well-off girl—each was met by the blank stare of a poker-faced audience. To add to her strain, there was the miscue: for one, Kokum's unbidden manifestations. Her grandmother's visitations often took Sophie by surprise. Sometimes the spectral sightings were so real they took up space in a kind of peripheral vision. Even now on the bus, Kokum blazed, bronze fingers plaiting sweetgrass.

Back at the bus depot earlier, the stink of cigarette smoke and burning motor oil assailed her nose. Mr. Garwin had led her past a brew of hair cream and lotion rising off the people who sat waiting in metal chairs. She hated stares. Sophie got into character. This time she would be an accomplished girl, a girl off to visit a wealthy aunt, a tall lady with gingery hair who called her "dear." She decided that she would act the day's scene out with Mr. Garwin as her uncle, since he had insisted on seeing her off. But then again, Mr. Garwin had just rushed goofily onto centre stage, confused. He stood in the middle of the bus station, his arms flailing and craning his neck. Strangers hurried to his aid. "The ticket agent is that way. You've an hour to kill.

Grab a coffee, why don't you?"

'First look, then move,' Kokum had said. The auditory hallucination caught Sophie off guard. She turned red. She momentarily lost her grip on her act. It seemed she could not escape reacting to the phantom presence, even though Kokum was more than two hundred miles away.

She revised the scene. Mr. Garwin, in farmer's garb or not, would be her chauffeur. Instantly she felt safer. Sophie might more easily now accept his offer of a soft drink, too. In line at the counter, she asked for an Orange Crush, please, and did her best to avoid the twinkling eyes of the Chinese Canadian at the till. But Mr. Garwin had not calmed down. He juggled dimes and quarters and a handful of rumpled bills as he paid for the foil-wrapped candies, Spearmint gum, Lifesavers, and a coffee. She knew from reading books that she ought not to be seen conversing with her chauffeur, and so she felt quite relieved when Mr. Garwin finally sat down at a table. From there, he gawked at other waiting passengers.

Despite the scene, Sophie spotted Kokum, stage left.

In fact, at that moment, with the bus roaring along, Kokum sat across the aisle from her. Each time the engine whined to a stop in a town, Sophie would force her mind back to the here and now, surprised to see the seat empty. Passengers boarded or left the bus, faces pouring sweat from standing out in the boiling sun, or dried to parchment from waiting indoors, fans blowing. At this stop, a student with an armful of books stepped off. A stocky farmer in overalls climbed aboard, embarrassed that his frail mother scolded him for letting go of her arm too soon. People held newspapers, soft drinks, chocolate bars, and packets of Chiclets. Sophie knew to hang on to her twelve dollars all the harder.

The hours wore on. Outside, golden evening light painted bands of sage and lavender across rows and rows of fallow. The sun's lengthening rays parlayed the bus's rectangular shadow against the furrowed field, tossing Guernica like discs and shafts into the air. A wave of loneliness thrummed in Sophie's chest. It was a shock for her to realize that she had not seen her grandmother in the flesh for almost three years.

Memories sprang up in what might pass for old curtain calls. Summoning up Kokum's wrinkled face, dark gleaming eyes, and the thinness of her build in a long black coat, Sophie began hunting in her bag for anything to stop an incoming memory: a small girl and her grandmother are in town, walking by a group of church women and farmers' wives on Main Street. Cold stares pummel Kokum's bowed head. Sophie jerked the curtain shut.

She realized that some things are worse than being poor. Danger lurked on stage right, stage left, backstage, and centre stage. But she had been lucky. She hoped her luck would stay. It might, if nothing gave her away.

A cool, vapoury peppermint took her back to that first day she arrived on the Garwin farm. It had grown past two o'clock in the afternoon, and they were at the final turnoff in the road. She became excited, as a tall white farmhouse flickered into view on the other side of a straight line of trees.

After she was shown upstairs to unpack, she placed on the bed beside her a pair of handmade sugar-bag panties, a pair of navy slacks, and a white loop-knit cardigan. No socks, she now realized, and no comb, no extra shoes, no toothbrush, and definitely no coat. Yet out on the open highway, riding in the Buick beside the jubilant reverend who had driven her here, she had thought only about how the miles took her away to a new life. She had felt that she lacked for nothing.

Sitting on the bed in the strange house, she was stunned. Had she been asleep? She recalled that back at home, she had desperately wanted help. She had no idea where stuff on the inside of the house was kept, since she was the one who did the outside chores. What went with what, and what was even hers to take? She had no idea what a girl ought to have with her when she left home. That morning her mother had lain silently on her bed. Leta, her younger sister, was nowhere to be found. A wall of dead air, with the clock ticking, forced Sophie to take matters into her own hands. She hurriedly packed a change of clothes.

Now she stared at her carton, emptied on the bed. She pulled her stomach muscles into a painful knot to stop the rising panic, her head and hair breaking into a sweat. After all, this was the room she would be sharing with her host family's younger daughter, she had been told. A clothes closet at the foot of the other twin bed was packed to the brim with the girl's slips, crinolines, skirts, dress slacks, dresses, and blouses. Pretty jars of cream and bottles of lotion stood on the night table beside the other bed.

There was no way not to tell Mrs. Garwin, waiting downstairs. The daughter, a tall teenager with strawberry-blonde pigtails, would soon learn Sophie owned no blouse, besides the one she had on underneath the oversize cardigan thrown about her shoulders. But she did know one good thing: she didn't have to worry about her sick mother now, or her little brother and sister, or her father—just herself. This meant the world had flung open the door and she could run into it, arms wide open. Startled, she caught a glimpse of Kokum fading into the ivory lace curtain at the window overlooking the yard. Sophie got to her feet, tossing her predicament aside.

Downstairs, Mrs. Garwin listened to Sophie's itemization. Sophie heard herself say, "All the same, I need very little, if anything, ever."

Mrs. Garwin was in possession of some new information. She had received a government statement in the mail, she said, and now understood that payment for Sophie's room and board barely covered costs. It certainly didn't cover school clothes. "I'll try to make the money stretch, however, and buy some fabric to sew you a blouse," she had said. It surprised Sophie to see how easy it all seemed. On the reserve, buying anything meant months and months of no, and no, for the last time. The Garwins gathered round, looking at her. Their faces showed they had been momentarily spooked. But here was relief. A fire stamped out.

The bus ground to a stop. A young woman climbed down, clutching three large parcels to her chest. Chin up, she crossed the highway and got into an idling truck waiting for her. The rusted vehicle was driven by a young farmer, smoke curling from a cigarette in his mouth, his hands on the wheel. Sophie was glad the young woman had not run across the highway's danger zone, although Sophie would rather be struck broadside by a truck than have any onlooker take her for a coward. New people climbed on board. This time, three frail old people, pale, unsteady, and thin-boned, gradually made their way to their seats. A farm couple stepped up next, a heavyset man with a boy's face; his wife, wistful. As the shadow of the bus lengthened, Sophie grew anxious. Would Uncle Regis be waiting at the stop, as stated in her mother's letter? Would she have reminded him? Sophie might find herself alone at the side of the highway in the dark, strangers eying her as they slowed to look.

She retreated into memories of Kokum during the years Sophie's father was away at war. Often she and her mother and siblings stayed overnight at Kokum's, where up to ten people or more found a place to sleep on any given night. Sophie's mother and children always got the tiny room upstairs with a mattress on the floor under a small window. Sophie loved looking out, elbows on the windowsill, watching ducks spin in tight turns and counter-turns below on the slough's glassy surface.

Checking the vacated seat across the aisle from her, she thought about how Kokum never scolded her. She could not think of a single time. But if her face got that blank look, Sophie knew...

Twelve miles to the bus stop home!

Finally Sophie was diving into the back of Uncle Regis's truck. She had already taken the time to pack down any feelings and had asked to sit in the back under a star lit sky. But she realized now that she had eaten but a single peppermint and soda pop that morning, yet felt no hunger or thirst. Dusk had turned the horizon blood red. Uncle Regis warned that her thin loop sweater wouldn't do, as it would be a chilly ride home. Sophie insisted she'd be fine, but then accepted his big plaid mackinaw. Tucked in behind the cab, she tried to guard her head against the wind that spun long hair into knots. The truck's jouncing, bone-breaking ride over rocks and holes in the gravel road was nothing like riding a galloping horse, a real horse that Sophie knew she would ride again in the coming days, breeze brushing her temples. Chances were, she'd be the one to chop wood and haul water, with Tony gone. She would also be the one to milk the cow and haul manure out of the barn, her eye-rims on fire, her nose numb with ammonia rising off the barn floor.

She tried not to think of her father's bouts of rage, or the countless times he had threatened to give her a belting across her arms and legs, drunk or not. She supposed she would have bruises and welts again, some time or another. She hoped not. Sophie remembered the first month or so when her father came home from the war, and how he had made them laugh. He did funny things, like ride a cow backwards across the yard for Uncle Regis's camera. But the laughter had long since drained away.

But then, all kinds of fears stalked her, like her mother's attacks of arthritis and those sudden nosebleeds.

Sophie tried to think of good things. She had grown taller. She owned a purse. She had money to give. Tears scalded her eyes—yes, she thought, and I will be back at school in no time. She tucked her feet under and pulled her uncle's mackinaw around her. Stars glittered in a pitch-black sky.

The drab familiarity of home reclaimed every space in her mind once she climbed down from the truck. She dodged her feelings, blocked mental getaways so that she might stay sharp. A throw-up feeling rolled in. But half-formed scenes began—make-believe props that made life lovely: lace-edged serviettes and tea in a cup, instead of in a jam can.

When she went inside, clearly no one wished to hear about her adventure. They forgot she might be hungry, the supper dishes having been put away. But Sophie had something up her sleeve. It made her smile. The cold in her feet and hands had not emptied her mind completely. Instead, a mental tableau popped up, showing her family inside a frame of red velvet curtains, celebrating. She had a card to play. In this scene she handed twelve dollars to her father. But first she would secretly place the purse on the kitchen table. She imagined the exact spot, too, on the stage, where her mother would cross and discover the purse. Sophie could hear the words she had practised saying: Dad, here is the sum total of my earnings. This is for you. Use it as you please.

But that night another reality intervened. The dogs barked. She and her siblings rushed to the kitchen window. Headlights jostled on the dark horizon. Finally a car lurched into the yard and stopped. Sophie's heart skipped a beat. Now she would see Kokum for real.

"Open the door, Sophie." Sophie's mother put the kettle on.

Her father, avoiding speaking directly to his mother-in-law as custom required, disappeared into the adjoining bedroom. Sophie's mother struggled to turn up the wick of the coal oil lamp atop the stove's small shelf.

The door opened.

Sophie held her breath. In the dim light, the visitors crowded in. Sophie saw their shadows on the wall; one stretched near to the ceiling, and the other was so tall it reminded Sophie of a sheet of foolscap creased down the middle. Finally, a stooped little figure came in. Solemn handshakes were exchanged. Kokum had shrunk, Sophie saw, but was dressed as always: black scarf wound round her head, long black coat, and torn canvas shoes. Kokum glanced briefly at Sophie, a spark of flint by lamplight. Sophie went to shake her hand. And in that glad moment, Sophie felt noticed for real.

Two young men stood in the doorway to the bedroom, joking with Sophie's father. They called him Old Bugger, and he called them worse. Curious, Sophie slid along the wall for a closer look. Dark eyes briefly held hers. Tar and gasoline fumes filled the room. The Lynx boys, Slim and Rodney. Their father had a home business, Slim-Rod's Auto Wrecking, where the sons used to work, and likely still did. They had grown tall. Their fingers were blackened with axle grease. Sophie could smell the stale odour of liquor, too. She backed away, wondering why Kokum was in their company at all.

"Where did Kokum go?" Sophie had not seen her leave.

"Maybe out to the closet, how should I know?"

Sophie's mother had used the word "closet" instead of "toilet." An outdoor closet, then, Sophie decided.

She asked no further. She wished to hang onto a good mood for when she handed the money to her father. The door creaked open. Moonlight streaming in cast Kokum's shadow onto the floor ahead of her. A draft of chilly air followed. Shivers gripped Sophie and a wave of fatigue descended upon her. Kokum drank the tea, but refused the bannock and salted lard. She made motions to leave. Sophie's mother alerted the young men. The Lynx boys, prompt and agile, thanked their hosts. Yup, they'd take the old lady straight home. The lamplight made a juggernaut of shadows that slipped across the floor and fled along the wall as the door closed on the moon. Sophie heard a Lynx call out from the dark, "We'll stay and eat next time, though, okay?"

Good-byes rang out like falling coins. The din of barking dogs died down as car doors slammed and night swallowed the car.

Light-headedness gripped Sophie. She thought to lie down, but agitation had overtaken her. Her mother blew out the coal oil lamp. Flickering lights from the stove lit a path for the children who went to their sleeping spots on one of four beds in the cramped bedroom of the tiny lean-to. Sophie looked around. Where was she to sleep?

"There." Her mother pointed to an open space beside the baby, a tiny, snarling motor idling under a puke-smelling patchwork quilt.

Sophie lay down in her clothes. She knew she ought to change out of the things she had travelled in, but into what? And where? Her carton didn't hold the pajamas she had borrowed from Lucy Garwin all last year. She lay listening to her real family summon a common sleep.

A dark bend in a road drew a picture in Sophie's mind. Almost drowning with fatigue, she realized that she hadn't exchanged a single word with Kokum. She didn't know even the Cree words for 'so good to see you.' Tears choked her. She needed to think before yielding to the pull of sleep. Then it struck her. Like a splash of icy water. She hadn't seen her purse! She sprang to her feet and ran into the kitchen, eyes sweeping the room—one, two, three. She hadn't realized that she had cried out.

Her mother, annoyed, stood beside her. "What's the matter now?"

"My purse! It's gone! They've taken it, Mom!"

Her mother was pale in the moonlight. "What did you say? You probably lost it! Or maybe you're just saying there's a purse."

"No! I left it on the table with money in it."

"Money?" Her mother stood still. "What money?"

"My money!"

"Your money! Where would you get a purse and money?"

"From the Garwins, Mom! It's twelve dollars I worked for! I saved it."

"Well, it's probably around someplace. Leave it till morning. You can look for it then. Get to bed!"

"But, Mom!"

"Get to bed. Don't make trouble. If it's gone, it's gone. No use getting Dad upset. Wait till morning."

Sophie relented. Her mother crawled into bed and fell asleep, snores recalling a lifetime. Sophie tried, but couldn't wait. She hadn't been to the closet yet. She tiptoed outdoors.

The night was crisp and beautiful. She inhaled the air. Soft, whining yelps of the dogs quieted down as she patted their heads. No hum from farm motors, no town lights vying for space in the night sky. Moonlight bordering the yard also carved a bright outline along the treetops. Frogs and crickets rounded out a basin of sound. No bears, skunks, or porcupines crossed her path, certainly not with the dogs at her side. After visiting the closet, she made her way back to the house. Surely, she thought, the purse had fallen under the table. Maybe it got kicked aside by accident. But wait, now—this setting, this quiet night proved too enthralling to pass up. In a twinkling, Sophie became a lady of means out on her grounds after dark. Her path was lined with a curve of moss sprinkled with dew, right there, along the base of an ancient stone wall where a cobblestone footpath lay between two wide lawns.

Then she spotted it: something—what?—familiar. A tiny white casket of a thing lying in the grass lit by the moon. She bent to see, heart quaking.

It was the purse, its zipper ripped apart. She shook it, turning it every which way. The money was gone. Gulping down silent screams and knowing better than to call her mother, she stumbled into the house on shaky legs.

She lay on the bed, quivering. Throughout the torment of the night, an owl hooted and coyotes wailed a hymn that expanded the space between the hills leading into the valley. She tossed and turned. Her mind sculpted a reprieve as fatigue and nausea rolled over her. She fell into a half-sleep where a dream pulled her, finally, onto a winding road toward Kokum.

The two ride horses, side by side. As Sophie rides, she also keeps watch. Kokum, in a black dress and black scarf over her eyes, rides a pony painted blue with white polka dots. Sophie finds herself riding sidesaddle in a long, green velvet dress trimmed in pale gold cord. It billows round her as she glides through an aureole of golden coins and falling leaves. Kokum gallops on ahead, her horse gathering speed over the rugged terrain. Her white moccasins, covered in red and green gems, cast an eerie glimmer. Meanwhile Sophie hurtles headlong toward a glassy lake, its reflective light pulsing where the sky assembles a torn, voluminous cloud. As Kokum dissolves into the dark, Sophie senses that she cannot avert a sudden fall.

Something Ahead in the Road

HAD SOPHIE AND HER PARENTS known of the coming danger, she might have been safe at home. But instead of dancing, there would be marching. At gunpoint.

Sophie's parents, Len and Sarah Stevens, had kept a sharp eye out for bad weather. The red sunrise had raised confidence in a bright, clear day. That is how it came to be that Sophie accompanied Stanley, her father's trusted driver, on a trip to the town of Broadview, twelve miles away, to pick up the sleighful of New Year's Eve revellers. Sophie was to take family greetings and two raisin pies to Old Sadie, who lived alone on the southern tip of the reserve, a mile off the main road near town.

The trip into town had been uneventful, but on the way back, blowing snow made Sophie nervous. The shrouded moon yielded a pale shifting light as shards of swirling snow whistled in the road. Stanley, cracking silly jokes, did his best to convince his passengers that all was safe. Sophie felt anything but, seated as she was in the back corner of the creaking sleigh, motionless as an owl.

Earlier in town, under the street lamps that shed a blue-green light,

Sophie watched exposed necks and eyelids flinch with pelting needles of sleet. The party goers, noisy with humour and exclamations, tamped down the straw on the sleigh's floor, a couple of the men stepping pow-wow style. An old blanket, old coats, and jackets were spread on top for seating.

Sophie recalled her mother's excitement during the preparations. This past week pies, cakes, and jars of pickles and preserves had appeared in the cupboard and on the windowsill in the kitchen. As her mother worked, she reminded her father again that she and the other women, most of them wartime grass widows, had gone without music and dancing too long. Now a dream of hosting a dance for friends was coming true. In Sophie's mind, it had to be that the women and the men, huddled under covers in an open sleigh, wanted to dance as badly.

The storm had begun erasing landmarks. Thick white snow scarves slanted across the road as the company watched, opinions unvoiced. Ragged trees loomed out of the dark and slid past like ghosts.

No one had taken any special notice of Sophie. For her part, she was glad to see the adults distracted. It meant she might freely view them. For instance, she disliked Stanley, whose eye, it seemed, had rested upon her on the way into town whenever her back was turned. He had no business looking at her.

Sophie settled on thoughts about Clara's overbite. She was Alex Babineau's girlfriend. Sophie's mother had told of a time Alex had used bad medicine to capture Clara, when she turned eighteen. He had stolen a lock of her hair and snuck it off to a bad medicine man that lived in the cold bush near the Mission. That summer, in the middle of hanging her laundry out on the clothesline, Clara had begun a mindless run to Alex, barefoot, her feet cut and bleeding. Sophie shivered and pulled the blanket up under her chin, forcing herself to look at the wheezing bulk sitting across from her, Alex Babineau himself. Thankfully it was too dark to see those sunken eyes and furrowed cheeks. Turning her head, she could see Clara's profile—a cat.

Off the main gravel highway, the sleigh squeaked over the snow and onto the reserve's mud road, a path the horses knew. Clara burst out laughing. "Someone just touched my bare leg this night," she said, "my left one to be exact, with a hand as cold as a frozen fish. And if that's what he's after, he'll still be without!" Laughter erupted. The Babineau boys, Alex and Norman, protesting, said that neither had arms long enough, even if cruelly stretched. The laughter went on, by turns muffled and then set free, as if the merriest among them, when facing into the wind, also turned to an invisible someone out there.

Sophie saw that Cookie, the city woman, kept to herself. It was said that Norman, her husband, spoiled her rotten, and that Cookie had grown to expect it. Sophie had also overheard Alex tell her father that Norman was out to prove he lived high on the hog, higher up than his big brother, at any rate. Alex let it be known that Norman had gotten himself a good-paying job in Regina, working on a city crew, by passing himself off as a Ukrainian; further, he kept the moustache as proof, despite Cookie's being dead set against it. Whiskers like Norman's, Alex said, called the family's heritage into question, and what did it mean for the Treaty? He had to wonder.

Tonight the storm pitched the barely visible landscape from dimmed light to utter darkness and then back again. Sophie had caught sight of Norman fingering his moustache. But when she could see again, he had stopped. He now spread a piece of tenting about him like a parachute. Soon his caramel voice rose out of the night. "I'm glad for this old-fashioned sleigh ride to Len and Sarah's. My own up-to-date Model T would have one dickens of a time roaring through such deep snow."

Clara's mocking laughter rang out. "Your Model T must be like you, a city slicker who wouldn't know a team of horses if they rang their arse in his face."

They all laughed like ten-year-olds. Cookie, however, dampened the fun, saying that she, for one, had no business out in the cold with such ignorance afoot. "I should be in my steam-heated apartment in Regina. Not stuck here with all this heaven-knows-what."

Sophie recalled her mother's having said that Cookie once visited her only to show off a permanent hair wave. Sophie's mother had seen Cookie's impatience that day. She had turned to her hostess, scolding, "Of course I wash my hair and the curls stay!" Sophie's mother, hurt, changed the subject to what steam heat must be like. She told Cookie that out on the reserve, keeping warm meant hauling in armloads of frozen billets that squeaked, sizzled, and spat in the flames. Cookie had replied, "Steam is what you either turn on or off, unless, of course, you're too ignorant."

Here in the sleigh, Cookie sat muffled in fur. Sophie had taken a good look when Cookie climbed aboard, and had glimpsed beautiful burgundy leather boots. In fact, both colour and polish had been dutifully admired by the others. The booted feet were now tucked under a roll of blankets. As for the other women, it was just their usual winter apparel: at least two summer dresses, a sweater under a man's suit jacket, and two thin sad coats over that.

Cookie dressed herself in fascinating layers, rich ones. When she and Norman visited her parents on a cold blustery day last fall, Sophie had a good excuse to sit near the stove with the guests. Cookie was wearing a grey tweed coat with a black fur collar that she had let fall around her. As the fur slid down her shoulders, a shimmery pink scarf, trimmed in fringe, slipped into view. As Cookie slowly pulled the scarf down, a free fall of blush fabric laid bare a string of pearls against a cream-coloured cardigan. Cookie undid three gleaming glass buttons on her blouse, red fingernails gleaming like kinnikinick berries. It was Cookie's perfume reaching Sophie, though, that was unforgettable—a crush of lilac, damp roses, a whisper of empty wine bottle, and faint skunk.

Sophie recalled her father's coughing fit and her mother's scolding after their guests left. Her father said that Cookie had acted like a showgirl in a mess hall, to which her mother said that since he could at least remember, he need never fear his mind betraying him. As for little Sophie, her one wish was to wear all of Cookie's clothes.

Tonight, Sophie caught a glimpse of a purple satin dress under the shining fur.

When Stanley was ready to set out for the reserve, everyone was caught off guard. The unexpected spectacle of Belle, a red-haired woman, climbing bare-legged into the sleigh, silenced them. She sang out that she, too, would attend the Stevens's dance. It was New Year's Eve, after all, she sang, and she hadn't been to a real fiddle dance since the war. No one had the presence of mind to object. Besides, she had already squeezed in next to a stung Cookie. The sleigh, practically in motion, forced cordial relations on everyone. After all, it was the season.

Sophie studied Belle. Her mother and friends often said that Belle liked men way too much, especially men who had gotten wicked ideas from overseas during the war—bad ideas like "making babies was now just a good time." The ladies had clucked, shaking their heads. They worried that Belle shared no family likeness to any of their relatives. This meant she couldn't be any of them, they said, especially since she wore tight dresses, her bare skin popping over the top of her dress, her high heels, and bare legs, year-round.

Sophie, tired from the cold and the lateness of the hour, wished to be home, and free of old conversations in her head: "Bare legs are dirty," Sophie's mother's voice says. "I, myself, can't see what's wrong with it. Belle must be happy not to have to wear rubber sealer rings to keep her stockings up," another lady replies.

The horses snuffled and snorted in their traces. Sophie imagined their muscles bunching and straining in the harness, hooves clobbering the snow drifts. Even if Stanley lost sight of the road, a hungry horse would take them home to the stable. Still, it was a comfort having a guide in the driver's seat, even if she disliked him—which was all the time, lately.

Alex's girlfriend, Clara, leaned her overbite toward Cookie's ear. In a lowered voice, she said, "Belle's got her eye on Stanley. Belle jumped into our wagon, not even asking, eh, sister-in-law?"

Cookie replied that it didn't matter to her, since she had no sister-in-law she ever knew of and didn't know Belle personally. "Add to that," she said, "as a city woman, I'm glad to see Stanley minds his own business and has the sense to keep it that way."

Failed at making a friendly exchange, Clara called out to Alex: Did he have chewing gum? He said yes, but he would have to dig for it. Norman joined in, adding that he might be able to produce a stick of Juicy Fruit, just for her.

At that moment the dark mantle of cloud overhead split as if rent in two. Bright moonlight turned the once invisible field into a band of sparkling diamonds set off by a tracery of small trees in the distance. The travellers, snug under covers, sat blinking, their solemn faces contradicting the laughter of moments before. Clara and Belle put on their widest smiles in the telling light.

"Who's looking after our driver?" The loud, smoky voice struck an odd note. It came from bare-legged Belle, of all people. She stared at Stanley's back. "Can I sit beside you, Stanley?" she called. "Poor thing up there alone on a night like this!" This was bold, Sophie knew, like her mother would say. Cookie cleared her throat loudly, reminding everyone that she, a city woman, was outraged.

But Stanley called out, "There's something ahead in the road."

Did he mean a team and sleigh, or stray cattle, or horses? Everyone craned their neck, trying to see over the side of the sleigh. A hulking shape ahead held its outline. Gradually the form loosened and split into three. The horses raised their heads, ears pricked forward. Sophie worried how a sudden noise or movement could unnerve the team and send them all plunging off the road into a field of hazards. But with ground being gained, the three odd shapes had not turned into bulls, or nasty-tempered heifers on the loose from the reserve's Indian Affairs experimental farm. Neither did a pack of coyotes stand slavering in the road. The gait of the horses and the jounce of their harness steadily closed the distance. Stanley turned to say that it seemed a child stood there, waving.

"Yup. And there's a big fella, too, and their dog, looks like," he said over his shoulder.

"Wonder what's up?" Alex spoke for them all. "Must be pretty damn near twenty below and no team, eh?"

"Pretty damn near, anyway," was Norman's city reply. Stanley pulled on the reins. Everyone stretched to see.

"Whoa!" Stanley called as one of the horses reared.

The dog hurled a volley of short barks and yips.

"Down, Sparky!" It was a child's voice.

"That you, Smoky?" Stanley held the reins tight. "What's the trouble?"

And at that moment, a tall, hefty man stepped up to the sleigh and pointed a rifle at Belle's head.

"I'll tell you what the trouble is," he growled. "You're the damned trouble! The whole damn bunch of youse. Not a goddamned soldier among youse!"

"What are you talking about, Ronnie? It's me, Stanley, your brother. What'n hell?!"

Ronnie ignored that. He wrenched the glinting barrel from Belle's head to Norman's heart. "I'm in charge! And I'm the major general! Right, Smoky?"

The young boy beside him squeaked, "Yes, sir!"

Sophie knew that something was horribly wrong. Stanley had tightened the reins at this odd reference to soldiers.

"Tell them, Smoky!" Ronnie ordered.

The thin boy, of no more than ten or so, called out, "He's the major general and he's in charge!"

"Tell them so they hear!" shouted Ronnie.

"He's the major general and he's in charge!" Young Smoky's voice cracked in the cold air.

Ronnie addressed the travellers. "Tell me I can't go to war! Tell me the army can't use me! I'll show you!" Spit flew from his lips.

Ronnie loosed a blood-curdling screech that turned moonlit faces ashen. Sophie shrank into a ball. Cries of shock and consternation were stifled in coat sleeves and covers. Ronnie's gun roamed to Alex. Stanley slipped the reins to Norman, who'd never held a team in check and clearly didn't want to now. He shook his head, hiding his hands under the folds of his parachute. But Stanley thrust the reins hard at his chin and leaped down to stand in the snow beside Ronnie. Norman took the reins.

"Come, brother." Stanley spoke in smooth, gentle tones to Ronnie, who lowered his gun for a moment. "Think of the women and kids all cold out here. And hungry, too."

But Ronnie's cry seemed to claw its way through churning guts into his lungs. He whirled around and put the gun to Stanley's head.

The horses jumped in their traces. Alex grabbed the reins. He sawed the bridle bit in the horses' jaws back and forth, bringing them to a standstill. Sophie had never heard such a cry from any human or animal. All the more frightening, Ronnie shouted at them to get the hell off the sleigh. Everyone but Sophie obeyed. She sat as still as a mouse, watching the passengers sink into the deep snow. They clung to one another in a road lashed with snowdrifts, a nearly invisible road stretching to nowhere safe.

Cookie's boots filled with snow. Belle whispered that her legs felt burning, real bad. Ronnie wobbled as he closed in struggling to hold a roaming rifle at eye level. Sophie caught a whiff of alcohol. Slowly, she heaped the blankets around her, trying to make herself appear like a pile of covers. The only movement coming from the boy and his dog were puffs of breath, rising in the air.

Knowing his younger brother, Stanley began to sing a Christmas carol. Sophie was shocked that he had even dared make a sound. His carol, softly sung, brought forth a tinge of Christmas: Angels from the realms of glory...

Stanley was singing just loud enough, it seemed, to reach the edge of Ronnie's crazed nerve centre without actually touching it off. Stop, Sophie mentally shouted to Clara, who nodded wildly and who might be stupid enough to join in. She did not. But now her man, Alex, took the opportunity to make a show of his complete and utter uselessness. He limped alongside the length of the sleigh, exaggerating what passed for a vastly shattered hip on his return. The sag of his cheeks and the drooping of his mouth signalled that he was in no shape whatsoever to endure a night of freezing cold at his age. Sophie saw at once that he cared only for himself. Not a bit for Clara, not for any of them. His hangdog posture proved that he was not worth so much as a stray bullet from so great a gun as Ronnie's. But Ronnie wasn't biting.

Norman came out with his city-crew reasoning. "This road ought to be ploughed, scraped, and cleared for traffic," he said, as though holding up a stunning example of something.

Clara's attempt at cheering laughter fell flat. She tried next to show how Ronnie was boss and she a willing slave. Her overbite was brimming with rabid smiles as she nodded and bowed. But Ronnie ignored that, too. It seemed he liked her fawning well enough. Still, Sophie felt sick at the sight of Ronnie's gun on his shoulder. It was all he needed, after all. And he had quarry.

She glanced at Smoky, a skinny boy in a man's parka past his knees. His teeth were chattering and body shaking. He appeared struggling against total collapse. It was obvious to Sophie that he and the dog were Ronnie's captives. The boy was too scared to be the ally of a madman. Ronnie, huge and weighty, was boss, no question. Sophie's stomach was a knot of terror when she realized Ronnie was bigger than his older brother. One look from Ronnie and Stanley's Christmas carol died in the night.

Sophie locked her gaze on the boy, as Ronnie pointed his gun at each adult in turn. She was desperate with horror to think she might be shot in the chest, or, worse, right in the middle of her forehead. Trying to divert a scream, Sophie focused her mind on poor little Smoky. Nothing could be worse than a helpless little kid under a monster's power. Yet there he stood, eyes shut tight.

Ronnie bellowed so loud it shattered Sophie's brain. "I want marching!" he yelled.

It was the beginning of roll call, he informed his captives. He, hereby, was giving notice that the word Private was the be all and end all. Anyone not calling him "Sir!" at the top of his lungs would be shot dead.

"Am I right, Private Clara?" Ronnie's rifle found her.

"Sir, you are so right!" Clara's overbite sputtered spittle. She'd nearly toppled at the sound of her name. She had flung an arm out, trying to catch hold of the wagon. Her smile was a death grin now.

The major general advised his troops that he wished for "proper protocol in speaking style, right up there with proper formation." He warned that there was to be silence in the ranks. "Not a peep out of any of youse. Just the sound of marching and proper answers or it will be the Lord's Prayer over youse, man or woman."

"Won't women be exempt?" Stanley asked.

A shot rang out in reply. The bullet kicked up a plug of mud and snow near Stanley's foot. The horses lunged in their traces. Beside the sleigh Alex steadied the team by jerking hard on the reins and locking his knees, his body leaning way back.

"That answer your question?" Ronnie's finger strayed to the trigger, in case.

"Yes, sir!" Stanley half-shouted. The moon glimmered on his sickened face.

Ronnie continued, "When I call you, state your name, treaty number, and regiment. Comrade Smoky, show 'em!" Ronnie cleared his throat and spat in the snow.

A high-pitched voice answered, "Private Smoky Smoker, Number 288, Regiment A1, sir!"

Ronnie laughed, pleased. He turned to his captives. "Now, the rest of youse, say it like Smokey! Step in line here, beside the sleigh."

The revellers fanned out alongside the sleigh and faced Ronnie. Norman, having long given up his treaty number to the government for a job, had none to repeat. He whispered his predicament to Alex, hanging onto the reins.

"Just listen for a number and add one," Alex whispered back.

Sophie feared for Cookie; she was enfranchised, too, like Norman. She would not be able to give a Treaty number, and she hadn't heard Alex's fix.

"You, there!" Ronnie pointed his gun at Stanley.

Stanley saluted, shouting, "Private Stanley Samuels, Number 99, Regiment A1, sir!"

Then, at Ronnie's command, Stanley marched up to Smoky and stood at attention beside the boy.

The gun barrel next found Belle. She almost jumped out of her skin. "Oh yes, sir," she cried. "Private Belle Stump from in town speaking, sir! Number Zero, Reginald A1, sir!"

Ronnie was taken aback. "Is zero a number?" he asked.

The troops answered in unison, "Yes—no!"

"It don't matter!" Ronnie yelled. "The A's have it."

At this, Ronnie broke into a spasm. He lowered his rifle. He hung onto Smoky's shoulder as a maniacal laughing fit overtook him. Sounds of strained chuckling rose from the captive troops. But Ronnie grew angry once more. He hoisted his weapon, eyes blazing.

"I need to go to the bathroom." The authority in Cookie's city voice strung ice crystals in the air.

"Who'n hell?" Ronnie stared in disbelief at Cookie. He shouted at her, "I said state your name, Treaty number, and regiment!"

"Private Constance Babineau, Number 24, A1, sir."

Sophie's heart thumped in her chest. Cookie had forgotten to say "regiment," she had managed only A1. But then, Belle had just got it wrong, too.

It was Ronnie's bidding now. "Private Cookie, you'll do ten push-ups for the misdemeanor of wrong-speaking and mispronunciation. One drop of pee and you'll do double the push-ups."

Cookie, trembling, removed her fur coat and laid it on top the snow. She sank to her knees and lay on the coat, face down. She reached both hands behind her back and pulled her dress down over her bottom. In the moonlight, the purple of the dress shone like aluminum foil from gum or cigarette wrappers. Cookie managed just one push-up, then burst into frantic sobs.

"Whazza matter, Private Cookie? Wanna get shot?"

"No, sir!" Cookie cried, her body shaking. Everyone stood in the grip of that pitiful, paralyzing sight. Stanley stepped forward. He saluted. He calmly walked over to Cookie and pulled her to her feet. He picked up her fur coat, shook the snow off, and helped her trembling body into it. Next he turned to Ronnie and saluted. "Major General, at your command, sir!"

Ronnie, pleased at this turn in the story, bawled, "Attention! About turn! In formation! Now, forward. March! Get a lick on! On the double!"

Stanley assembled a lineup. He would take the lead, he said, followed by Clara, then Belle, then Cookie, Norman, Alex. They formed into a line, one step behind the other, and faced town.

Grabbing the reins from Alex, Smoky climbed onto the sleigh. He sat himself down, across from Sophie. He stared unseeing as he covered himself and his dog, the reins held tight leading back over his shoulder. Sophie didn't move. She could hear the boy's teeth chattering and his soft mumbling.

Ronnie, marching the adults up the road, yelled at the top of his lungs, "Okay, youse guys! One, two, three, hup! Two, three, four, hup! Hands on heads! Hup! Raise those knees up! High-er! High-er! Hup! Hup!" Their forms disappeared into the dark. It grew still.

Sophie's mind and bones ached for home. She didn't dare suggest she and Smoky make a run for it to Old Sadie's place, maybe a couple of miles or so across the field. There'll be pie, she'd tell him. But she didn't know if she could trust him. Or the dog. But then, the boy was shaking so hard with the cold, he might fall and not be able to get up.

Had Sophie known her parents were watching the road for any little sign of her at that moment, she would have felt protected --- enough, at least, to distract herself with thoughts of a dance. But she had no knowledge that Les Musiciens had already arrived at the house, fiddle and guitar in hand; and that they had already taken rosin and guitar picks from their pockets a few times to practice. In fact, by eight o'clock they were exchanging maybes with her parents: maybe the dance party had thought it best to wait out the storm; maybe the horse was lame and had to take it slow; maybe Norman and Cookie had arrived late from the city.

Then Sophie saw the marchers looming out of the darkness. They chugged back to the sleigh. Ronnie had gotten tired—obvious by his stumbling gait—and had been talked into standing down. Once at the sleigh, Stanley gently offered to hold the gun for Ronnie, who flung his bulk onto the sleigh and plunked down beside Smoky. Still, he made a grab for his rifle and laid it across his lap. The captive foot soldiers, exhausted, cold, and wordless, climbed in and covered up. Mad cries and howls rose from Ronnie as the horses pulled in their traces and set out for home.

Belle spoke, "We should help out our leader, eh? After all, he deserves it. Tell us what you need, Ronnie, I'm here for you."

Belle's pretend little-girl voice sent shock waves through her fellow sufferers. Sophie could not move for trying. Clara and Cookie clung to each other.

"Easy," Stanley said, as Ronnie stared at Belle. His hand had swarmed to the trigger, but then he relaxed.

Sophie's words resounded in her head: Shut up! She felt she might lunge at Belle.

They travelled in silence. Finally the sleigh squeaked to a stop and Sophie could let herself believe she was home. She felt nothing. Strangled sobs from Ronnie rose and fell. Sophie's father and the men, including Old Solomon, came rushing out the door and began to pull, lift, and all but drag Ronnie Samuels out of the wagon.

"Don't hurt him!" Belle called, reaching a hand out.

"You! Get inside!" Stanley was no longer obliging. He thrust Belle's hand off Ronnie. Cookie and Clara grabbed her by the arms. Struggling, the three fell into the house. The men were finally able to commandeer Ronnie's dead weight into a straight-backed chair in the big room. Now, held in place by Le Musiciens, he hurled meaningless syllables at the stunned host and their dumbfounded friends.

Sophie's mother looked her over and motioned her to stand by the stove. Three silent, shivering women pressed in beside her. Confused and crying, Belle tapped a finger on her leg. Cookie's mascara sketched trails down her face. Her small, trembling hand held the front part of her wet satin purple dress away from her body. As for Clara, her overbite now held a calm, permanent smile.

Ronnie found words. "Not fit to go to war, they said! But, see? I got my platoon back alive, what?! Where's my comrade?"

Sophie's father said, "Make room for the boy, Sophie." Smoky shuffled to the stove, Sparky wagging pitifully, lay down beside the boy.

Throughout the next hour, Ronnie went from tears to shouting to saying crazy things. He cried for his mother. He cried for the dead. And he cried for Smoky and Sparky, "my two little bags of bones." And then he cried for himself. He wrestled off anyone who touched him. Sophie feared he might bite Belle when she ran to him and stroked his face as she whispered in his ear. Looking at her through bleary eyes, he babbled swear words. Sophie's mother, wanting to do something, ran up and dabbed at his face with a damp towel. Still, his lament went on and on.

Len, Sophie's father, turned to Old Solomon, his former army comrade. "It looks a lot like shell shock, eh?" The two had seen action. They knew the signs. Len had lain in the trenches, soaked in the dark sucking mud that drove cold and dread into the bone. He had lain alongside the dead, puking like his buddies. "When you think of it, Ronnie's talk about war shows no respect."

"You can't always put a name to it," said Old Solomon. "He doesn't have the soldier's thousand-yard stare, is the difference."

Disgusted, Sophie suspected Ronnie had no wound. Yet, here he sat, screeching his head off. "The priest said I'm substandard! Not worthy of our queen!" His legs kicked out. Loud gurgling arose in his chest. The men grabbed him by the arms and pinned him in his chair.

Sophie's father insisted, "You are worthy. You are a treaty man."

"That's telling him, Len." It was Belle, her eyes overflowing with feeling. She bent toward Ronnie's ear again. This time the men ignored her, including Ronnie.

They might still dance, Sophie thought. Ronnie had shut the spirit down but now he began to drowse his way to a deepening sleep.

The door opened. Stanley stepped in, a cloud of cold around him. He had unhitched, fed, and watered the team, he said. Sophie took a real look at him. She had to admit he had tried to protect them. On their way home, he had made up a play starring Ronnie as a major general. In the play, the major general was to hold the barrel of his gun pointing down and set it upon knees held wide—to make him look mighty, as Stanley said. He had added the aside, "And you don't need a cigar." A strong major general needed but a show of good posture to lead his troops out of enemy territory. Stanley had also signalled the moment they came upon a dangerous war zone, a place where the major general must keep a sharp eye, here on this deadly stretch of road bound on one side by the government's experimental farm and, on the other, by a platoon of imported Nazis. Thanks to Stanley, Sophie realized, she and Smoky had remained safe in their roles as lookouts with Sparky, their attack dog.

Now, standing at the door, Stanley hung his head. His brother had spoiled things. Yet, Stanley's work was not over. "The horses are okay," he announced. "When things are dried out, we'll head back."

Turning to the women, Sophie saw that Cookie, in her stocking feet, stood on a folded red towel beside the stove, staring at the flames. Burgundy boots steamed beside the wood box. Belle whispered that white spots covered her legs and that her toes hurt, really bad. Cookie pulled her closer to the stove as Clara made room. Smoky and Sparky had fallen fast asleep, curled around each other on the floor by the stove.

Sophie, warm now, went to sit by the window. Coming dawn dimmed the stars. One glittered like cold water still, above the trees. She turned to watch her mother handing round sandwiches, cakes, and preserves as take-homes. The adults whispered their thank-you's, so as not to reawaken Ronnie. Sophie's mother nudged her father. He raised his cup to the party of exhausted friends at the door and said in undertones, "Happy New Year!" People kissed and shook hands. Tightening their layers about them, and nodding one last gentle approval at the trio asleep by the stove, they tiptoed out into the glittering cold. They climbed silently onto the sleigh and slid away in a soft turn.

PART TWO:
While Looking In

Adam's Tree

I

I WOKE IN A HOSPITAL BED. White walls. White bed. White pull curtain. I was drained and dead tired. In the middle of the night I had settled on names for my newborn twins. "Adam" came easily for my first-born. But my daughter's name was what I lay awake struggling with. Finally, I had it. "So-Small," I said. My twin sister, Johanna, in a chair by my bed, tried to smile. She had said earlier that if I had a girl, I should give her my name, Imogene.

"So-Small, no other," I said. I could almost see the nurses joining in, trying to make me find a better a name, a real one, to them. But this was the name I wanted. It was me putting So-Small up for adoption; I had no choice. When I told the father, Mr. W, that I was pregnant and carrying his twins, his eyes went blank. He did not want us. I could see it right away.

My twin sister and I sat in the chilly hospital room, two eighteen-year-olds, our heads down. Johanna said, "We have no money to go back to Cowessess, Imogene, to ask the Elders to name the twins beforehand, I mean ..."

She was the spiritual one. Elders gave names to guide the spirit. It was not lost on me that Johanna was thinking ahead. But, to me, the name "So-Small" sent a signal. Her future mom's heart would fill with love the minute she saw a baby girl and heard her name and touched that tiny mole above her lip. Tears stung my eyes. But I hid the signs. I didn't want nurses saying I had it coming—saying I had committed adultery and deserved pain. Their snotty looks said enough. Everything had to be about Adam now, my son—the baby I would keep.

I saw fear flash across Johanna's face then. She told me that she had just recalled a vision she once had. She was forever painting a picture for me, so again I listened. In the vision, a huge tide swamps the fields back home. Reserve roads lie flooded. Cowessess mothers flounder in a torrent that sweeps all kinds of things along: radios, parts of cars, whole trucks and tractors, sports gear, fishing tackles, rakes, disks, harrows, lumber, polished tables, furniture legs, glass door knobs, ladies' fans, bedding, dishes, headstones, framed pictures, vases, and clothing—the likes of which, in all our days, we have never seen on the reserve.

This vision was so real, Johanna said, that her heart pounded in her ears. I told her it didn't make sense. All that stuff. Think of it. But we were soon to learn that a flood was already tearing at us, leaving a jumble behind it. That flood had begun to pour down on us a long time ago.

In Regina, Johanna and I lived on our own. When our adopted mother died, we were fourteen. Our adopted father sent us to live with his sister in the city, on Halifax Street. A few years later, our aunt got sick and moved to Winnipeg. We seventeen-year-olds stayed behind. We hunted for jobs, telling future employers that our grade eight certificate proved we could read and write. We claimed to be strong, we never got tired. Johanna finally landed a job as a cleaner at the hospital, and I found work as a maid. Even to this day, I sometimes see myself in Mr. W's house, dusting and polishing shiny wooden floors in rooms with green velvet curtains and tall ferns in heavy ceramic jars. If I ever let myself, I could still smell his shaving lotion—the scent that made my knees weak whenever he snuck home from work, his wife away.

Johanna said yes, we could raise the baby boy together, she and I.

I told her, "I should never have held him. One sniff of his breath and I'd kill anybody who'd try to take him from me. So-Small, though, I was too weak to hold her right away."

I caught sight of myself in a framed mirror across the room. My face looked as dry as a prune, my mouth a purple twisted stain against my white hospital gown. I had been struggling during the night with how we might keep both babies. I told Johanna, "Last night, I asked myself just who from our reserve might take in So-Small. Who are our relatives, anyway? I could think of nobody."

Johanna said nothing, but took a comb out of her pocket and tried combing out my long, black tangles of hair strewn across the pillow. The mirror caught deep shadows in my face, a face that once laughed at boys, but stopped when that married man ripped my heart in two.

"Even our parents aren't ours for real, eh?" I said. "I asked Mom lots of times about our real mom. She always said it's a long story. Your relatives got lost in the Red River flood, long ago, she'd say. And all those times I did the farm work with Dad, you'd think he'd open up, but no."

Johanna said to keep up my strength for the boy. "So-Small will have a good life, like we did with our adopted mom and dad. Someday she'll come to us. She'll find us. You'll see." I could see Johanna had her doubts. She quickly turned her face away and stared onto the street below, where dust devils sanded cars in the hospital parking lot.

Johanna said, "I wonder if Social Welfare will find parents in the city for So-Small. She's a prairie girl, after all." I understood that she wanted to put a hopeful picture in my head for when we left the hospital. But I heard myself cry out, "I don't want them to take her to another land!" It was too much. We fell together in a heap on the hospital bed, sobbing like orphans.

When we arrived at our place, baby in arms, trials began.

Adam was colicky. I was torn with grief for So-Small, and nervous about handling Adam. Mr. W's lean face would pop uninvited into my mind. Johanna was often dog tired.

On top of it, the apartment was stifling. The July sun beat down all day. I scolded Johanna like it all was her fault. "Look at his shirt—stuck to his back! His hair is wringing wet." But then, that winter, freezing cold clawed inside the apartment each time the furnace quit in the building and the janitor had not come around yet. So now it was, "Look! See his breath!" Johanna would poke her head from under the covers and peek to the foot of the bed, where, against the wall, tiny wisps of breath rose from Adam's little heap of blankets in his dresser drawer straddling two kitchen chairs. Still, no matter the weather, we got little sleep.

I began to see now what Johanna saw. We were poor. Our one-bedroom bachelor apartment felt closed in. The walls echoed Adam's cries—and my weeping. That first week, a heavy-set woman, chest heaving, and an elderly man with white hair knocked on the door. The two blasted mean remarks directly at us and threatened to report us to the landlord because of the noise. On edge after that, Johanna and I took turns walking Adam. It was back and forth between the burnt-orange kitchenette cabinets and chipped enamel stove and sink and the red chrome-legged table and squeaky chairs. By day the bay window threw a yellow-grey pool of light on our scratched-up wooden floor. No velvet curtains here.

The apartment made us feel safe, though. Our building was close to the hospital. Johanna, the breadwinner, had only to run across the street and parking lot to go each morning to her cleaning job there. But our money began running out faster and faster. It was plain that I had to find employment, and soon.

Johanna took the awkward step of asking patients at the hospital if they knew women from the reserve, in the city, who might be willing to babysit. "He's a very good baby," she'd say. But each woman we talked to claimed Adam was too young. I told Johanna we needed someone like Mrs. Sarah Stevens, an older woman who raised children of almost every age. Johanna had to remind me that Sarah lived more than a hundred miles away and had no car. It was the same with our aunt who had looked after us after our adopted mother died. In Winnipeg now, she was too sick to return.

I clutched at straws. I told Johanna I was going to try to get my old job back as a maid. I would walk those fifteen blocks, easy. "Then our worries will be over," I said. I knew my sideways mention of Mr. W shocked her. But as far as that went, I had never felt so dead inside. Johanna said that even if she worked overtime mopping floors, washing windows, and hauling bedding to the hospital's laundry centre, the money would still not go far enough. Diapers and baby food were expensive.

Still, I was shocked when she announced one Saturday morning that we'd be moving back to Cowessess. "We'll live in Mom and Dad's old place beside the reserve," she said. She tried to paint a bright picture. "Just think for a moment, Imogene. Hear that bobolink? When you were little you used to say its song lit the inside of your head with blue. Remember?"

I gave her one devil of a stare. Trying another tack, she said, "One time I heard a bee so clear, my nose smelt honey. Even now, it tingles with wood smoke and sometimes that smell of bark in the woodpile after a rain. Try it."

"That'll be the day," I said.

I said no more. But then, at dusk, gloom slunk into our room. Shadows darkened corners and crept out from under the chairs. I went to sit at the kitchen table with Johanna to explain why I balked. "I won't leave my baby girl alone in the city!"

Johanna stared at the floor. Finally she said, "A baby girl, with that tiny mole, will always be alive here, it's true. All the sidewalks, iron gates, and fences connect our apartment to that little breathing chest." And so we talked and cried. We weighed it all. Toward dawn a pale greenish sky lifted some of the dark and I agreed to move. But deep down inside, I felt helpless and angry. Even Johanna had turned against me, it seemed.

Out on the reserve, word had already gone around that we were returning to Cowessess with a baby. And that we'd be living in our adoptive parents' old house, next to Cowessess. I pictured our old little grey house just across the gravel road from the reserve, where we used to go and visit. When our adoptive mother died, our adoptive father boarded up the house. "You're big now," was what he said, his blue eyes sunken, his shoulders slumped.

It was said that no one was more excited about our return to Cowessess than Vitaline, a boarding school pal who had returned to live on the reserve. She was single, living alone, and bringing up a toddler called Seth. Whatever the story, her secrets would soon be ours.

Vitaline made us a nice homecoming. As soon as she found out, she said, she sent word to Tilly, a tomboy in her twenties who lived twelve miles away in the town of Broadview. Tilly was the one who had out-boxed Vitaline for the right to be our friend when we were kids. She agreed to help Vitaline with repairs to our house. She did one better. Travelling on foot all over the reserve, she invited people over to join work bees and to make donations of furnishings. Our childhood yard and house had become a real beehive, she said—Tilly in the lead, her red plaid shirt sleeves rolled up, hammer ringing.

And so it proceeded, broken window-panes were being taped up, mouse droppings swept out the door, tall wild grasses yanked out of the yard, floorboards nailed down and sanded, spiders caught and flicked into the bushes behind the old house. In the city, our one bay window, greasy in the glare of sunlight, pitched a hard rectangle of light onto a floor that no longer showed any sign of twin sisters and a baby called Adam. I wept in the back of the bus, sitting beside Johanna, holding onto Adam for dear life.

II

WE ARRIVED ON COWESSESS in the afternoon, around three o'clock. It seemed unreal to be sitting with our two old school friends, Vitaline and Tilly, at our newly sanded wooden table, eating bannock and strawberries and sipping tea out of jam jars. I was tired and numb, so I said nothing. Johanna, free from city worries, said more than enough grateful things for the both of us. Happy faces beamed at us.

Tilly, dressed in a man's work overalls and plaid shirt, was proud to show us around, the repairs to the door and to the ceilings. Pointing to the bed in the big room, she said, "These mattresses aren't new but they're clean, although really thin." A second bed, also covered in patchwork quilts, stood under the low, slanted ceiling of the lean-to. We crowded in the doorway of the bedroom to view a shined-up brass bedstead that had once belonged to our parents. Tilly turned to the big room. "See?" she pointed with her chin at the whitewashed walls. This room held two iron-frame cots, one to be used as a sofa and the other as a cradle, where, at the moment, Adam lay fast asleep beside our bundles with blond-haired Seth on the other side, also sound asleep.

I was so dazed from the trip, it took Johanna to realize that we were in the middle of a reunion. Didn't the four of us use to play together in this very house? In this yellow kitchen—before boarding school? In this yard!

"And that fence and that tree …" Johanna stopped.

I turned a blank eye on it all. I stared out the window. An iron band had tightened around my head. Heat waves blurred and shimmered in an open field. "I'm going back, me, with Adam," I said, my chest hurting like I had just run a mile.

However, it would be years before I would draw that one deep breath, accepting that I was on Cowessess to stay.

Johanna and I were summoned to Vitaline's place. She had something to tell us, Tilly had come to say. When we got there, Vitaline came right out with it. "Seth is the son of my stepfather, either him or his white friend." The men, drunk, had come home late from town and raped her. She had just turned eighteen. "My eye patch is the giveaway. This eye is blinded. It makes me ashamed." She described a terrible night of flailing legs, horrible screams, fists and knuckles on sweaty faces, knees thudding stomachs. "Look at the proof," Vitaline said. "Seth's blond hair and silver eyes." She said that whenever she saw Seth speed-crawl across the floor, it made her queasy. It made her think of a dragonfly she had once seen tangled up in a spider web, dangling from a tree branch over a scummy slough. "What chance has the boy, with all that in him?"

Vitaline said she was only too glad Tilly had decided to stay on, to live with her and Seth in their little mudded log house. Tilly added that she wanted to help raise both Seth and Adam. I didn't mind. The more help, the better. A punchy outdoors girl, Tilly had no wish to marry; she had apparently said, laughing, that no man was her equal.

The wonder was that the four of us ended up living but a short walk apart. Johanna always said that, morning or afternoon, an amble through the stand of flickering poplars, with the scent of sweet grass and tiger lilies in the air, was beautiful. As for me, I saw it all as if through a dark piece of dusty blue glass, any time of day.

And that is how we lived. But even the hope of those years soon fell out from under us.

Our boys were taken. Tilly and Johanna cried like we did, the real mothers. Adam had just turned five; Seth, seven. Without warning, a truck from the Mission pulled into the yard. Two school authorities loaded the boys into the back and left. We knew what was happening.

The second they turned the last bend in the road, the stillness got to me. I grew frantic for the sound of Adam's voice. I wanted to see his little hands, see where he placed them, how he held them. Did the wind blow in his hair? Were he and Seth sitting together? It seemed that wherever I ran, whether through field or bush, the boys' voices cried.

Vitaline, Tilly, and Johanna wondered, like I did, if the arms of strangers would be kind. Like the arms that now held So-Small.

It was plain that, as time went on, strong-hearted Tilly missed the boys, what with the wrestling, arguing, and play-acting as Superman and Robin. A broad-shouldered, boxer type of woman, Tilly had taught them sparring. I would watch her arm-wrestle them, or their foot races and stone-throwing contests. Whenever she made a little extra money from picking rocks off farmers' fields, she would walk into town, which meant she came home with a comic book like maybe Superman, Tarzan, Dagwood, or Little Orphan Annie. She made up games that suited her temperament, too. Over the years, we would hear her say to the boys, "One day, you'll be strong enough to run down Hog's Back hill, make a turn, and run up again, full speed." Hog's Back was a long, steep hill connecting the reserve and valley. Stones, some large, and thick berry bushes lined its path. "Look after each other like brothers," she'd say, "because that's what you are."

One day Tilly brought up a troubling fact. She had been to see the Elders, where it was said that schoolbooks were breaking the children's hearts. Reserve kids shouldered a rock they could not put down, was said. I pricked up my ears. I disliked any talk pointed at Adam. It sickened me. It made my arms ache for So-Small, on top of it. The Elders had also apparently said that kids from boarding school had dead eyes, like those dots of black blotting paper left by the two-hole-punch on the Indian agent's desk. One Elder had said, "They don't know who they are."

I curbed my tongue. Tilly had better not be trying to say Adam was like that.

"Our boys' eyes are bright," Johanna, always quick to spot my temper, hurried to say. "Just like the Stevens girls', eh? Sophie and Leta skip and sing! They play, same as Adam and Seth." That stopped me lighting into Tilly. Besides, I knew it was different with the Stevens's girls; their parents had kept them out of boarding school altogether.

Once and only once, on their visits home, did I overhear Seth and Adam speak of hunger and fear at boarding school. It shook me so bad my body went into a kind of fit. My joints locked and I found it hard to breathe. I called Johanna. She held my hands, promising me that our eaglets would always soar far above steeple and agency, wings unclipped. Years later she confessed that she knew our boys faced a cruel world. Still, she had no idea that worse was on the way. Neither did I, and I was the mother.

We often studied old photographs of the boys over the years. Vitaline, Tilly, or Johanna would clear the table and spread out the pictures. They would then compare the boys' gain in weight and height, year by year. They would swap memories: look, here they were three ... six ... ten ... fourteen. I dreaded these times of their trying to pin down the past: we bought the boys new shoes, that year ... showed them how to make a slingshot, eh Tilly? ... the time their voices broke ... took them stooking ... the time Johanna and Tilly ran alongside when they first drove a team of horses ... that powwow ... the Stevens's Thanksgiving feast, that time ... Christmas concert. I didn't need pictures; I saw it all like it was yesterday. The whole time, I grieved for So-Small. I couldn't take it. My heart beat too fast. I would jump to my feet sometimes and run outside. Tilly, Vitaline, and Johanna called these times "Imogene's pains."

One day Johanna said, "When the boys get back, let's take a real hard look. See if they're happy—not all jumpy and hiding something."

We readied ourselves, or thought we had. When the boys walked in that summer day, they were as tall as men. We could hardly believe it. Adam, seventeen, and Seth going on nineteen—they were not skinny boys anymore. Their boy frames were gone.

"Hey! You look like warriors!" My mouth got away on me. What did I know of warriors, except from comics? We women jumped up and hugged the boys and felt their muscles. Tilly shoulder-checked them and punched their stomachs. They only laughed.

"Try wrestling us now, Tilly," Adam said.

"Watch us chase girls, you mean," Seth said. We four women clapped eyes on him. He lost the grin the second he saw. But we had already caught a whiff of disrespect.

At the time we said nothing. Seth's silly remark had been taken in, however, especially by Johanna. She said that Seth's reference to girls marked a time of truth, like in Genesis in the Bible.

When the boys went off on one of their rambles the next day, Johanna told of another vision she had had: a wheel up in the sky came rolling closer and closer, ready to strike. Johanna summed it up, saying the past is always alive in us. I summed it up, too. Johanna always read the Bible like it was now.

III

AFTER A CLOUDBURST one morning, Johanna came in, face perspiring. She set down by the woodbox an armful of small twigs she had gathered for the stove. "Oh my!" she said, "Baby frogs leaping all over the wet grass out there—you should'a seen!" She threw her head back and laughed. Vitaline and Tilly, at the table drinking warmed-over tea with me, joined in. We had seen this dazzling sight a few times before.

But today Johanna meant business. She wished to discuss trouble brewing on Cowessess, she told us. "Married couples are breaking up all over out here. It's way too many. Think about it."

Surprised, we agreed. "Think," Vitaline added. "More children are being held in the arms of strangers, eh? It's not right, this mix-up."

Not thinking about putting people in their place today, I handed round a dish of strawberries I had picked earlier that morning. The mist and the stillness outdoors had calmed me. But now my voice began shaking again. "Relatives are not strangers. We always know. And always will!"

Johanna, keeping an eye on me, said, "What I mean is people have more reason these days to ask who So-and-So's mom or dad is."

It was true. Fewer people had stayed a couple and fewer still were parents of the same children. "People like Sarah and Len Stevens up the road are rare," Vitaline said.

"The war, eh?" Tilly offered a guess.

"The Mission school—although—" Vitaline struggled with her thoughts.

My temper boiled over. "Old bedbugs!" I was thinking of Mr. W, who hurt us still.

"Whatever it is," Johanna quickly said, "we have to think of our boys."

Vitaline spoke. "Who'll our boys marry? Lots of girls have kids already. Take Sarah Stevens's girls, Sophie and Leta, they won't stay on the reserve, I bet."

The women's faces filled with alarm. A chill ran down my spine.

We settled on one thing. We'd throw down a fiery border and a barrier of thistle piled sky-high to protect our boys. Yet, we had no idea that greater danger lay in wait.

"You know," Johanna said, as though reaching for the right thought, "there is a thing called a 'family tree.' And we ought to make one."

I sensed what Johanna was thinking, often before she spoke, but lately I didn't see everything. More and more, I missed what she meant. I burst out, "Wah-hie! In school that time, the teacher gave a big belly laugh. He said Indians are impossible."

"Never mind him," Johanna said. Again, she wanted a different kind of discussion. "It's not the time to be thinking school," she said, mostly to me.

"Let's make that tree, anyway," Vitaline offered. "Our boys need to learn their relations. They're ready to marry soon."

Jaws dropped. Marry? That was years away! We steadied ourselves, hands and bellies against the edge of the table. Oh yes, we said, oh yes, we had better get at this.

"If we start now and put our minds to it, we'll get it done before the boys come in to eat. They must have stayed overnight at Butchie's after the dance, eh?" Vitaline wondered.

The tree was a step into madness. Trouble began the minute Vitaline adjusted her eye patch. She made it known that any tree she'd be asked to draw wouldn't be a chestnut. "Imogene and Johanna, them, they seen one. But me, I never seen it. And I don't want to use a poplar—too many twigs. Another thing, elms are uglier'n anything, and I won't draw it."

In the end, we remembered an oak at the edge of town. "It has fat arms and a long life, after all," Tilly said, hiding her amusement.

No sooner said and Vitaline drew an outline of a tree on the reverse side of a piece of cardboard cut from a large carton, with printing on it that said Protect from Freezing. She drew it in such a way that there were as many roots as branches, "and space for more." It didn't go well. Our thoughts got tangled up like knotted strings; besides, our mind kept getting stuck between some kind of unholy spirit and some big seeing eye—or maybe, more between the living and the dead. To make it worse, a sudden memory could stake out a wrong claim on the tree.

So we argued about where to place the names. Vitaline asked, "Is it proper to put old people in the high branches, or do you put only young ones up there?" We could see what she was getting at. Elders, after all, were the centre of a good life.

"We hold them high, but what is respectful?" Tilly asked, biting a thumbnail.

"Well, is it dead ones only who go to the roots? Or live ones, too?" Vitaline held her pencil in the air, waiting.

Arguments went on for over half an hour. We all swayed in our chairs, cleared our throat, and brushed at our laps, hands sweaty. Finally, we ended up saying that, really, what mattered was the oldest person—and close family members—"all in one branch and one branch only, with extra twigs, in case."

The muddle irritated me. I said it was stupid, what with that yellow stub of a pencil of Vitaline's and the layers of ifs and buts showing through dirty erase marks. The more I said, the angrier I became. I smacked my hand down hard and practically shouted out what was needling me. "Do any of you have a head for adopted ones?" I asked. "Look! Vitaline has put Seth next to Tilly! Shouldn't there be two branches, seeing you think he has two moms? Or doesn't my life count?"

Now it was Johanna. "After all, I am Adam's second mom, since no one else is Imogene's twin. If Seth can have two branches," she said, "so can Adam."

The words let loose a live wasp into the room. "Even if the law says Adam is my one twin," I said, my breath coming so hard and loud I could barely stand up from the table, "I want a spot for both." In fact, I wanted a spot up high for So-Small, the baby adopted out these seventeen years. I yelled louder, "Seeing as how it's all going, I don't think Adam should be on this dead tree, any which way!"

I felt bad afterwards. Especially since no one fought back. Sighs and moans told how badly they wanted to finish the tree by noon. They knew enough, now, to make So-Small's name stand out. But with all the erasing, writing, and re-erasing, the pileup of black tracings looked like a smudge had been set alight for mosquitoes. Vitaline said the sight reminded her of a spider's web drifting on cloudy water. To Johanna, it was a spill of living tadpoles from the sky. As for me, I saw only So-Small and Adam, in the upper right-hand corner of the oak.

The room erupted. Adam barged up to the house. He stood outlined in light at the open door. He must have grabbed the wash basin from its spot on the step outside and baptized himself. Johanna spread her hands to protect our tree, what with Adam's shaking his wet hair out. Voice trembling, he shouted out, "Seth took my girl!"

We got the story out of him. He and Seth had had a fight at the dance, down at the Mission. Adam had pointed out a girl to Seth. The girl had stopped and looked back at Adam, a little crooked smile and a scar above it. But Seth had already taken to her and so led her onto the dance floor. He flirted with her, making jokes all the while. Adam heard him say that the girl's bony face and gleaming eyes reminded him of a cat—a bobcat, actually. That had got her going. She punched him, calling him a lynx with the clumsiest paws ever to try a two-step. So then Seth grabbed her by the wrist and waltzed her down to the lake. Where they stayed. Furious, Adam ran up Hog's Back and waited for Seth. Later that night, Seth came rushing up, dodging rocks and washouts on his way, his frame lit by moonlight, to where Adam sat waiting. Seth said, "Fair is fair, brother." So Adam put a fist to his head.

Fists or not, I managed to keep my mind straight. "What girl?" I asked.

But now Johanna was firing questions. "What's her name? Where's she from? How old is she?"

Pain in my chest, I could only watch him—shoulder against the doorjamb, pretending interest in a scraped knuckle. Adam had said too much, and he knew it. Steadying his eye on my forehead, he said that the girl was not from here. "She has a long name," he said. "Adele Something-Something. Anyway, I don't give a damn."

"Then what do you mean, Seth took her away?" Tilly's tone warned she meant to shield Seth.

Adam raised his voice. "Adele is my girl! Seth cut me off—him and his goddamn yellow hair!" With that, he turned and ran into the trees across the yard where his rambles had always begun with Seth. His manner of speaking, never mind what he said, dimmed our day.

Tilly smacked her fist into her hand. "Adele? What girl would dare push her damn way into our life?"

Vitaline, a mother caught between two sons, tried to find words. I knew she didn't wish to call Seth's origins to mind. But she said, all the same, "Ee-a-how! Why would Adam scoff at Seth's hair so all of a sudden?"

I tried to turn our muddled thoughts back to the family tree. "What in heck kind of name is Adele, anyway?"

On the table lay our scribble of a tree, looking oddly threadbare. Unspoken things began shifting their weight in our mind. My decision was made. There was no way I would ever speak of Adam's father. Mr. W had no business in our world. I would never raise his name to fresh air. As for Vitaline and her story, she said nothing about Seth's father, either. Why would she? Devils had to be stepped over.

IV

JOHANNA SPOKE FIRST, "Sarah and Len Stevens—they're steady people. Sarah might know a few things about a young female stranger, eh?"

Tilly said, "I, for one, don't feel right going around asking cheeky questions."

"We're strangers," Johanna added. "All of us. We're like the dead to Cowessess kids, especially the ones just born and the ones yet to come. Look at what we're dealing with. We have to straighten out our boys on—on pretty near everything."

Vitaline swallowed. She said it might make people mad at us, were they to find out who belonged to what bunch. "But then again," she said, "a new generation is stepping up. Yet, Tilly and I, who have lived longest on the reserve, still know only a few relatives." Her words made me realize how bad it was for all of us to have had no guiding light from a real mother.

We agreed to ask Sarah Stevens over right away.

"Mind you, Elders don't know every detail." Vitaline spoke from experience. "Even if they did, could they really say? They don't like making trouble, as it is." Then, sadly looking at her hands spread out in front of her, she said, "Lots of girls, nowadays—they pin their hopes on boys who never knew a mom's love, let alone a dad's."

I sent my chair crashing against the wall. But the women ignored me. Now, suddenly more than ever, I knew our boys came first. That I had to take charge of myself.

Sarah Stevens hurried on her way over up the road. We could see her trying to keep up with Tilly's man-like strides. We sat her down in the big room. She mopped her brow, brushed her greying auburn hair off her face, and drank from the jam can of cool tea handed to her. Tilly had said nothing to her on the way over about the tree, which, at the moment, stood behind the open door.

Sorting out our questions, Sarah Stevens said that a girl had arrived on her doorstep just recently. The signs were that she had ridden in the back of a truck. "I mistook her for a little old lady at first. She stood on the step blinking, skinny face covered in dust and streaks."

We pulled our chairs in close, knees practically touching. Sarah looked uncomfortable, even rattled. But we paid no mind. We behaved in a way Elders called "putting our own needs first." After prodding, Sarah pitched us a fact: the girl, after washing, was quite pretty, pointy cheekbones and bright eyes. We pulled our chairs into an even tighter circle. Sarah went on, "I told her that she didn't look more than twelve, and so what was she doing on the road alone, this time of day. I asked her name. She said she was eighteen and not a kid. And that her name was 'Crystal Brooks Delima Olive Adele Lynxleg.' Adele, for short."

"Adele!"

We clung to our chairs. I nearly fell off mine. "Didn't Adam just say—?"

Tilly, her mind on track, asked, "So many names? How can that be?"

Vitaline leaned in, but Sarah sat palms up, empty. She had scoured her mind. Still, I stared in a barefaced way at her. Sarah would say later that she sensed the near strike of a hawk, its injured young nearby, each time she looked my way.

Tilly dug into her floral shoulder bag for the eraser. "A happy life for our grandchildren is in danger, Sarah."

Johanna scraped her chair on the floor and wiped her hands down her dress. She spread our family tree on the table, smoothing it flat. Looking straight at Sarah, she said, "If we are to sleep nights, we have to figure this out. Otherwise, it's going to be always just dread in our mind."

Someone tapped on the door jamb. Sarah Stevens, having a clear view to the door, which was propped open to the breeze, cried, "Adele! Adele Lynxleg!"

"Adele!" We spun round. Sarah Stevens, flustered, said, "I mean Delima-Olive-Adele. No, Crystal-Brooks-Adele. No, Delima! What am I saying?"

"Come in!" Vitaline had found her voice.

Questions burst from us. Yes, her name was Adele. No, she was not a runaway. Yes, she'd gotten left in the valley. Yes, she was looking for her boyfriend. No, he had only forgotten to come for her. No, she'd stay standing, thanks.

Something like an Imogene-of-all-Imogenes came over me. I took aim. "You have more names than all of us put together!" But the girl did not drop her gaze, even when spoken to by an older lady. I felt ire rising. She thought she was somebody.

Vitaline had managed to stay calm. She took up the pencil, flicked her eye patch, and said, "We're listing the names of all the people we know. I'll write yours down, too. Say them again, but go slow."

Adele, likely sensing we'd been talking about her, watched Vitaline's careful hand. I looked the girl over, taking in details: skinny, yellow and green checked shirt over a mauve dress, long hair tied with green ribbon, deep brown skin like Johanna and Adam, and a scar above her lip. She was quick to react, a real smarty-pants.

Vitaline repeated, "Crystal, Brooks, Delima, Olive, Adele Lynxleg."

"Where did you grow up?" I was impatient.

"With my parents 'til I was three, then Grenfell."

"Who are your parents?"

"I said I don't have any … now." She spoke in town-speak, curtained off, truth's full wings clipped.

Johanna asked the question on all our mind: Who brought her up, and where?

"Sadie and Bert Jones," was the reply.

"Never heard of them. White people?" Tilly had come right out with that.

"How old are you?" Johanna took a different tack.

"Eighteen—well, almost, anyhow. Seventeen."

Johanna raised an eyebrow at me. But losing all patience, I demanded, "What do you want with our boys? That's why you're here, isn't it? Men leave girls, you know. Oh, they do!"

Dismay gripped the room. I had crossed the line between child and grown-up. Everyone heard me. I heard me. Respect had flown out the door. "Yours was one hawkish dive," Johanna would later scold, even if I had never meant to say such a thing.

But Adele had squared her shoulders. "I have one boyfriend. And if he went and left me on purpose, I'll tune him up."

The other women covered their mouth, but I cut the nervous giggles short.

"Starting with your names," I said, "the whole bunch of them—are they from an aunt, then? Say, by the name of Crystal Brooks? Or a cousin called Olive? Or Delima? Somebody like that?"

The girl stood her ground, tears springing. "I lied," she said. "I have only one name! I wanted more. Not just the one my mother gave me when I was born. I took names out of books."

"Is Lynxleg made up, too?" I pushed hard now.

"Lynxleg is the family I stayed with, summers here in the valley. But they've moved to Sakimay. My foster mom, Sadie Jones, wants me to get to know Indians before I'm too old."

"Is Adele at least your real name?"

The girl muffled a sob.

"That's enough!" The voice belonged to Seth, entering the house.

"My heavens!" Tilly's face dropped at Seth's manner of speaking. Johanna was to say later that it felt as if a beautiful tree in the clearing had been cut down.

"Leave her alone!" It was Adam next, stepping over the door sill. He might as well have thrown a cape of bristling quills around his shoulders. His stance got my goat.

"Shame on you, Adam!" My voice rose louder than even Tilly's. "And you, Seth—fighting like that—and speaking rough in front of your family and our neighbour here, Mrs. Sarah Stevens, in case you forgot. Not to mention this stranger, this girl."

Seth stepped up, arms held out. "Adam and me, we're not fighting. Not anymore. We talked it out. Adele is free to choose who she wants."

Seth looked at me. "If she picks Adam, I'll still be his friend, and brother." He turned to Vitaline and Tilly, choked up.

But Seth's silvery eyes had turned grey. His chest sank. His glance took in the girl, so small, yet so strong, holding her place by our door. Adam's face held such a mix of hope, of fear, and of joy that my heart quaked.

Adele's gaze fell on us all. "I choose Adam," she said.

That's when someone screamed, as if losing ground to a flood.

Focal Length Quandary

OUR SUPERIOR AT THE DEPARTMENT asked me to stand in for Jerrod Henley, senior officer on the Saskatchewan file. Jerrod had grown suddenly ill and couldn't make Thursday's flight to the prairies on assignment. I was hardly the one to take pictures of Indians, much less negotiate budget information and transportation, once out on a reserve. I was a hobbyist photographer with no field experience. I was a university graduate, but it was my first year as a temporary policy reviewer in the Indian Affairs federal government office in Ottawa. My peers and my immediate supervisor, Eric Cline, knowing I was green, made jokes at my expense.

The file on my desk that Thursday morning contained brief instructions: Take a dozen realistic photos of domestic life on the Cowessess Indian Reserve, July 1948.

I had been privy to the initiating meeting and knew the pressure was on. Tensions in the building were high. This year's intergovernmental report centred on the question: How are tax dollars being spent on our Indians? The growing presence of World War II veterans, strapped for cash and assistance, had given legs to the long-simmering question. It was my job to come back with unique proof. Make that "proofs."

Derek Cline, supervisor and mentor, had said only, "You arrive tonight in Regina. Tomorrow you meet your first Indian, a Mrs. Sarah Stevens. The Indian agent out there, Hugh Passmore, will pick you up at the airport and drive you to the reserve, about ninety miles due east. You'll spend the night in the Passmore home, at the Indian agency on the reserve. Hugh Passmore will drive you around Cowessess—well, to the Stevenses' home—in the morning. After that, she's all yours. Take it easy on those women, buddy! We need you back here Monday."

The remark drew laughter from nearby consultants, causing Derek Cline, master of office levity, to swagger back to his desk.

Think smart! Work smart! My mentor had suggested that I aim for a permanent government job with benefits, as early as next year, for, he insisted, here was golden opportunity.

Camera, logbook, toothbrush, Gillette razor—and I found myself on the Passmores' couch in his basement office, my stuff spread out on a government-issue chair beside me. I drifted off to sleep, phantom ground below turning from forested hills to a patchwork quilt of variegated fields of green, black, and gold.

Mrs. Stevens was adamant. Her children were not to be aware that she and they were being photographed. Their grandmothers might say that their souls had been taken. It was a duty to them. Also, her son, home from boarding school, would not like the attention. I agreed and apologized for waking her so early. She had been dreaming, she said, shuddering. As we sipped tea from glass sealers, she told me that she had dreamed about a garden of roses, blood red spilling over a greenish-black trench. She'd lain by a gutter surrounded up to the chin by stiff grasses. Shrouded in fog, a ghostly palisade stood beside flat stones piled alongside an enclosure. A wedge of light had harrowed in through a slit in the wall.

I was intrigued by the description, like a photograph. One I might like to take.

Her breath came in short bursts. "There were these glimmering lines and angles. Near ... what, a fortification? A ditch? An ochre cloud hung over rows and rows of Old Bloody Warrior in parade ... And alone on guard is Len, my husband, in uniform." With a sharp intake of breath, she added, "Anyway, it's probably just my tooth. It's been bothering me on and off lately."

I felt a real sense of sympathy toward her. My grandmother had suffered from anxiety nightmares, too, during and after the war. And something of the mind's registry of detail, call it what you will, had rubbed off on me.

I found Mrs. Stevens willing to help. I had to take twelve pictures that day, carefully selected, this while keeping out of sight, yet close enough to get the shots. It would slow me down. However, being agile and having just turned twenty-eight, I was confident I could trust my camera, despite the conditions.

My mind had already taken in Mrs. Stevens as a whole. She was thirty-five years old, or younger, clear skin, balanced features, nicely shaped brows, auburn hair, and slender. The vulnerability in her face recalled an American impressionistic painting I liked, Julian Alden Weir's "Ideal Head: portrait of a young woman." It shimmered with light and feeling. It would be a coup to get Mrs. Stevens to pose out in the sun, but anxiety flicked on and off in her face. A pinched, anxious aura might queer the result.

I had also to bear in mind that there would be cold inspection of my work back in Ottawa. I could almost hear Jerrod Henley's stentorian voice decry the fact that my snapshots conveyed "an obtuse, dangerous quality"—his favourite expression lately, particularly at lunch counters in downtown Ottawa. Candid shots were called for, I knew, but I tended to like the sheer liveliness of portraiture—the devil with government prerequisite! If only...

Inside, I snapped my first shot and entered a note in the

department's official logbook: *Subject 1—Maternal iron bedstead with rumpled bedclothes Jul. '48: Cowessess.*

Let the day begin. I sensed that her odd dream, likely brought on by the night's sudden hard rain against the roof and window, found Mrs. Stevens struggling to conquer aftershock as she woke the three older children. I had agreed she would take them outdoors before the sun got high. "It'll boil away the mist," she said, "a real lotion for the face and neck."

I went to the back of the house to await my cue. Sweet smells of grass and freshly dampened soil filled me with such a deep sense of peace that, for the moment, Ottawa had drained from both mind and body. A bee buzzed and probed at the side of the house under the eaves, the only noticeable sound. I sighed deeply.

After a breakfast of milk and bread, mom and kids stepped outdoors. I peered through the open window into the empty room. Bread crumbs on a red oilcloth covering a small table near the window would make one trim photo, I knew, but, alas, it could represent anywhere. A toddler, asleep on the bed in the corner, surrounded by a rolled blanket, made a great image. But take it? I considered. Everything about it said no.

I heard Mrs. Stevens say, "Let's go see the flowers waking up."

I slipped along the wall of the house toward the front. There stood the rest of my subjects: a fine-looking boy of about seven or eight, quite sturdy but, oddly, showing signs of tension, and beside him a little girl perhaps four years old with dimpled cheeks, clearly the youngest, and pouting. Her stance told how she might test all kinds of ambitions. The middle child, a thin girl of about six, in a red dress, had a disconcertingly objective, though perhaps not a totally dismissive, gaze—a photographer some day?

Mrs. Stevens told them they were off to the cold bush, the one with leaves flashing blue and silver. The children took turns walking beside and behind her, bare feet dodging clumps of tall, showery grasses draped with glistening beads.

Speaking softly, she gathered the children round. A lady's slipper, she said, nestled here, and if they looked closely they might see tiny air sacs clipped tight to its heart. As the children peered at the orange-yellow petals, I dove for a spot, the sun at my back, and snapped three rapt little faces. For another shot, I knelt in the weeds. Wet declared my right knee. But before I could snap the shutter, my subjects were off. I quickly wrote an entry: *Subject 2— Siblings, two sisters and boarding school boy Jul. '48: Cowessess.*

I could have kicked myself for neglecting to establish a signal that would let Mrs. Stevens know when to stay put and when to turn and move on. Raindrops gleamed on thin brown legs as the four tramped on ahead. I wanted this shot—cropped. The convergence of angle, light, and form was perfect. But now the spectre rose of an unappreciative Jerrod Henley at the office, summing up my photo as "entirely too artsy." Only practical shots, I scolded myself, and none that hinted of wastefulness. Policy, I knew.

Fronds of mist in soft veils skimmed kneecaps and stroked the children's waists and shoulders. I took aim, intent on catching a sudden absence of strain in the boy's face. But Mrs. Stevens, turning, got in the way. "Leta, Tony, come, Sophie, let's find another and look into its face." Here was the boy again. I snapped the picture. Confidence soaring, and remembering to maintain accurate government records, I wrote a second entry in my log: *Subject 3—Morning atmospherics, close-up of Tony, approx. eight years old Jul. '48: Cowessess.*

Tony, hair falling in his eyes making him blink, was a nervous observer; and, as I was to learn later, on the ride back to the Regina airport, he had been taken from home as a five-year-old by church and school officials. Hugh Passmore, Indian agent, said that, so far, the girls had escaped going at all. About six-year-old Sophie, he said, "She has an exacting manner, that one." The younger girl was self-assured, he said, and, he sighed, heaven knows, there was the one-year-old baby boy.

As the group made its way toward a bush of flashing leaves, their mother, tapping each child on the shoulder, told them that they needed but three important things: sharp eyes, total stillness, and a sharp memory. "Can you?" she asked.

"We're big now, and Tony is back from boarding school." That was Sophie.

It was Mrs. Stevens's first real smile of the morning. Her teeth had a greyish cast and might not photograph well, but her features more than compensated. I realized that I had grown so relaxed I was actually enjoying the fresh, bright morning. I stepped all the more quietly now, too, silent as a fox.

Mrs. Stevens put a hand to her cheek as she drew the children into a semicircle. "Here is a snapdragon," she said. The children, kneeling, heads bowed, marveled at its green iridescence. I closed in, camera clear of the tall grass. Mrs. Stevens cautioned the children, "The shine disappears if people touch. So be careful." Each child touched a leaf only. "That's the way," she said, sunlight lighting her face. I snapped the photo. At that moment, I could care less who said what in Ottawa. I wrote the entry with a strong hand and a flourish: *Subject 4—Mrs. Stevens, as her husband might see her Jul. '48: Cowessess.*

"Here's a sweet pea patch," she called. The children's eyes, so packed with wanting to see, seemed to be flooding. They gathered around. The light alone was pure Karsh. I was stunned. But my shutter finger froze; and so entranced was I by the image, I missed a family shot that would have gone down very well in Ottawa.

"Their petals form a hug," she was saying. "Look. There's a place for a tiny seed inside, like a baby. Just like you were once, remember?"

"I do!" The children called out in unison, which made their mother laugh.

She looked toward the house, the baby asleep there. She put her hand to her cheek again—the tooth, I guessed.

She pointed out a cowslip this time. "See this blossom, it's as if it's carved from an orange cone and curved round a tiny hole, no seam at all anywhere, see? And, careful, they fall easily. Pick up only the tumbled ones. Mind, don't knock the plant. Or it will signal the others and they will all drop way too soon."

His mother's hand on his shoulder, Tony's face had brightened. Had I known his full story, I would have watched for, and possibly even captured, that boarding school sadness, gone for the moment. My entry said only: *Subject 5—Close-up of mother and son showing family connectedness Jul. '48: Cowessess.*

I decided not to add, or subtract, a single word.

Mrs. Stevens said, "Wee Doco will be waking up." The one-year-old slept seconds away, at a run. Heading to the house now, she answered Tony's questions: yes, there were good things about boarding school. "We learned new names for old, old flowers. We learned other new words like scissors, paper, pencil, and eraser." Best of all, she said, she loved words like "lavender," "ochre," "rust," and "lemon yellow." She winced.

She told Tony how she had wished to know the names of all the flowers in the world. Instead, she had learned mainly vegetable names from weeding and hoeing in the boarding school garden, like all the other children. But, she said, she had seen a picture book of a real English garden once. It was labelled with hard words like "rampart" and "column." It made her curious, she said, and made her wish to learn. "Just like you—a schoolboy."

I summed up my catch: *Subject 6—Children, close-up Jul. '48: Cowessess; and Subject 7—Older daughter, Sophie, about six Jul. '48: Cowessess.*

"Why didn't you stay in school?" Tony asked. "Were you scared?"

"When I passed into grade five, I was put back into grade one. We had to start over again, with the same books." No, she didn't know why, she said. Oh, some things scared her, all right. When the dentist came to the school, for instance, he put big, clunky tools in her mouth that, when turning and spinning, tunnelled and growled right in her head. She laughed again.

Taking a roundabout way, I was the first to reach the house. I waited out of sight, outside by the open window. I took a wide-angled shot of the inside, and wrote: *Subject 8—Inside the home, a small lean-to to the left, woodstove, cupboard, table and chairs Jul. '48: Cowessess.*

The four quietly entered the dim, drowsing house. Mrs. Stevens stood stock-still, struck by something. "That's funny. A pain's tapping in my tooth."

She patted the side of her face. "Early this morning, when I got up to give Wee Doco his bottle, a sharp pain jabbed up here. Tony, get up on the chair and hand me Dad's toothache drops from the top shelf."

Tony climbed onto the creaking chair, hand outstretched. He felt around on the highest shelf of a cream-coloured cupboard, its green trim fading to beige. Sealers and plates lined the middle shelf. From the top, he handed down a tin of salve, a bottle of baby Aspirin, a blue jar of Vic's VapoRub, a bottle of green liniment, and a vial of toothache drops. My eyes roamed the lower shelf: two Old Dutch and Ajax cans stood next to a stack of frayed tea towels. Tony held up the vial of drops to the light. He shook his head. Even the smell was gone.

"Hand me the vanilla instead." Pain creased Mrs. Stevens's face. She peeked at Wee Doco, who was stirring.

"When's Dad coming?" Tony's face revealed tension again.

"In a couple of days. He's on foot, mind. People might give him a lift in, though. When he buys the tractor, it won't be more than a day, maybe."

I wanted to get a close-up of the cupboard's contents but had to cut my losses. The angle was impossible, and I had given my word that the children would not see me. The last thing I needed was trouble.

Then Mrs. Stevens screamed. She grabbed her face and fell onto the bed. "My tooth!" she whimpered. The children rushed to her. She tried to speak, but Wee Doco was screeching and flailing his arms. The children stood dazed. It was their mother's sudden guttural cry that propelled them into action.

I willed body and mind against jumping in to help. I had put my camera down. Pulling it back up by its strap, I watched Leta dip a small piece of rag in a saucer of vanilla and hand it to her mother. Sophie lit a fire and then set on the stove a small amount of water in a pot and began crushing two baby Aspirins between spoons, adding drops of water to make a paste. Tony grabbed up a flat-edged rock from the woodbox and crushed kernels of clove on the cupboard counter. The girls tied the bits up in a corner of a dishcloth, which Sophie then dipped into the heated water.

Mrs. Stevens pressed the Aspirin paste to her gums and, after a minute or two, her hands turning red, then white, again and again, she squeezed the clove mixture to her gums. Eyes shut, she howled. She screamed at the children, "Leave! Leave! Get away from the house! Go!"

Leta grabbed the baby, handing his empty bottle to Tony.

"Go!" This sent the children fleeing across the tall grass to the far end of the barnyard. They ran behind a greyed haystack leaning toward a mudded stable. Hands trembling, I raced to the side of the stable to keep them in view, took the picture and scrawled an entry: *Subject 9—Children running, toddler looking back over shoulder of big brother against barnyard, stable, implements Jul. '48: Cowessess.*

Wee Doco grew all the more fretful. Tony broke into a run back to the house. He returned with a coat from the porch. The girls, in the meantime, took turns gouging out a ledge in the haystack for Wee Doco to lie down in. Their mother's wailing reached here, too. Again, Tony ran to the house, this time returning with the sugar bowl and a sealer of hot water from off the stove, for the bottle. He said their mother was on the bed, her head all covered up.

I knew I should, but I could not make myself go back to the house for that one revelatory close-up of the cupboard and its contents. I stayed put.

I was amazed at the children's dexterity and their quickness of thought as they handled the boy. Leta poured warm water into his bottle, as Tony eyed what a teaspoon of sugar is. They removed the toddler's diaper, saying that if they held him at arm's length, he could pee on the ground. Looking at Wee Doco's bright red cheeks and sweating hairline, Tony said, "He's way too hot."

"Let's take him down to the well," Leta said. "He can sit in the shade."

They headed for the well. I followed at a safe distance, ducking behind a grey-weathered shed, and then a rusting plough, a beat-up buggy, and a lilac bush. I wanted to kick myself for missing these key photographic moments. But the children were running headlong down a steep hill, the toddler bouncing on Tony's shoulder. As they disappeared, one by one into the trees ahead, I stepped onto the hill. A small clearing came into view below. They had gathered near a wooden contraption. I crawled within hearing distance.

From his perch on Tony's arm, Wee Doco looked around. My shutter finger was itching, but I ignored it. The cries from the house had grown dimmer, the lower I descended. Finally there was silence. The sun blazed overhead. The hillside where I lay was abuzz with insects that had flitted up at my every step. They now tickled my sweating neck, ears, and nose. In the tall grasses, a host of grey-green, metallic-looking grasshoppers shaved their heads, tweaking scissor-like appendages up and over. It occurred to me that I might better try my luck as a nature photographer someday.

I studied the lay of the land. Water ran in a V down the ravine, dividing the stands of birch and poplar. It ran over rocks and gravel that fell away to lowering land, which, further on, linked the ravine to a valley. At the water's source, abutting the side of a hill nearest me, leaned a squared-off corral of planks. In a kneeling position, I had the perfect camera angle. I was relieved that here was opportunity, the chance to depict the Indians' use of lumber as an example of a modern adaptation. I took the shot. My entry, in concrete terms, added weight. *Subject 10 — A homemade, half-full, well in fitted plank-surround. Navy and white flecked enamel dipper on spike, with birch and poplar in background Jul. '48: Cowessess.*

Tony set Wee Doco down on the coat in the shade. The girls placed diaper, bottle, sugar bowl, and a sealer of water at hand. Tony made a little heap of pebbles for the toddler to play with, while Leta and Sophie counted 'five giant steps' to the well, from where a gravel bed of dappled stones lay under a sheet of burbling water. They stood listening to the water prattle over their feet and ankles. Tony joined them. He grabbed the dipper off its spike and, scooping water from the well, gulped it down. I aimed my camera at Sophie, red dress bright against the green of poplar leaves, but she stepped behind Leta, thence out of focus. Leta said Wee Doco must be thirsty. They filled his bottle, but he refused it. Upset, Tony threw a stone in the direction of a crow cawing like a sick baby up a tree.

"He's hot. We should cool him off," Tony said.

"How?"

"We could pat water on him."

"He won't like it."

"We'll take his shirt off. And when he's not looking, pour water on him," Leta said.

As for Wee Doco, he seemed listless and confused. The tall grass around him made him look tiny and sad. I decided I would take no picture, even if a government job depended on it and it alone.

"Let's just take his top off," Sophie said.

Wee Doco didn't object, but refused his bottle. The children went to stand in the cool stream. Leta again said, "He's too hot." With that, she walked to the well, scooped water up in the dipper, and strode over to Wee Doco.

"Hey!" Tony hollered.

Too late! Leta dumped the full dipper of cold water on Wee Doco's head. At that, the little one sat very still, hair a shiny cap, eyes shut. Then his body convulsed and he threw his head back. Tony swept him up. Wee Doco's mouth was turning purple. Tony jiggled him. Panicked, the girls tugged at his limbs. They blew breaths at his mouth. I jumped to my feet, but at that second, Wee Doco drew in a long, agonized breath. Finally he howled and howled. Sophie grabbed up the diaper, dried him off, and put his shirt back on. Her hands were shaking. Tony ripped off his own shirt and wrapped the little trembling legs. He placed the boy on the coat. The three dropped on the ground in front of him. Wee Doco, dazed, stopped crying. He flapped his arms and started cooing happily.

Of all things, at that moment Tony buried his face in his arms. The girls joined him, and all three began sobbing wildly. I decided that, in a photo with their heads down, it might be said that they were playing hide and seek. I snapped the photo and managed to write, for the record: *Subject 11 — Siblings seated on the ground, heads on knees Jul.'4: Cowessess.*

"Why are my children crying?" Full of cheeriness, it was Mrs. Stevens coming down the hill opposite me. I was never gladder to see anyone in my life. Shadows of poplars played against a beautifully lit lavender and floral dress as she strode up to her children. The girls ran to meet her, telling her what had happened and what they had done. She looked Wee Doco over, top to bottom, and kissed him.

"We all had a bad scare today," she said. "But think. Wee Doco's fine. My silly old toothache's gone. There's something nice to eat. Dad's likely on his way home. So, let's do a special thing to remember our beautiful morning." Carrying Wee Doco, she led them up the steep hill near the top of which was the house. I stepped into the clearing behind, from my vantage point on the opposite side of the valley's dip, and pressed the shutter. Later, when I was rereading my notes, I reminded myself to use precise technical descriptors. I had erred on the side of poetry this time: *Subject 11 — Mother and child in light descending Jul. '48: Cowessess.*

I moved to the open window after they went inside. Mrs. Stevens, eyes swollen, stood at the stove, stirring a mixture of flour, water, and sugar—her famous flour porridge, she said. She promised that the porridge would be a treat, as if tasted for the first time. And, she said, their father might pull into the yard as early as today. "It would be just like him to head home in the middle of the night."

She told them about the slow tractor he'd be driving home. "It's more powerful than all our wonderful dear old dead horses put together."

"Stronger than Fanny and Star?"

"Yes, there was real power in those two," she said. "Horses can think and remember. Tractors can't."

"See my arm!" The children showed one another loads of goose pimples. They had imagined mindless power, it seemed. I experienced sympathetic goose flesh myself, oddly.

Mrs. Stevens noticed me at the window. She raised her eyebrows. I held up one finger. I needed a family picture inside the house, and maybe another, for luck. But I realized, as I watched the little family making a diorama in a shoebox, that the shaken mother wanted foremost to help her children forget their fright. I pointed my camera, scribbled a note, and left. *Subject 12 — Indoors, in afternoon light, newly constructed diorama lit from w. window, family in mix of silhouette and frontal views Jul. '48: Cowessess.*

Hoofing it up the dirt path to the crossroad, I took a shot of the gate connecting a length of barbed wire demarcating the reserve boundary. For *Subject 13*, I decided I would wait and think about my entry wording.

It was an Ottawa wind ensuring that I gripped to my chest, a brown envelope of newly developed, enlarged photographs. Trepidation hounded my every step into the boardroom. I needed a permanent job. My photos would either help me reach that goal, or lose my prospects.

Not five minutes later, the black and white photographs were being passed from hand to hand. Seated round the boardroom table was Jerrod Henley's team: Kent Haultain, mild-mannered regional coordinator, heavyset, smartly dressed as usual in shirt and tie, with a cardigan and dress pants 'for the road'; Jessie Dukes, a brunette with strong brows, department research consultant, sharp as a tack and sharper of tongue, as people often said; Derek Cline, my quick-witted, earnest mentor. Rounding it off were two hawks from Finance: Warren Mays, still fairly young; and John Markham, obviously headed for wisdom.

The five sat around the table, assessing my work.

Jerrod Henley, our superior and the chair, raised his head. "So, what'll it be?" No one answered, for the moment.

"Kent Haultain!" Jerrod liked to hurry results along, voice a prod. A regional coordinator, oriented in field-based thinking, usually stopped dead short of all precipitous decisions, so I was not too worried. Abashed, Kent Haultain fudged his assessment. "I don't see the point of these, frankly." Lifting beefy shoulders, thick neck reddening in too tight a collar, he looked directly at Jerrod.

"You don't? Why not?" Jerrod scowled like a school principal, homework yet to be turned in.

Kent Haultain, flustered, threw in a storyline. "If you look, say, at this photo, it's of a lad. Now, if he were at least holding a toy gun ..."

"Okay, so we're missing the Lone Ranger's pistol. Anyone else? Jessie, anything to add?"

"I was wondering," she began, "whether these shots of Mrs. Stevens, lovely as she is, add anything to a report we have in mind?"

My face reddened. Were it my place to butt in, I would make it clear that Mrs. Stevens was a fine mother who had suffered horribly that day, but it would show me up as being defensive and unprofessional, a bad thing all around.

Jerrod leaned back in his chair, "All right. Two down. What else have we got?"

My hands broke into a sweat. Derek Cline, bless his soul, intervened. "Hang on, people. It's going to be what the public thinks, in the end. I see the sympathy. I also see … ah, look here, Subject 9—nice action shot, the children running, a toddler looking back at us, and the … the stable and implements. There's money in them thar hills!" Laughter eased the tension somewhat.

It occurred to me that even a trained eye might not ever deduce the facts of Mrs. Stevens's second-hand belongings. Out on the reserve, I thought her circumstances all so apparent. But then, these were photographs taken by a hobbyist—his future in the balance.

Jerrod turned his attention to the young accountant, Warren Mays. The stone-faced, post-Mussolini-cum-actor, pawing through the photos, now withdrew Sophie. In that particular shot, the family was on its way to the house from the garden. Sophie's mother had just turned to Tony and said that, yes, she really had wanted to learn. But when she passed grade five the people at school put her back to grade one. It was then Sophie stepped into the light and I pressed the shutter.

Nonetheless, hope dimmed when Warren Mays began speaking. "The kid has a thankless expression. That says a lot. For me, at least," he said. I bit my tongue.

Jerrod took hold of the picture and squinted at it. He pursed his lips, considering the remark, likely wondering, as I was, if the accountant had gotten himself stuck on a criterion of his own particular brand of bias. But his senior accountant, John Markham—thinning white hair, and wearing a grin like the toothy profile of a whale—leaned in, the better to see. "Sums it up nicely for me, too. Shows how we in government manage to be both frugal and fruitful in our grants contribution."

"And, what about this one?" Derek Cline, winking at me, held up the photo that went with my log entry: *Subject 12—Indoors, in afternoon light, newly constructed diorama lit from w. window, family in mix of silhouette and frontal views Jul. '48: Cowessess.*

As the picture made its rounds, I recalled why I had wanted that picture.

Mrs. Stevens had sent the children outdoors to gather up bits of natural objects like bark, twigs, stones, and burrs, "no glass or tin." As she waited, she got a shoebox out from under the bed. She mixed flour and water in a small pot and set it aside. Then, with a damp washcloth, dabbed on a bluing cube, she 'painted' the inside of the box. Scurrying back in, the children and Mrs. Stevens placed the findings in neat rows, on the kitchen table. "We are going to make us a little world," she told them. The result of that hour's activity was a diorama, a landscape of interlocking birch bark strips and a straw sun, rising from a golden horizon.

But it was only a beginning. Glued inside the box with the flour and water mixture were red berries, small twigs, pieces of perhaps dog fur, a mix of colourful feathers, and dappled stones. Stillness had embraced the children while their mother built what turned out to be a surprisingly captivating miniature scene. I felt compelled to raise my camera, but stayed my hand for the moment. Instead, I allowed my mind to 'find and lose boundaries' as I always did, and always loved, about still life paintings. I imagined the children experiencing the same sensation of relaxed control and rising wonder as they grew tall, then short, at will. In fact, this was another reason I loved photography. Experience told me that the children were seeing themselves as both big and small, near and far, inside and out of the box, not always at the mind's choosing ... It was then I took the photo.

Jerrod Henley got into traffic management mode. "Jessie, as you were saying?"

Startled, Jessie mumbled, uncharacteristically. "Well, it's all a bit of a jumble, isn't it? I mean, where is the eye to rest? This shoebox landscape stuff—I never was good at the world-in-a-drop-of-sand thing."

Her attempt at humour hid sarcasm's unruly snout. If anyone could knock a thing—like say, a job with benefits—down quietly, it would be Jessie Dukes. To quell my rising panic, I retreated to the artistic world of the diorama: its bits of bark had become hills, horsehair a tracery among branches; kinnikinnick like fire, striated birchbark a field...

"Warren!" The young accountant jumped at his name. Jerrod could use his voice like a bullhorn, without trying.

"Well, let's see," began Warren Mays. "The cupboard and kitchen furniture are okay—I mean 'representative.'" John Markham, his senior associate, nodding sagely, took a hard route now. "It's a well-stocked cupboard and a pretty decent table, affordable, obviously."

Replete with toothache drops, my mind said.

The young accountant, obviously finding his feet, dropped all hint of a velvet glove. "What do you say to the assertion that this expensive junket for pictures of Indians belies all notion of government thrift?"

Jerrod did not blink, even if our trip west had just been poked at with the business-end of a crowbar. In fact, he spoke like he had heard it all before. "Governments hire people like you and me to see through a reporter's eyes; especially when we consider the people with whom we have deep constitutional relations. 'Thrift' is but a relative term, dollar for dollar."

Jerrod turned to my mentor. "Derek, tell us what you think about the evidence, budget-wise, please." Jerrod, ignoring Jessie's chomping at the bit, was heading the team toward closure.

All heads turned to Derek Cline. "Well, it's a family, a healthy, nice-looking family enjoying … recreation. And living a decent, well-ordered life. That's the human side of it, if I may say."

"And you think the photos answer where the money goes?" Jerrod likely wished Derek had been a bit more explicit and more to the point.

Derek, looking at me, shrugged a half shrug. He seemed to be hoping I'd speak up in defence of my work but, all things considered, that would be out of line.

Wasting no time, Jerrod concluded the meeting

As the consultants stood to leave, he turned to me. "Got a minute?"

A distant voice and image burst into my mind: "One more thing," Mrs. Stevens is saying as she dips her slender fingers into a cup of water and flicks tiny droplets onto the little world. Dew settles on the moss and polishes the stones. At that moment a lake, a green meadow, and a stand of trees are a firmament sprung to life—exacting its own focal point.

Cutting Deals

WHEN OUR DAUGHTERS WERE going on seven and eight years old—Leta the younger one and Sophie the older—and still not in school, they knew little about how things worked in the world. To them, trade had to do with farmers' wives nearby and us women on the reserve. The girls came along each time I went to meet a farm lady at the fence where reserve and farmland touched. She might have eggs; I might have a duck. But trade in town was a whole other thing that day. It was one-sided. Len had tried to protect our horse. And I had to think of the girls.

Mr. Brottin lived in town. He dealt in horses. Len had no collateral, so he couldn't borrow the money to buy horses from Mr. Brottin. Disease had killed our best ones, and now we needed a new team in the worst way.

From the beginning, our puny savings went to Len's dream.

As soon as he got home from the Second World War, he made a plan. He wanted a racehorse in the worst way. Horse racing might bring in money. Len said that in England, horses won big. Men there were their own boss. They lived in mansions. So right away Len took on work as a farmhand. Add to that, he farmed his own land and hunted and sold grain and muskrat furs. He worked hard. Still, a four-year plan was hard on me and the girls. We went without.

Like all reserve women, I expected more when the men got back. I had been stuck on the reserve alone too long. No money to get around. No nothing! Money Len sent didn't go far. I couldn't work, what with the kids. Besides, it was a rule those days—Indian women and white women lived separate lives. The boarding school drummed it into us Indians. Churches drummed it into the whites, I suppose. Nobody knew. Nobody asked. We trading women just looked the other way whenever we saw one another in town. That was fine with me.

The soldiers had their problems, too. It got around at home that there had been women overseas. These women had nice things, like good dresses, nylons, and perfume. Our husbands overseas ate good food, too, at real restaurants. Us, we ate from the garden and from hunting, and if there was butter you could trade for it. We picked berries and Seneca roots around the valley for eggs and sugar. Now here it was going on ten years and Len had yet to buy me that silk blouse. And there was no Tangee lipstick or a new yellow cinch belt, like he promised either. Too busy recounting our cash.

There was trouble at home that time, too. We had to face our girls' getting schooled. When Len came home, our boy was taken away to boarding school. The authorities came for him. Tony was just five then, and he was scared and cried when he understood what was happening. When that truck pulled out of our yard, I screamed and screamed. One minute, our son had been playing in the dirt in the yard. The next, I was hurrying to wash his face and hurrying to change his clothes. He kept smiling at me as I hurried. I couldn't look at him. Next minute, he was gone. Even now I can hear him. I think that's why I got so sick for so long. Len didn't speak for many, many days.

Next they wanted our girls. Len said to me, "That'll be the day. When money rolls in, we'll buy time from Ottawa." Until then he and the other dads kept up the fight for a school here. The Indian agent got into a temper but the men held their ground, and the federal government grew real quiet. Not a word from the Indian agent, anyhow.

A racehorse was our one hope.

It was in June, on a day before our noon lunch, when Len actually brought a racehorse home. A pretty three-year-old bay with a black tail and mane. She would be our money-maker. More than that, we would come to see her as a member of the family.

We named her Bette. I couldn't believe she was finally home. Here stood this young, fine, quivering horse. Her nervousness worried me, but Len said she was just high-strung. She'd learn to manage her objections, he said, because she was intelligent. He told me to watch her ears to see for myself how they responded to his voice. She needed training, Len said. Then Bette would do what she was bred to do: race and win. The girls said Bette smelled beautiful. And she did! Like fresh grass and that fresh early morning air.

Len's four-year plan began unravelling the day he said, "It's time to go in to town. We need a team to haul grain, to haul wood and stones, and to pull the plough."

At the mention of town, the girls' ears pricked up. They held their breath. Our trips to town were few and far between. Still, I should have known. Might have paid attention to what I felt. But I was anxious. I said to Len, "What's the use? Nothing comes of it." My voice had no energy. I couldn't push things. Partly because I didn't want to have the girls looked down on. They were smart now, and knew what looks meant. Nevertheless, their eyes just now were bright as stars. Still, thinking about the tough time we were having, and with Len wanting to escape life in a shoebox, like he always said, I hated to see the girls suffer disappointment. We had only so much choice.

"Mr. Brottin from the livery stable wants to look Bette over. Swap a team for her," Len said.

"Not Bette!" I said. I loved that horse. She was the only horse for miles around that wasn't a nag or a big-boned sawhorse. I liked her shiny coat. Such a rich sheen against green fields! She was something. These past two summers she brought in good money. She won races at fairgrounds around the reserve and down in the valley.

"Mr. Brottin wants her bad," Len said. "Word is out. Bette is that good. He stopped and talked to me right out on the street in town the other day."

"I'll bet he did. So, what about next year's winnings, like you said?"

"Bette can still make money till fall. We need a team. Fanny's dead. Luc's hoof is going. Just think for a minute—we need to haul wood before winter. Then there's grain to haul for next spring's quota. The Indian agent says it's opening up." Len's eyeing me meant I shouldn't be questioning him in front of the girls.

"I see," I said. I tried to make my face match hope. Still, Sophie and Leta got teary-eyed when they found out we might leave Bette in town. At least she would still be living, I reminded them.

The girls had seen our horses die. A horse would be fine one day, its head up whenever Len crossed the field. The next day it would be on the ground like something had struck it down. Groaning, eyes glazed—even the girls saw how it gave up. In fact, all that summer, the girls faced many a day of rotten air wafting off dead horses. They found Fannie, our mare. That one reminded me of my old auntie. Fanny was down. The girls called and I ran to hold her head up. We scooped water from a rain pool and poured it down Fannie's throat. We used one of Len's high-top rubber boots Leta had on. Fannie's breaths began to rattle and she died. The girls were shaking. But they took it.

I asked Len, "What on earth's wrong with our horses, anyway? It must be something!"

"Could be when those planes were spraying last year." he said. "It's happened before."

"What? Farmers spraying?"

"My parents said that, back in their day, the hay fields were expropriated. Reserve land had been divided up for farmers who had their crops sprayed. My father said a plane would fly in over the fields, passing back and forth, again and again. A few days later, fish floated dead to the top of the lakes around here. Something like that is the cause. It's not natural."

Len got up and went to water and harness the team. We were going in.

I had to agree, we had no way out. Whatever the cause, out of a dozen horses, only five were alive, a sorrel mare and her colt, a bay with a bad foot, our dappled grey gelding, and Bette.

Now everything fell on her.

We had been so happy and hopeful those two short years. Len liked telling about the first time Bette approached him. She had whinnied and kicked but grew steadier as the morning went on. Len gave credit to Benjamin, the jockey we paid. He was the trainer. He had moved into the barn that spring, sleeping nights near Bette. Up at dawn, he'd feed, water, and groom her. Len said Benjamin was a master jockey. No false pride, stuck to his work. Bette fought the saddle, though! She took the bit, then she took the blanket, but when Benjamin tightened the girth strap, she bucked and bucked. Benjamin was finally able to mount her. He bent close to her ear and told her the story of her life, Len said. That helped her find her place. That same day, she walked up to Len and nuzzled his shoulder. "Benjamin is one hell of a jockey," Len liked to say after that.

Len was busy, too. He made a racetrack. He ploughed over a big oval shape in front of the barn, and then harrowed and disked the furrows flat. Back and forth he walked, over the track, again and again, dust rising at every step. By evening, the sun going down, he looked as if he were walking in a haze of gold. I was proud of him. He was a thin man, but he was well built and very strong. And when he wanted something! Well, he even picked pebbles, dozens and dozens of them, and filled gopher holes. What a worker! A few days, and the track was ready for Bette and the jockey.

The girls and I kept an eye out for Benjamin. Near us, he stood aloof. He ignored the giggly little girls who had a crush on him. He was a young Métis man, fair-skinned, blue-eyed, and blond. The works. He'd come up to the house, bowlegged, wearing cowboy boots, and stand over the wash basin out in the yard. He'd throw handfuls of sparkling water on his face. Then he'd give a hitch to his jeans and step into the kitchen. He never sat down to eat. He'd tilt his head back and swallow a soft-boiled egg in one gulp. He'd finish this off with a dipper of water. Then he'd nod to me and stride off, not saying a word.

After dishes, the girls and I would go to the track and watch Bette stamping the ground, prancing sideways. Round and round the track she went, led by Benjamin. Every once in a while, he'd stop to pick up a stone or a pebble and hurl it into the bushes. Finally it was time. The training now was about racing. About speed. Benjamin mounted the horse. The cantering around the track turned into a trot. Then pow! The horse burst into a gallop, and away they went, faster and faster, dust clouds churning. The two made a wonderful sight!

Our girls squealed and clapped. On the home stretch, horse and rider were just a blur. Loud pounding hoofs and sharp snorts rose and fell at each turn in the track. In a blink, Bette's hooves slammed to a stop and Benjamin jumped down to walk her. Like I say, it was one beautiful sight. For me, it always felt a bit awkward being so close to the horse and jockey then. It was the sharp smell, too—sharp as salt in the mouth, or sweat off hair. It was pure happiness, as if hope had come rolling in from a good strong place. And to think, these were only practice runs!

But soon a trade was coming. Len's face said so when he came back in and sat down at the table. I went over to the big stoneware jar under the kitchen table to get out a cotton bag of sugar. I had to show Len how low it was.

"I have the team ready," he said. "We'll tie Bette to the wagon. The colt will be fine at home for the day." Len told me how the business would go in town. The girls and I would wait in the wagon while Mr. Brottin's men looked Bette over. While waiting, we'd eat the sandwiches I packed. Then, with the ten dollars Mr. Brottin would give us for bringing Bette in to be seen by him in the first place, we'd hitch up our new horses, tie our sorrel and gelding to the back, and make a turn for home. Leaving Bette. On the way out, we'd buy a few groceries and a soft drink for the girls. This made Sophie and Leta smile a little.

"Will Mr. Brottin be good to Bette?" Sophie asked.

"He'd better be." I told her. "He has a good stable and lots of feed. Bette will like it there with the other horses."

But I could see there'd be no hiding us. The livery stable was just off Main Street. Town was small. The picture we made shouted Indians of the old horse-and-buggy days while their picture said modern cars and trucks. Anyway, we had to take the stares. Some were clear-eyed. Some spread smears. Some flashed lightning. I told the girls not to stare back, and they tried not to, even Sophie.

I was about to bring out the sandwiches, but Mr. Brottin was coming down the street, red and huffing, round and bossy. He growled to Len, "Bring 'em to the house. Leave your team with my men."

He wanted to talk in private, he said. Len reminded the girls to answer questions, but not to ask any. It was a short walk up to Mr. Brottin's house. Inside, he sat wheezing in a large wooden rocker that stood beside a reddish-brown wooden table. The room had dark-stained cupboards standing opposite the table near where we sat, and an iron pot-bellied stove in the middle of the room. Mustard-coloured drapes hung in front of sheers in the front window. The table reflected oxblood red on Mr. Brottin. The girls stood side by side, beside me. Len and I were sitting on kitchen chairs facing Mr. Brottin.

"How old are the girls?" he asked, tilting his head at them.

"Turning eight and nine," Len said.

"In school yet? Heard you Indians are holding your kids back."

"That's right," Len said. "They're staying home till we get a school on the reserve."

"Not any time soon though, eh?"

"We'll see."

"Any other kids?"

"A boy in boarding school in Birtle, Manitoba."

The girls nudged each other, noticing that this time their father had not told how Tony cried about that place. When I looked, the girls seemed so small and skinny in their little bleached sugar-bag dresses. I always did my best on their dresses. I caught Mr. Brottin studying my hair when I took off my kerchief. I always wore it to keep road dust off. Mr. Brottin got very rude, all of a sudden. He said, and what was worse, in front of the girls, "Got a bun in the oven?"

"No." Len answered for me. I felt my face burn. Len laughed, but not in his usual easy way.

Mr. Brottin belched into the room. "I like a good pony."

Len nodded, his eyes down. "Bette, yes."

I had the impression Mr. Brottin had the girls in mind. He stared at them as he spoke about Bette. I didn't like the tone of voice. "Nice shaped head, good teeth, strong little legs, long mane, smooth flanks, compact haunches, fine, fine tail—the kind a man likes to ride. Bet you like to ride, eh, Len?"

Len had difficulty getting his words out.

Mr. Brottin's eyes roved like icy silk up and down Leta. His eyes seemed to be gobbling wrists, knees, and ankles. I felt faint. Bad breath, like wind drifting over rotten carcasses, filled the small, airtight room. I pulled Leta closer to me. She was used to stares. On top of it, she was more forward than Sophie. And, sure enough, she began forgetting herself. She smiled at Mr. Brottin. Len, too, noticed that the horse dealer was distracted. So, as if he were back in his soldier's uniform, he said, "Bette's a good racer. Young Benjamin LeRou is the jockey. A fine young man. Give them a racetrack and the spirit shows."

But Mr. Brottin, in control, said nothing.

Len asked, "Do we have a deal?"

Mr. Brottin started. "Well, now, I've been thinking. Seems to me there's no guarantee your pony will stay healthy and strong enough to win anything. I'm hearing you people's horses are dropping like flies."

"I have no guarantees, either," Len said. "Could be your team will fail as workhorses. Bette, though, is young. She's trained and fit to race. Today."

Mr. Brottin smiled. "How can you be so sure she won't sicken on me?"

"I've kept her corralled. Whatever is killing horses kills them in the pasture and out in the open field. Bette drinks well water, hauled especially. The rest drink from the slough and creek."

Mr. Brottin let on as if he'd made up his mind. "Okay. It's a deal."

I hung onto Leta's hand as she jiggled with impatience.

"Tell you what though, Len," Mr. Brottin leaned forward, his rocking chair creaking. "In six months' time, I'll give you an additional horse if my horses die. But I want something in return."

"Let's hear it."

"It's about those able-bodied daughters of yours, your little ponies, there."

Again, Len's voice choked up. "What about them?"

But Mr. Brottin turned to Leta. "What's your name?"

"Speak up," Len said. He taught the girls army manners.

They answered one after another. "I'm Leta."

"I'm Sophie."

"Do you girls know how to work?"

Len spoke for them. "They know what work is."

Mr. Brottin, ignoring Len, spoke again to the girls. "Well, one of you can live here and help keep house. Besides, you should be going to school. It's the law."

Now Mr. Brottin turned his eyes on me. "She'll go to school, like the law says, here in town. There'll be light housekeeping. No cooking or laundry. She'll have her own room."

I felt Leta's excitement. I knew what she was thinking—a room of her own. A bed with real sheets and a pillow. A window all to herself. I squeezed her hand hard.

"Sorry," Len said. "My family stays together. That means us and our daughters."

Mr. Brottin's pink face turned to stone. "You mean to say we have no deal? You people should use your head! You'll have to turn your racehorse into a dray, hauling rocks and stuff all over hell and damnation, instead of racing—call that good?"

"Bette's a racer," Len said. "And she'll stay that way."

"Well, let's hear what your daughters want. How's that again, Leta?"

Leta's eyes sparkled, bright. "Me? Yes, I will!" she called out.

I almost fainted, but Len caught my arm. He pulled me to my feet. He herded me and the girls out the door ahead of him.

"Just a minute, here," Mr. Brottin was hollering. "Talk to me! Talk to me, I say. Come 'ere, here!"

"By the jumping Jesus!" Len said, voice rising.

He pushed us out onto the sidewalk and hurried me and the girls down the street and onto the wagon. Bette, red coat shimmering, flicked her ears forward.

White Wash

WINNIE STOLE MY HEART. Loving her meant that I had to move to an Indian reserve. I was twenty-nine and jobless, half French, a man following his heart. I was also white among Indians, and a World War II army reject, due to poor eyesight. Indian boys much younger than me went overseas. Not that I was blind—far from it. But the army saw it that way. It didn't matter that I spoke three languages, a major thing in war. Also, a necessity in St. Boniface, heart of Métis country, where I lived those days. I couldn't find a job and so went looking in Saskatchewan, stumbling across the girl of my dreams.

Winnie had just returned home from residential school—seventeen, a redhead with ideas. I met her through a buddy of mine, Len Stevens, before he went overseas. The moment I laid eyes on her, I trailed along, following her and Len and their pals. I loved the catch in her voice and that musical laugh. She was bold, too, bolder than me, anyway. I came to realize much later that if anything could get me kicked off the reserve, it might be my association with her.

"Julien," she would say, "why did you duck out of sight back there? I see you everywhere the whole time. Scared of me, eh?"

She teased me. And if she laughed at my expense, so what? She warmed my world. One day I asked her to stop and talk. She just looked at me, long strands of windblown hair across her narrow face. I asked her to marry me. She doubled over, laughing. Then she straightened up, a major cloudburst darkening her eyes, and then, I have to say, she ran away. She stayed away that year and most of the next, sometimes on her reserve, or near town. Word was, she went dancing in and around the valley, at the Mission, down the hill from her parents' place. She had gotten married, common law, but it had not worked out. I didn't want the details.

My heart had gotten the better of me. I could not hold back. It did not matter that I was an oddball, like the dislocated half-breeds who arrived from the flooded Red River area in Manitoba a few years back. I wanted a life with Winnie. Finding no work and my rent money in town running out, I talked my way onto the reserve. Len Stevens's folks stood for me. They also pitched in and helped build me a mud shack. I took a spot across the creek from Len's parents' place and waited there, hoping to see Winnie. After a few missed chances, I cornered her one windy day, and I talked and talked. Winnie agreed to live with me. Marriage was out, she said, because she didn't want to lose her Treaty status.

She set some rules. We would live common-law but in separate houses. Otherwise, it was no. "And I don't care how hard you cry," she said, not laughing, "I want my own life. Even if I say I love you, don't get any ideas and go all stubborn on me after. And don't try to baby me just because you're old. You're not my dad." Both her parents were dead. I had no wish to replace them.

I promised. I built her a little house, part log and part lumber, about fifty paces from mine. Other than that, we lived like an ordinary couple. She was not short on energy, and I watched her chase her ambitions. One time she got ahead of herself. She caused trouble and it hurt a lot of people.

I suppose her stubborn ways began when she was little. She told me that in boarding school, when she heard The Lord's Prayer for the first time, a clothesline had popped into her mind, a pure white sheet hanging from it, bright against a blue sky. "My best dream," she said. I thought it a bit odd, but held my tongue. She had a mind of her own. I might have seen trouble coming, might have called the warning, but there it was, I wasn't her father. And it wouldn't have made any difference, anyway. Not with Winnie. Her spirit and her brain simply took off, like a puppy's nose on a scent.

As she flew around each morning, getting her housework done, I hauled wood and carried water for her. Most days, after the woodbox and reservoir were filled, we'd have a cup of tea out on her doorstep. Later I would round up one of the horses Len loaned me. This way I could ride around doing odd jobs for his parents and for older folks whose sons were also overseas.

During that first year, trying to get to know Winnie, I built up a name for myself: I was a kind and careful man, a man of many skills, a man who kept his word. I worried that some bad actor might try to get me barred from the reserve—a terrible act not unknown among half-breeds on Indian land. I had to gain people's confidence and hold it. I was fair-skinned and blue-eyed, after all.

I made my rounds. People began with saying, though not directly to my face, that someone, like maybe Winnie, had started gossip. A rumour was hurting entire families, it was said —and this to benefit herself. I worried. I heard the tale and, silly as it was, it had found ready ears and willful tongues. Word had it that two elderly ladies, Kokum Stevens and Kokum Arthur, were on the warpath, their kin lined up on opposing sides. Perhaps in telling me, people expected me to confront Winnie, straighten her out, and make her apologize. But I said nothing to her.

Talk grew. Each of the two old ladies, it was now being said, had vowed to prove herself the best housekeeper on any reserve. People were outraged, the insult taken to heart. Few could afford a bar of soap, let alone soapsuds and bluing. Still, the old ladies had agreed, it was said, to a contest in place of a face-to-face knock-down battle. I kept my ear to the ground as I chopped wood, cleaned wells, and hoed gardens. The tale upset me. My own mother had been called a "dirty foreigner," and, what's more, in a world of broken English. Gossip hurt the boy in me. I felt for those old ladies.

I discovered that Len Stevens's mother knew nothing about the rumour. She and her daughters said not a word about it when I stopped by one afternoon to replace the ripped tarpaper on their roof, and to mix mud and straw to patch the chinks in the walls of their mud house. Kokum Stevens, warm and kind, was her usual self.

As for Sarah's aging mother, Kokum Arthur, on Kahkewistahaw Reserve next door, I would see her in town sometimes, slight of build and sure-footed in her traditional moccasins, going about getting sugar, lard, and flour. I had no idea what the talk might be doing to her.

One morning after a fine rain, there in the clearing between our two houses, I saw Winnie come high-stepping over the tall wet grass, holding up the hem of her faded purple dress, her red hair spun with fire. She told me that Sarah Stevens had gotten wind of a rumour going around, likely from her seven-year-old daughter, Sophie. I said I saw how it could happen. Little Sophie's job was to take messages back and forth between the two women, almost daily. But now, Winnie said, it seemed Sarah suspected her of something. "All I ever said was that I'm the enemy of dirt. And that's altogether true, isn't it, Julien?" I nodded but said nothing, hoping to keep a lid on things.

Sarah Stevens spoke to it briefly when I went to check her potato cellar for mice. She said she didn't care what people said—as long as they kept her mother out of it and, of course, Len's mother. It was sad to see Sarah in pain. She had small children, and missed Len. Plainly, gossip had raised its ugly head. Plainer still, it was spewing muck on the innocent, as usual.

Sarah must have felt caught up. Old ladies of fine reputation, now in their seventies, were being smeared. She told me that people had said that her mother ought to know better. They said that for Sarah, as the daughter, not to mention daughter-in-law, to have brought such talk down on her family had to mean that she, herself, was a dirty housekeeper, didn't it? And didn't it mean that her whole family must be like that, even if they lived on Cowessess now? I agreed with Sarah that the least of her worries had to be mice in the cellar. There being none, in fact, I left, shaking my head.

A storm was on its way. Still, it was hardly my business. It did seem, however, in some way, to be Winnie's.

I did not want there to be trouble between Sarah and Winnie. It could hurt us all eventually. I knew that there was true affection between the two. Sarah told me on my rounds that she and Winnie had become fast friends after boarding school. As young women they had spent hours sharing dreams and listening to Sarah's scratchy shellac gramophone records that Len sent from England. The girls, Sarah said, imagined owning houses with lace curtains and colourful blooms on every windowsill. Each of them would have lovely French petticoats in a range of soft colours, and silk shawls sprayed with English Lavender. Lately, though, I noticed there was no mention of such things from either, save the times Winnie grumbled aloud to herself.

Whatever the case, I had to keep my distance from any form of mischief; otherwise I might get myself barred. And Winnie risked losing her rights were she to leave the reserve with me for good.

From my doorstep, one early July morning, I could tell she was up to something. She came over, whistling "Yankee Doodle," her hair like wild fire in the sunlight. She asked if I had any black paint. I did not. I did not ask why she needed it, either. Later that afternoon she rolled into the clearing, driving a sorrel hitched to a peeling black buggy.

"Uncle Charlie loaned me," she called out, laughing as she drew up, "for over the summer, eh, Julien?" I nodded and wondered what the devil she had up her sleeve.

All the next day I watched her give the borrowed gear a going over. She greased the wagon axles and checked for the soundness of the horse collar, the halter, hame straps, and reins. She came to my place dangling a piece of frayed harness. "Julien, can you mend this halter for me?" I did. I asked no questions, even as she watched me poke holes through the leather strap with an awl and then flatten a row of rivets with my hammer. She left happy, but told me nothing. I heard her singing inside her house: "Don't Fence Me In."

It seemed that not a day had gone by when a white banner, flapping in the breeze, came into view—half a bedsheet, actually, lettered in charcoal saying Whiter than White. Without a word she hitched up her sorrel, pulled out of the yard, and clattered down the stony road. People reported seeing her driving her outfit up and down the reserve road, her red hair flying. She waved and called to everyone, laughing at every little thing, her white banner billowing.

But after a week or so, she grew glum. She came to over to say that her banner had failed to attract clients. "It's only Sarah, so far," she said, sniffing. I was pleased that she and her old friend were speaking, even if Sarah might be tending the friendship for old time's sake, and on account of Len. On the other hand, it seemed Sarah might only be Winnie's guinea pig. Sarah had accepted a sample jar of a Winnie's homemade cleaning solution, a kind of foaming powder that she had labelled White-and-Whiter.

Winnie, upset, said that people kept telling her that all Indians on-reserve could make no money. "The nerve!" she said, eyeing me. "It won't get me down. No siree." She had apparently told Sarah to her face that she would prove people wrong. I did not have the heart to say to her that the doubters might be on to something, all things considered.

"You'll see!" Winnie's colour rose in her cheeks. My face, an open book, had just said too much. I tried to take her in my arms but she whirled out of the house.

She began her business campaign by turning her wee house into a spotless showcase. When I arrived for meals, I noticed towels and sheets ironed and stacked in an open-shelved cupboard that she had pulled into her big room. The entire house smelled of washing and ironing—scorch mixed with soapsuds, tinged with lye. But when people dropped by, they didn't take it in. They said nothing about Winnie's polished stove, the scrubbed pinewood floor, and the firewood lying straight in the woodbox beside the stove. Our closest neighbours might have asked how she kept it all up. But then again, those days, ordinary curiosity was often sidelined.

Take the picture I gave Winnie that past Christmas. She hung it in plain view on the wall of her big room, a fair-sized print in a gold frame. It gave her joy, she said, and inspired her. It was of four lavishly dressed dogs—a border collie, a basset hound, a bulldog, and a red retriever—seated in chairs and pulled up to a round oak table where they played a game of cards. To Winnie, they looked like rich men from town; and as she said this, she laughed and did a little jig. Her happy excitement filled my heart.

Little Sophie liked the picture, too. She would stare at it while she waited for Winnie's return message to Sarah. It was no wonder. The dogs wore eye-catching clothes. The jackets alone were of velvet trimmed in gold braid and shiny gold buttons. What's more, the dogs sat on pink and gold striped cushions on polished oak chairs. The bulldog, at least to my eye, smirked at us over its crystal goblet filled with a pale golden drink. It pleased me that Winnie and little Sophie liked the picture.

Sophie, though, had apparently told her mother one day that she thought the bulldog mocked Winnie. I could see why the child might think so. Day after day, Winnie could be seen bent over a steamy washtub in the middle of her big room, her reddened hands scrubbing at piles of wet clothes, sweat pouring down her face, all for an income.

She did too much, I knew. As for the dogs, they sat easy in their game. Winnie didn't see it that way. In fact, I overheard her say to Sophie, "If dogs can be rich, so can I."

One day Winnie hinted at trouble brewing. Something was going on, she said. It was as if people had stopped talking. "They used to poke elbows and snicker when I was around. Now, nothing."

I said it must be a relief. I asked her if it pleased her. She spat like a cat. "You don't understand, do you, Julien!" With that, she churned the dust home to her house. I had no idea what upset her. I wanted to know, but she gave me nothing to go on. I received only snippets, and in a roundabout way at best.

Then I, too, sensed something underfoot. I kept an eye out. Besides, it was time I put new putty on Winnie's windowpanes.

That morning she had hauled rainwater in from the barrel under the spout of the roof out by the door, to fill the washtub and the reservoir. Water sloshing in her pail, she appeared stumbling and, maybe, even anxious. Now and again she stood still and peered across the yard, like an owl weaving its head as it stared through the trees. She seemed to be waiting for little Sophie with a message from Sarah.

Sophie was easily spotted on a sunny day. She would skip down to the creek, where she might stop and play, before running up to the house. I watched for her, too, today, wanting news. Of course, I kept busy scraping and chipping off cracked pieces of putty from the window frame in the big room. Winnie hardly noticed me. Soon a little blue dress in slatted light rippled through the birch trees and poplars. I wondered if Winnie saw, but I held my tongue.

In no time Sophie stood at the door, barefoot as usual. This time she had run straight up to the house. In a flash she stood waiting in her spot by the kitchen stove in the big room.

Winnie said, "Well, if it isn't my best-est friend!" She grinned like a ten-year-old.

Sophie turned her gaze to the dogs. But Winnie kept it up. "Look!

Look at us, both in blue dresses!" Then, without any forewarning, she asked, "So, who do you think's gonna win the contest, Kokum Stevens or Kokum Arthur?"

I nearly fell over.

Sophie must have heard the talk. She stood for a moment, open-mouthed. The bulldog in the picture had scoffed, all right. At this nutty thought, I shook my head. But Winnie, not seeing the girl's reaction, pushed harder. "You mean you haven't heard? Didn't your mom tell you about the competition? Both your kokums almost came to fisticuffs, eh? About who will win that certificate—The Best Housekeeper Certificate, courtesy Whiter than White!" Sophie ran out the door, leaving no message and taking none.

A certificate? I glanced at Winnie. The half-smile meant her mind was already on the chase. "My clients!" was what she said, half addressing me. "All those relatives from Cowessess, Sakimay, Kahkewistahaw, and Ochapowace."

Danger reared its head. Sophie's mother might put two and two together and then send a letter to Len. Winnie didn't know fingers were pointing her way—and that Len's could point my way. Without a second thought, I dropped my putty knife and ran madly after Sophie. I would tell the little girl that Winnie was only joking. I would say there was no way Winnie had caused any grief.

But it was too late. Sophie had outrun me. She and her mother stood talking in the kitchen. I sat on the doorstep, my usual place, waiting a moment before knocking and asking what I might do.

"What? Quit your tattling, Sophie Stevens! I told you, no tattling! What's wrong with you?" Sarah scolded the little messenger, claiming also that she had carelessly tracked dirt into the house.

But Sophie held her ground. "It's true, Mama," she said. "Whiter than White is picking a winner!"

Losing her way as a mother, Sarah now asked an adult question of the girl. "What did Winnie mean by that?" The little girl had no answer. "Besides," Sarah, in her ire, added unfairly, "you have a big mouth sometimes." I thought I should to go inside and say something humorous, like maybe people had gotten mixed up about the upcoming fight on the radio, between the famed champion boxers Joe Louis and Ezzard Charles.

But Sophie's mother hollered, "I know who's at the bottom of this! And she won't get away with it!"

A scuffle of shoes and Sarah burst out of the house, pulling Sophie along behind her. It was headlong down the path to Kokum Stevens's place they rushed, dust puffing out from under Sarah's shoes. It was time for me to hurry off to the doorstep at the old Stevenses' house; by now my sitting on doorsteps looked normal. Today I took a shortcut, dashing like a boy through the tall weeds and through a clump of bushes and burrs, my heart pounding. Beating the pair to the Stevenses', I sat on the step, hands dangling from my knees.

Sarah, head down, charged up. She stood for a moment, catching her breath. Sophie, face crammed with uncertainty, fingered clusters of plaited white onions and purple corncobs hanging from rusted spikes on the wall just outside the door. Sarah's eyes met mine, but she did not really see me. She pushed the squeaking hinged door open, pulling Sophie inside. Len's female relatives fell silent. I could hear the dried vegetable husks whispering against the house in the breeze.

I turned my head. Sarah, trembling, stood before her mother-in-law. Seated at the table were three sisters-in-law: Ena, Mary, and the oldest, Gina, on a visit from Calgary. Any other day I would have stepped inside for a taste of those hot homemade buns with butter and raspberry jam. But today, entering even out of politeness would make their business my business. I had to keep a distance, for Winnie's sake, and for mine.

The old lady reached for a cup. "Come, Sarah, come Sophie," she said happily.

But Sarah was not there for tea. She wasted no time in squaring off at Ena, a tall, angular, mild-mannered woman known for her graciousness.

"Shame on you, Ena! You have the nerve! Putting Winnie up to dirty tricks!"

Ena got to her feet. "What are you talking about, Sarah?"

"You know very well! That so-called contest—my mother and Len's mother—your own mother, for shame! You and Winnie spreading lies and gossip!"

"Pardon? What lies? What have I to do with Winnie? She's your friend." Ena was confused and seemed to be trying to cover all bases.

My heart sank. Winnie, absent and so unaware, had just been pushed into the centre of a showdown.

Sarah Stevens's voice shook. "You live for gossip. You dance a giddy step when you think you've got somebody. You'd call down your own mother. There's proof!"

Sputtering, she grabbed Sophie by the shoulder and spun her out the door, then hurled a final insult at her in-laws. "I'm taking the kids to my mother's, to Kahkewistahaw. Len's going to hear about this. I'm sending a letter overseas today!" Tears gushing, she rushed Sophie up the path and away.

Ena called from the door, "But I don't know what you mean, Sarah! Sarah!"

But Sarah was beyond turning back.

Just before dusk that day, I spotted Sarah Stevens hurrying across the shallow end of the creek, straight to my door. She told me that she wished to apologize for not acknowledging me and for letting her mouth run away on her. Her face was bleak. There had to be a misunderstanding, I told her, and she was not to blame. She thanked me and asked if I could please take her to her mother's on Kahkewistahaw next day, say around one o'clock. I agreed and she left. She had not as much as glanced at Winnie's little door, ajar.

I wished Winnie would come and see me. But she did not that

day. I would not have known what to say to her anyway. She might already have guessed that Sarah had asked me to take her to her Kahkewistahaw family.

At about one o'clock the next day, Sarah, Sophie, the baby, and I set out. Earlier I helped her load boxed clothes, baby food, and bedding onto the wagon. I put my saddle on board, too, in case. As custom required, I leaned a short pole against the outside of the door of the house to give notice to passersby that no one was home. Then it was four miles of bone-rattling travel ahead of us. The clanking steel rims of the wagon wheels striking on the stony path filled the entire trip. I took it slow on account of Sarah and the children.

In spite of this, Sarah was wrung out by the time we arrived. Sadness etched her face, so I tried to cheer her up. "Things will turn around," was what I said. After all, I told her, here was her childhood home, a nice two-storey, whitewashed house, and looking like a friendly lady sitting by a slough. And didn't the sun's late afternoon rays cast a wonderful light over the yard?

Then I saw them. A row of children and grown-ups of all ages and sizes, in a line outside the door of the house, happy and excited to see us.

Sobs choked Sarah's voice as she entered the house. "Len's family is against us! They claim we're dirty."

I sat down on the step, heaving a sigh. Sophie came to sit there, too, hugging her knees. She took quick peeks at Kokum Arthur through the window, who was seated in a chair, examining the end of a braid. The old lady, speaking a mix of Cree and English, reminded me of the old days in St. Boniface. She was telling Sarah that being clean meant moving one's tipi every two days to a fresh place filled with sweetgrass growing near fresh water. It meant washing clothes in rainwater and spreading them over bushes to dry all day in the sun. "A house, him, you can't move," she said in English. She also claimed that clean minds stop bad stories. With those simple words, she snuffed the fire out of the rumour Sarah and I carried over. There would be no more talk of it. Little Sophie looked disappointed. Or did I just think so?

I had a job to do. I unhitched the team and saddled up the roan. She had pep in her still. I told Sophie to let her mama know I would be returning early next morning.

I felt a strong urgency. I had to let Len's mother know that Sarah and the kids were fine. Besides, I needed time to think. The roan and I took it slow, taking shortcuts across open fields where ducks and mud hens carved circles on ponds and slough that reflected the red and gold of the setting sun. I felt comforted by the soft air and the gentle rhythm of the roan. I wondered if Winnie waited at home, and what she might be thinking. Sometimes, without warning, I felt lonely for her, as though something divided us, or might. I knew I could never ask her to forego her Treaty rights. If it came to that, it would have to be a clean break.

I got to Kokum Stevens's house as dusk fell. Walking up to the door, I could see the Stevens women through the window, a lantern on the table casting a yellow light. They were at supper. The women sat, elbows on the table, chins on hands, eyes downcast. I tapped the door lightly, went in, and stood in the middle of the room. Cooked vegetables lay limp in their plates. Boiled potatoes had settled on a grey slick in a square blue dish. Before I could say anything, Ena quickly pointed out that she and her sisters had played no role whatsoever in hatching any scheme against Sarah's people. Gina, Mary, and she were incapable. They would rather die. The very idea of such a contest was graceless, she said, and not worth the mind their dear old mother gave it.

Kokum Stevens, pulling out the empty chair beside her, spoke. "Consider what Len will think—his own mother fighting the mother of his wife. And his little family running away. And him in battle overseas."

Ena poured me a cup of tea. As innocent targets of Sarah's displeasure, Ena gave me to understand, they knew next to nothing of the sorry situation. Nothing had been said against Sarah over at Winnie's the other day, Ena insisted. This surprised me. Winnie had not said a word about Ena's having come by. But then, lately she rarely told me anything. So I really listened now.

In fact, I held my breath. Ena began, "Winnie said she plans to pull together a gathering—a big gathering, in her words. It will be a crowd, more people than at a wedding or funeral—again her words. Why? To show off her cleaning products! Winnie spread a sheet on her bed to show me how white it was."

"What else was said?" The loud smoker's voice was Gina's, heavy arms folded across her broad chest. Her tone had turned a question into a command.

Ena, staring at her older sister chewing gum ever so slowly, replied, "Well, I told her that the washing was whiter than the cloud of white butterflies flitting in among the shrubs outside her bedroom window. That's all there is to it, Gina. And you can chew all you darn well want."

A giggle escaped Mary. Her painful, arthritic joints seemed to keep her nerves on edge.

Kokum Stevens turned to me. "Julien, get word to Sarah right away. Tell her we'll pay her mother a visit tomorrow, as early as we can get to Kahkewistahaw. But first sit down and eat something. Here, have some tea."

Before dawn I returned on horseback to Kahkewistahaw, arriving just as the sun rose. My message ignited panic. Sarah began to holler. "Len's family is coming! They'll see everything! Hurry!" I glanced around. The room was packed with people asleep on the floor. Sarah shrieked at her slow-waking relatives. "Get up! Get up! Len's family is coming! They'll say his kids are living like pigs!"

I looked more closely. Cousins, aunts, and uncles roused themselves from their slumbers, and began dazedly gathering up jackets and coats that had been rolled up for use as pillows, along with the odd blanket or two. Sarah, clenched hands held tight against her face, pleading, told them to put everything out of sight. But difficulties mounted. Eager hands found nothing of cupboard, dresser, trunk, or even a bed with space underneath. I felt a bit sickened and so sat down on a small bench, the room's only extra chair, save Kokum Arthur's. Were these Winnie's clients? I rested my head against the wall and exhaled.

Kokum Arthur set everyone to work. The adults around her pitched in, translating. "Clean the firepit!" At that, a boy of about nine, snot running down his face, carried a smoking pail of charcoal and ashes around to the back of the house. "Shake your clothes and bedding outside!" Little dust storms broke out all over the yard. "Wash the kids!" The bigger aunts and cousins dragged screeching smaller children off to the slough.

The old lady stood beside her daughter. "Sarah, you scrub him floor."

Sarah, hands covering her face, moaning, came to her senses. She addressed no one in particular: "Where in all the king's land is my husband?" She caught Sophie by the sleeve. "You'll have to help me." She rolled an unclaimed jacket to serve as a broom and handed it to Sophie. "Come, get busy and sweep."

I watched little Sophie make quick, short strokes across the planks, pushing ahead of her bits of gravel, twigs, small dried leaves, and dust. Sarah lifted down a pail of water from the stove. Placing it on the swept part, she began to scrub at a mantle of grey on the floor. Steam rose off the planks in the heat, immediately making the room feel close and muggy.

But time had run out.

Wheels clattered outside. Kokum Arthur's young family went out and stood in a line...

Sarah shook her head in despair and said, "Look at us."

I had to agree. We were a sight in our un-ironed clothes, buttons missing, old sweaters full of holes, grey, ill-fitting dresses, and a couple of youngsters, noses running anew. The team and buggy made an outline of itself in the already wavering heat in the road. The Stevenses' outfit pulled up all too suddenly—from shimmering in the distance to team and buggy at a full stop before us.

Soon I would witness an unfolding story first-hand. I moved aside, however, thinking to stay clear of being too noticeable, but close enough to see and to overhear. Winnie, be good, my mind pleaded.

Sarah, stone-faced, had led the visiting ladies inside to the only seat, a short, sturdy bench that I had vacated, now placed in the middle of the room. Kokum Stevens and Ena sat down on it, side by side. Stacks of folded clothes and blankets on the floor lined the wall behind them. Across the still damp pinewood floor, dry patches began to show up, giving off a heavy smell. I hoped no unthinking child would fling open the door to the mottled blue pantry standing in the cooking part of the room. Sophie had done so earlier, and a fit of coughing sent her reeling outside. A strong blast of mould and mouse droppings had given my nostrils one devil of a twist. Windows and door, thankfully, stood open to the breezes.

Ena kept her gaze contained. Familiar scents of the Stevenses' home, a mix of Camay soap, liniment, and newly ironed clothes fresh off the clothesline, reached my nose. I wished Winnie were with me. I could almost hear that beautiful laugh, that little catch in her voice. The nerves in my stomach trembled.

Kokum Arthur's older girls set to serving our visitors tea, in dull-looking quart sealers. Silence remained unbroken. Indeed, Sophie's gaze was busy tracking a fly buzzing around the room when, without warning, the Stevens women began to weep soundlessly. I had to think Winnie really ought to have come; she might know what to make of this.

Finally the hosting Elder, Old Lady Arthur, spoke to her opposite number in Salteaux while Sarah interpreted. "Why do you want to win against me, Mrs. Stevens? We have no money and no soaps."

Sarah, I noticed, translated with feeling, though not exactly matching her mother's.

Old Lady Stevens raised a tear-stained face. It broke my heart. I didn't know what I thought, but I knew I really wanted Winnie. In part, I wanted her to witness undeserved pain in the two old ladies, in these kokums to so many children. Their obvious distress made me angry. And I had to fight down rising doubt.

Len's mother, Kokum Stevens, said in English, "We don't want a contest! We don't do things that way. We heard maybe you did. Or somebody did. We're here because we want Sarah and the children to come home."

"But I am home!" Sarah's outburst was out of line. This earned a sharp glance and an even sharper rebuke in Cree from her mother.

Ena reached a hand out to Sarah. "Sister-in-law, the house is lonesome without you and the little ones. I will talk to Winnie. Come home."

I dared not breathe. Sarah looked at me, her face colouring, and said, "I have no worries with Winnie!" But perhaps knowing Winnie better, she added, "She wouldn't own up to it, anyway."

I knew I ought to absent myself, but Winnie's hand was in this somehow.

In a very painful discussion, the two elderly ladies agreed to take a healing walk to Winnie's. Upon hearing this, Sarah asked me to harness the team and load up. She would return home to Cowessess, taking Kokum Arthur, her mother, along. Once there, Kokum Arthur would be joined by Kokum Stevens and would cross the creek to join her, so they might walk together early next morning.

At Winnie's the morning sun shone all around. It was a prairie summer on full burn. Winnie was already up. When I asked for tea, she said she had already had hers. I saw that she had brushed her hair and must have spent time polishing the glass front of the picture of gentlemen dogs. As I admired it, she reached up and straightened the mirror beside it, now also gleaming. The dishes had not been done, and I could see that her bed was still unmade. Her face was smudged and her dress was rumpled. This was so unlike her that a part of me wondered if she had always had the odd untidy spell.

"Julien," she said, taking but brief notice of me, "one day, I will have a green satin dress with glass buttons and a silver comb. There'll be cash, Julien. Piles of it, I'm telling you."

I didn't argue. "I have some puttying to do on the window," I said, and also watch the goings-on inside. I knew better than to say anything. If things got out of hand with Winnie, it might be said I had interfered in Elder business.

A dog barked up the road.

"That's funny, someone's passing by," Winnie said. "It's still early."

Sweat had gathered on her brow. She wiped her hands on her apron, put a length of her loose hair behind her ear, and opened the door. Two old ladies, arm in arm, were walking toward the house, their windblown dresses flickering blue, red, yellow, and white against the green of the bushes. Winnie squinted. She wiped her eyes with her arm.

"Oh my!" she said. "Old Lady Arthur and Old Lady Stevens!" She slammed the door shut. A cold light seemed to be flickering in my head. Should I warn her? What did I really know? Or want to know? Or need to?

Winnie quivered like a puppy in a thistle patch. "Dear me! Am I seeing things? Why are they acting like old friends?" She sank into a chair near the table, voice camouflaged with nervous chuckles. "This is bad! Let me think ... I should call out that I'm under quarantine." She leapt to her feet.

But the knock came first. Another knock rattled the door in its frame. I slipped out through the window.

I heard Winnie open the door. Her cheerful voice rang out. "Come in! Come in! Come in and sit down!"

The old ladies entered and waited. There was no place for both to sit down. Winnie had yet to spot the greasy frying pan she had left on the second chair. She stood paralyzed. Finally she quickly removed the pan, then stooped to brush the chair seat off with an arm.

The ladies sat down. Kokum Stevens began. "We want to talk to you."

Kokum Arthur came to the point. "Us, we no like him, contest."

Winnie paled. A smile died on her face. I wanted to rush to her side and catch hold of her hands or get her a drink of water; but I stayed put.

"Oh-h-h, the contest!" Winnie's laugh sounded different; it expressed neither joy nor fun. "You mean the cleaning contest—the one dear little Sophie has been talking about, right?"

The grandmothers gasped. My head reeled.

Winnie said, "Oh, I don't think she really meant anything. You know how kids are. They see a contest in everything, eh?"

I nearly fell over, even as I sat. The child was not present to say any different.

The old ladies' faces dropped all sign of patience.

Winnie tried backtracking. "I mean … all I know is, one day, Sophie didn't let me explain what I meant about cleaning—like a winner, mind. She ran away, eh, Julien?"

But I was outside.

Winnie tried another tack. "She might have had something to do—about how everything got twisted. That's gossip for you, eh?"

It I felt as if an unshakable shadow had gathered itself inside the house. The old women met her remark in silence.

Winnie had exhausted all exits. She threw her hands in the air. "What's the matter with me?" she asked, but then she turned around and took it back. She blamed phantoms. "They wanted a contest for best housekeeper." She had turned the problem into a trifle. "Things can be taken so wrong!"

I wished I could have watched their faces more closely as the old ladies talked. I might have seen the truth's real face at last. But they got up to leave.

Winnie cried out. "Wait, I'll make us tea!" But they left; tea was not important right now. "There's a way to be clean, you know. And it counts for everything."

They headed out the door, I hurried alongside the house back to the window. Winnie watched the departing Elders, two colourful dresses disappearing into dappled trees. She rushed around, erasing all signs of messiness. I scraped at the putty, trying not to attract her attention just yet.

Winnie clunked dishes into a dishpan of water. She pitched out a jam can of dead daisies from off the sideboard. There was the bed to make.

But then my young beauty charged and flung the laundry from the chair to the floor. She grabbed the end of the table. But, seeing the dishes piled on it, she made a lunge for the back of a nearby chair and knocked it hard against the wall. The picture of the dogs in their world of luxury came crashing down onto the tabletop, their glass front shattering.

Winnie cried out. Hands shaking, she reached for the picture. Glass splinters rained onto the table and down onto the floor. She took a deep breath and made herself look. The picture was all right. Only the glass had broken. "Yes! My dogs are fine ... their coats buttoned, goblet full ... monocle ..."

She caught sight of herself in the mirror. She was as white as a sheet.

A Banner Year

I ARRIVED AT THE SCHOOL, a fast sprint from the teacherage. I was out of breath. My pupils watched me, a blond exclamation point, struggling to get the words out. Finally I could speak: I'd gotten us a spot in the school district's annual field day. Yes, their school, Lakeside Indian Day School—an "okay" from town. I basked in the moment. This was big.

"Like a coronation," I said, though more to myself. "This is your chance to put a face on. That's if you know how to run and jump with the best." I let that sink in. "And have no fear," I said, "I'm in charge of your training." Twenty-six years old, I'd made many a silk purse in my hometown when it came to sports. The children took peeks at each other's skinny arms and legs.

It was my second year of teaching on Cowessess Reserve, most students from last year with me again, in this one room school of "all grades." I, Mr. Keith Ready, had yet to enlighten them on a major point: I was the one to thank. And they ought to be proud.

Last year the kids clapped when I got a telephone line connected to my temporary home, a small white teacherage with pink trim and two of the smallest bedrooms known to mankind, with an all but useless porch. I had asked the able-bodied male volunteers, fathers and uncles of my pupils, to string telephone wire over miles of treetops on the reserve, beyond the outlying farmers' grain fields bordering the highway, to a final destination: a sun-bleached pole at the edge of town.

Getting connected was my first step to Out and Up.

I hadn't invited my pupils into the teacherage to hear the telephone ring, as they'd hinted I might. Instead, I bored my eyes into theirs, one by one, row by row, until they got it though their heads. "The RCMP will charge anyone caught touching the wire," I said. "Tell them at home I said so."

The school lay on the south side of the reserve near the Indian agent's pale-yellow house. Set in a thick hedge, the house was surrounded also by a wrought iron fence with a gate that opened onto a cluster of sheds and a larger building. That first year, the Indian agent, Hugh Passmore, a big, bluff, older fellow, showed me around inside the agency building with its supply of tools and implements, and small shelf of medicines.

"I figure the agency must feel like a town to your pupils," he said. The agent and I got along.

I warned the class that the agency was off-limits, and whatever lay inside the two-storey house was none of their business. I said there would be no peering over the fence and no long stares in that direction, either. I reminded them again, for good measure.

For a good part of that spring, the schoolyard felt as hard as rock underfoot. The lake, within sight of the school, clung to its gunmetal grey shards of ice. Although the snow had disappeared in an unexpected chinook, the cold blasted our face with icy gusts that stung the nose and made the eyes water. I longed for the scent of warming earth. At recess the children huddled alongside the building in coats that never looked new or warm. But a single cawing crow staking out claim in a naked tree—well, that would be a real sign of spring, at last.

And I didn't need an Elder to tell me.

In the meantime I worked my plan. The first thing was to get my pupils' physical skills on par. Fathers and uncles would build us a high-jump stand and mark off a racetrack in powdered chalk. I needed jumping pits dug and the sand hauled into the schoolyard.

These days, the air around me crackled with energy. It was time. Time for the big race. Time to make the big leap.

After "God Save the Queen" at the end of the day, I said to the class, "Tell everyone at home there's a meeting at the school tonight." My pupils nodded, putting away their exercise books, erasers, and pencils. "Seven o'clock sharp. It's a big opportunity, hear? Everyone needs to get behind me. Got that? Repeat after me, 'It's a huge community opportunity!'" They said it in unison, voices low-key, as usual.

I would find out, as Hugh Passmore did in his time, that as long as the community didn't meddle, progress could be swift. But let people start asking questions ... I needed their help, not their direction.

For me, success was spelled *w-I-n*. I knew that with a field day of winnings under my belt, I stood to receive handsome praise in the provincial school district. My abilities would shine in front of the school officials; that is, my intestinal fortitude, my skills, and my pure talent. On a clear day, my tall frame, chiselled nose, Pepsodent smile, and qualifications would do the rest, I had no doubt. After all, I had talked my way into bringing ten little Indians into the district's home space, had I not? An educator with negotiating ability—me, Mr. Keith Ready!

Not that Hugh Passmore hadn't tried. But there had been the stranglehold of the Depression, the Dirty Thirties, and World War II - I empathized.

And there was no way I was going get stuck teaching in a one-room school on an isolated Indian reserve for the rest of my life. I would fight. I would use this colonial experience to prove I was a man of serious ambition. I felt certain that my having served time here would cut me a path straight into a provincial school district, a district rife with connections. The way I saw it, a regional directorship could be mine in fairly short order. I had ambition. And I knew the route: become a school principal and, fast on the heels of that, secure a superintendent's position in the system—then, if need be, put in time as a consultant for the federal government.

I checked things out with Hugh Passmore. He agreed that what I needed now was a share of the limelight under which to show my competence. "After that," he said, fair eyebrows twitching over his glasses at me, "who knows what might befall that leonine head?"

He advised that I fatten up my resume as a brag sheet. It got me thinking. I had done pretty well in Normal school, particularly in sports. I was liked by my instructors and by my peers, though I had my share of detractors. The sticking point was that I lacked a surname that heralded connections, along with ties to land, money, and influence, never mind an established professional network—all the stuff that ensured pull once I was inside the structures. A small-town boy lacked credibility unless he came from a political family. Poverty and isolation be damned! Just get that foot in the door!

Incredibly, my future boiled down to a classroom of dark-haired, brown-skinned Indian kids, grades one to seven. To me, they showed potential as victors, hence my thinking in terms of a field day—with the benefit of strong, excellent coaching provided by yours truly. Those sweet ribbons of victory: white for first place; blue for second; and, should the fates insist, a couple of reds for third, all pinned to the lapels of my pupils, would be a personal banner of victory.

What I failed to see was how queen and community might have a say in the matter.

Len Stevens, chairman of the board at Lakeside Indian Day School, was the father of a boy called Tony and two younger daughters, Sophie and Leta. The children's case was typical. The boy, in grade five, had recently been released from the Indian boarding school in Manitoba.

The girls, ages ten and nine, had not been to school at all; that is, until Lakeside Indian Day School was built and opened on the reserve. The three were in the same classroom: mine.

As I reviewed my present teaching assignment for inclusion in my resume, it was plain to see that, compared with my counterparts in town, I had it rough. In the town of Broadview, grade one meant, for the most part, six-year-olds in the same grade. A teacher there said goodbye to last year's kids. And to last year's mistakes. Out here, my pupils were a mixed bag. Len Stevens told me that the community had fought hard to get a school on the reserve, and so I did not complain to him. Neither did I ask, for instance, why ten-year-old Sophie had had to start school the same time her nine-year-old sister did. In any case, one did not ask about or share such concerns, if Hugh Passmore was right.

As a World War II veteran, Len Stevens had seen the breadth of almost half of Europe, or at least enough of it to hope he might see it all again someday. He said, when we first met during parent interviews, how he hoped relations between the reserve and the townspeople might move beyond a stubborn winter impasse—despite there being a few icy roads left to surmount, in and around town. The children from Lakeside School had to attend high school there soon enough, he said. I liked the tone of the man. He'd seen things, been places. He appreciated discipline. What's more, he kept a tight rein on his children.

As for the meeting tonight, I decided to tighten my grip on the future. Getting Len Stevens onside would help my cause, should any headstrong parent get stubborn. After school I soon cut a path to his home in my rusty old Pontiac.

Len Stevens reflected on the news. "Lakeside School invited! A thing like that! I'll bet it has to do with the coronation last year. How could they not ask— in the spirit of the coronation, I mean. They're veterans' kids, and Treaty, after all."

His voice held a strong note of soldierly pride. He had served his monarch, the late King George VI, deceased father of the newly crowned Queen Elizabeth the Second. I could tell that Mrs. Stevens felt a real bond with the monarchy. Mention the Royal Family and Mrs. Stevens's face brightened in childhood loyalty to the new queen and, as was often said out here, "in faithfulness that comes from the Elders, and the Elders' Elders."

Sarah Stevens cleared her throat. "It's a way to honour the queen, to make sure the day is special for the kids."

"No harm in that!" I said, at a loss for the right thing to say.

I was glad when Len Stevens and his family came to the school early on the evening of the meeting. As we shook hands, Sarah Stevens grimaced and said it was good to stand. Seven or eight other women, heads in kerchiefs, accompanied by children and older folks, hurried across the windy yard into the schoolhouse. The yard, surrounded by last fall's dead twill grass and flanked by scrub brush and stands of grey poplar and red willow, felt like late October and the onset of winter, not a late spring.

I saw with satisfaction that Len Stevens had joined the circle of men congregating near the steps of the school. The lot of them waited, as usual, to participate in the old formalities of handshakes all around and lively ancient salutation. As for me, I stood beside the steps, counting heads, assessing who had arrived and what influence each might exert one way or the other. Of course, I could never be sure.

Parents and guardians, some fifteen in all, squeezed themselves into the children's desks, or sat in the three extra chairs that were pulled noisily into the large circle of desks. My pupils sat on the floor, backs against the wall at the far end of the room, while I stood by my desk up front.

I swept my gaze over the parents and came right to the point. I said I had a list of expectations and that these boiled down, basically, to their signing up for committees. "After all, they're your kids," I said.

A pall descended, as I expected it might. But I had to show who was boss. I had based the decision on my discussion with Hugh Passmore, a successful, if long-suffering, Indian agent. "Make no exceptions, and give no special consideration for those oldsters," he had advised. "Let it be all suit and tie as you work your agenda."

I knew one crucial step was to instill ownership of responsibility in the community. Stroking my blue tie, I meant to make this clear. "Jumping pits and a racetrack are mandatory," I said. I also told them that, as the teacher, I was obliged to look after the training aspect. People nodded, and I could have done a little dance to, of all things, the Marshall Wells Paint jingle in my head: *Oh, any time, inside or out, really fine …*

I had made good use of the tactic of starting the meeting on short notice, too. This would cut back on the time needed for the contemplation of a veto. Hugh Passmore said the veto was always a possibility, a time waster without legs. But Len Stevens, chairman, quick to grasp the lay of the land among the assembled, announced that the Elders had to have their say, with time for Cree translation. The growing hum from the Elders stopped. They let it be known that Old Favel, an interpreter for many years, would translate. I hadn't seen that coming.

I nodded to Old Favel, a frail-looking, elegant old man. He made his way to the front of the room, a green and brown plaid jacket buttoned snugly on a tall, thin frame. A red neckerchief brightened his solemn face. Old Favel fixed his gaze to a spot at the back of the room and stood inert as a crane. It vexed me that he held himself at a distance, as though locked inside a glass box. The Elders now said their piece in Cree. Old Favel summed up, eye on the same spot at the back of the room. "Our Elders want the children to learn all about the new queen," he said, "before they go to town in a rush."

Hearing this, my pupils craned their necks, doubtless trying to gauge my reaction, their heads weaving behind coats and jackets hung on the backs of chairs. Reacting to Old Favel's words, my hand had shot up.

He ignored me. His voice began setting the tone—at least, that was how it rang in my ear. "Our young queen is a gracious spirit. Her smiling face is like the fresh rain filling our rivers and streams. She is the sun warming the land. Great King George VI has passed on. Queen Victoria, of generous breast, has gone ahead. Our children must know their queen. This is the training. Not sports and big jumps, so much."

Cringing, I saw that Sarah Stevens, of all people, fluent in Cree, joined in the nods of affirmation. She exchanged happy smiles with the women in the circle. It irked me to think my cause had gained no solid ground in her mind.

As for me, I ignored that it was bad form to interrupt the contemplative silence following an Elder's words. Anyway, it was my meeting. I was the one who had called it, after all. I leaped to my feet. "Hang on here!" I said to our translator. "It's sports training, I said!"

But Len Stevens had quickly stepped to the front. He leaned toward me and spoke under his breath, "Treat Mr. Favel like an Elder, or lose them."

I glanced at my volunteers. Lose their help? Me—shovel in hand, digging ground that was frozen solid? I sat down.

At that moment, Old Solomon, a Métis man, rose. He steadied his weighty frame against the classroom shelf. Short and broad-shouldered, he looked strong. Knowing Cree and French, I had long heard, he was considered a respecter of heritage among the parents of the school. Apparently, people liked his summations, too. Tonight, ignoring a crosswind of feelings, he said, "Our kids has got to learn our root of mutual honour. Their majesties started this. So help us teach the kids, is what."

I was irritated by the applause. Old Solomon was as blue-eyed as I was. Half-breed, indeed! The ovation was misplaced, if anything.

"We'll get to it in the coming weeks," I said.

So now obligation hung like Damocles' sword over me. Be that as it may, a winner knows when to take a new tack. The use of jargon, an old trick, had always revved up the engines of provincial regulation. So why not for me? I began, "The time required to teach the instructional objectives, in their entirety, as outlined in the provincial curriculum, is limited. At the end of June, the children will face final exams, a time almost upon us. Physical education, a foundational objective of primary and utmost importance, system-wide, requires practice, as a top priority, in all district-wide competitions."

I had to admit it was a curve ball I threw Old Favel. I knew a translator worth his salt wouldn't attempt even a summary.

Not so, Old Favel. "Time is needed in two places, sports and books. A third thing has no time left. Our queen." He now gave his summary in Cree.

The Elders averted their gaze.

Sarah Stevens got to her feet. "I speak for us mothers," she said. "The kids can make scrapbooks on the queen in art period. That way they can learn on their own. Moms can help now and again."

Elders and mothers murmured their approval. I sawed my thumbnail between my two front teeth, trying to think of a way to turn things around. I was about to speak, but Old Favel was summarizing for the crowd before launching into Cree. "Scrapbooks is a good way to learn the queen. Time can be stretched out over this, with help." he said. He spoke in a direct, impersonal way, as from a distant realm. Then he added, "Our children know running. They're fine jumpers, too."

I resisted the urge to pound on my desk. Mr. Favel had chosen to interpret the room's feeling. He had not stuck to exact wording. Surely a translator worth his salt ...

I spoke louder than necessary. "They need physical training! Besides, how are we to make scrapbooks? I believe you know well enough that there are no books around here. No library here! Look here! See for yourself!" I held my arm out toward the little shelf under the row of windows holding some fifteen books—likely the sum total on the entire reserve and not a single one of them new. "None on the queen!" I said.

Old Solomon, Mr. Blue-Eyes, rose again. "Chaskwa mahka!" he said, impatience raking gravel in this throat. "We agreed! Everybody makes his own scrapbook!"

"Including the boys?" I was unwilling to give in. Boys, I knew.

The old people consulted briefly.

"Yes," Old Favel said. "All."

A decision, quite possibly injurious to me, had been made under my nose! That night I tossed and turned, struggling with a recurring dream wherein I was forced to select what was worse: Indians, Elders, or England. The dream hadn't resolved itself by the time dawn punched through my bedroom curtain.

At the end of the day, I sent word for Sarah Stevens to come to the school. "It's about the scrapbooks," I told the Stevens kids, Tony, Sophie, and Leta standing in front of me, their faces one big question mark.

Within the hour Sarah Stevens appeared, accompanied by her friend and consort, Winnie, the two laughing nervously like schoolgirls climbing the school steps. I decided to let them do the talking—the better to sleuth my way out of the scrapbook project. After all, it was already the first week in May, and June 18 was rounding the corner. We hadn't even begun practice, let alone prepared the grounds.

"So where do we find pictures?" The question was put by Winnie, as though casually to her friend. I kept my mouth shut.

Sarah Stevens answered, "Len said magazines are everywhere in town. The coronation was only last year, come to think of it. Len thinks we'll need help gathering up newspapers and magazines. He plans to buy Regina's *The Leader* and the *Winnipeg Free Press* for Tony and the girls, and the Broadview and Whitewood papers, if there's any left. He has a little money from last winter's muskrat pelts."

I half-nodded once. If they wanted to gather papers, it was their lookout.

Sarah Stevens glanced around the classroom, face bright. "When the kids sing 'God Save the Queen,' it will mean something," she said.

I thought it odd that she expressed so much feeling for the Royal Family. The answer, however, was at this moment being laid in store, doubtless for my gain.

"I wonder if you remember my saying," Sarah Stevens began, her remarks directed at her red-haired partner in crime, "how Tony, as a baby, was touched by the queen's mother when she was queen. Remember when I said that, in June, the train carrying the queen and King George VI stopped for the people waiting along the railroad track by Melville?"

Winnie, not meeting her gaze, replied, "Yes, I recall you said they stepped off the train, just like that." She shifted in her seat.

"She came straight to us. She said Tony was a beautiful baby."

This meeting was way off track. I had loosened control and now had no idea how to stop the train. Sarah Stevens spoke of royalty as though she and they shared a bond. "The other day, Len said that the king and queen stayed with the soldiers as bombs fell on London." She made it sound as if Len, stationed in London at the time, had stood within speaking distance of their majesties.

"Rubbish!" I wanted to say.

But now Winnie asked a question that no doubt had only at that very moment popped into her head. "So what was said at the meeting last night?"

"Good gracious! You should have heard Old Solomon. Everybody clapped when he said the queen is the centre of the field day."

"That means we've got our work cut out," said Winnie, eyeing me.

I got the scrapbook project rolling the following week. Magazines, pamphlets, and newspapers were brought in—by me. Townspeople had been only too happy to help. My pupils were now caught up with hunting for pictures of the Royal Family, stacks of magazines on the windowsill growing dog-eared and tattered by the minute.

As I studied the bind I was in, it had struck me that a little competition wouldn't hurt. So, in the middle of the yeasty smells rising off paste jars, and the snarls of paper clippings strewn like squirrels' nests on the floor, I had held up the work of little Lucy LeRou, second grader. "Look at what Lucy has got done, already!" I emphasized already. "Little Lucy here is ahead of all of you. Her work is excellent! Right, Lucy?"

Little Lucy LeRou, small for her age, donned a look of smug satisfaction. Later, at recess, I overheard Sophie and Leta say that Lucy had flipped her long hair at them, galling even the older girls. I had their attention, all right.

The boys said Lucy had taken her scrapbook home at the end of the day, and that she had returned the next morning with more pages done. I cannot say I gave it too much mind. I held to my plan: come next year, I would be gone. So I took heart and had pushed my young athletes hard in scrapbook period, my voice tight as a tin drum. "Oh, come on! Look at Lucy's, here. Lace edges on Princess Margaret, here. See that?"

The little Stevens girls, Leta and Sophie, chided each other: *Why didn't you think of it?*

My method was taking hold.

The weather had grown warm enough for the children to practice most days without jackets. Early heat phantoms danced and shimmered in the grey fields near the schoolyard, which received only the rare blast of cold wind now.

On this day, while the men dug jumping pits and drilled holes for high-jump posts, I went to see the mothers meeting in my classroom. The chatter was full of commas, dashes, and exclamation points, what with the hammering and the sawing outdoors echoing off the agency warehouse near the window. The fresh scent of lumber filled the air and lifted my spirits. But I had to close the window on the noise.

Wouldn't you know! The women had a request. Deportment had to be addressed, they said. Irritated, I listened to their appeal, purportedly based on the Elder's recommendation: that, once in town on field day, the boys and girls stand tall, speak gently, and keep their clothes, hands, and faces clean, as representatives of the queen. I nearly fell over! I nodded curtly and stomped out into the yard, with no choice but to go to see my all-male work crew. I breathed a sigh of relief when the men agreed to oversee softball. In fact, I even gave them controlling rights. Softball on field days was mainly about demonstration games, all just hip-hip-hooray—with no ribbons.

I might have guessed. Len Stevens, board chair, said that he had been thinking about the Elders' recent advice and had come to a conclusion. Softball would be played "the right way." In other words, a kid aimed for accuracy and consideration both. A kid pitched easy if the batter was small, had a hip problem, was new to the school, or had a mental disability. So there it was. Were it up to me, we'd flatten the enemy, no questions asked. Or die trying. Still, it was their game now.

I climbed the steps back into my classroom. I had neglected to discuss a small matter with the women. "I need someone with a sewing machine," I began, "a steady hand to sew seams on our school banner." I underlined my points using my best straight ahead, get-on-with-it tone. Arms outstretched, I added, "I have a banner in mind, three feet high and four feet long with extra inches for hems for the carrying-poles at each end. A couple of kids will carry our banner in the big parade of all the schools, in town."

The women bent their heads in thought.

I went on, "I'll supply the material."

I soon had reason to regret sharing this task with such busybodies. Trouble started when one of the women asked what the banner would say.

"'Lakeside Indian Day School,' what else?" I asked, feeling defensive.

"Will there be a picture on it?" one of the mothers wanted to know.

"Well, yes, there will. A little red schoolhouse, beside a blue lake … and … and a green tree, of course." I hadn't really given it any thought. But now I surprised myself.

Silence again. The women thought differently, obviously.

"No, that won't do," one of them said. "We already discussed it with the Elders, eh? There has to be a queen on there."

"A queen!" Just let me spring up as one devil-of-a-fire-dragon with a fierce blast of steam and ash—and I'd blow the lot of them clear out the door!

"Yes, Queen Elizabeth the Second." It was Sarah Stevens, turncoat.

"Now wait a minute. I don't think so!" I didn't care if I they thought me rude. They had no right of decision here.

A woman named Vitaline, who had no children in school but who showed up to almost everything anyway, flipped out a substantial mane of black hair with almost her entire arm before speaking. Her booming voice had an edge to it. "For the queen it should be big, eh? At least four by five, right, Mrs. Sam?" She turned to a sweet-faced, thoughtful-looking lady on her right.

"Yes, that should do it," said Mrs. Sam, though perhaps nursing a doubt.

I restated the facts. "The pressed felt is regulation size—three by four. That's it. No more."

But now I made a fatal mistake. I allowed an opening for maybe when I added, "Besides, where can you get a big enough picture of the queen? They don't grow on trees."

"That's for sure!" Vitaline sprang to her feet, agitation alive in a quivering mane. The women knew this side of her. I sure didn't. Vitaline sounded like one boxcar striking another. She jerked her kerchief off a shoulder and snapped it at an imaginary fly—what's more, killed it on the spot.

I tried to speak but a coughing fit choked my attempt. Another woman, rubbing her elbow in the cup of her hand, stepped in. "Mrs. Sam, over here, she's an artist, her. She could draw a queen." Next Vitaline tapped the shoulder of the woman in front of her. Dumchill, a shorter lady with grey hair held up in a hairnet, taking the cue, said, "Mrs. Sam is the best artist on the reserve. She can draw a rose without trying, even with no single rose to copy in her whole house. And draw a real picket fence around it, too—the rose."

Hoping to gain a foothold in female minds run amok, I informed them that no other school in the district would go so far as to have the queen's image on a banner. It was a school event, after all, not a federal case.

"This is more than school." Dumchill looked at me over her small round spectacles, temper rising. "It's our reserve—to show what we stand for!"

So I found myself, next day, seated in front of Mrs. Sam, lauded artist. She began with a complaint: were she to sew together the two small pieces of felt that I had just handed her, the queen would have a line running across her face—an outrage and an insult. But a single piece would be too small; the Elders said so. In the end I agreed to buy a white bedsheet as a substitute. That was only a beginning. Mrs. Sam now said that the matter of the crown had to be considered. Real jewels were needed, "the realer the better." I pleaded the cause of the Indian agent's limited budget. However, according to Mrs. Sam, Dumchill, the others were dead set against cheap glass beads. "These turn brassy on a white sheet," she argued. I finally relented, just to be free of her. There was no way out. Jewels it was. And so, with the dexterity of a long-armed monkey on a monocycle, all over town that week, I saw to it that Mrs. Sam gained a small fortune in old brooches to dismantle.

That banner signified a further undoing, I was to learn.

The day of days arrived. Lakeside Indian Day School was ready. I smelled victory! I counted my athletes, twenty-one in all. Their white shirts and blouses had been bleached by the sun or shocked into brightness with bluing. I noted the crisply ironed creases and collars.

In the midst of all the children's excitement in getting ready to board the truck for town, Len Stevens came over to tell me that the banner had not arrived. "It's well in hand," he assured me. "Mrs. Sam has sent word she'll meet you in town by the underpass. She's had some trouble with the crown. Thumbtacks or something."

I fired up the truck and we were off, my athletes over the moon.

As we approached the outskirts of town, the children spotted Mrs. Sam. She and her team of horses waited at the underpass. She handed me the folded white bedsheet like it was holy raiment. She also handed up two peeled poles and told the boys to place them flat on the floor. Nodding my thanks to her, I geared up and we pulled out. The truck growled through weeds onto Main Street.

A multi-windowed brick building of the town school loomed into sight. It was down to business at last.

A sea of smiling faces greeted the athletes of Lakeside Indian Day School. The sight of so many schools standing in line across the lawn was awe-inspiring. Classroom after classroom stood in precise order, short to tall, section after section, each row more razor sharp than the last. I was as taut and jittery as a bow and arrow in the wrong hands. So much was at stake.

I hurried to confer with the officials assembled outside the front steps of the school. Yes, we were in the right spot at the right time, and good luck. I ran back to my athletes, and scolded them under my breath to get into line, for crying out loud. They were a tangled mess. I had forgotten to practice lining up, and so now by dint of scowl, sleight of hand, and sheer wizardry, I got them into four rows. In the nick of time, I remembered to send off the banner carriers, my sturdy grade-five boy, Chuckchee, and, of course, tough little Lucy LaRue. The grand troupe of banner honorees was about ready to start its advance. Chuckchee took off, a white-knuckled grip on the poles. Lucy, flipping her hair, clutched the sheet to her belly and ran after him. "Hurry!" My voice cracked. For a moment, it was all 'my kingdom for a sheepdog,' but somehow, the two got into position and, raising our banner to the sky, goose-stepped behind the troupe to the beat of the drum.

"Where's the queen?" one of my grade ones asked, mistakenly thinking the real queen was approaching. The children hushed him.

When the bugle blared, the banner-carriers began marching out from their end of the field and around the yard, passing in front of the officials and the schools. On my left, I observed a precise line of superintendents, principals, and teaching staff from the district. Theirs was a straight, tight line of power and promotion. Banners of every colour blazed under their noses; I saw the names of schools in tall bright letters, each with a unique symbol against a contrasting background, flapping in the wind: a stiff golden sheaf, a white and blue schoolhouse, an oak tree, an angular flamingo, a grinning dog, and a fluffy Churchillian hand of victory.

But where was Lakeside's banner? The children and I craned our necks.

"There!" My whisper rasped like a goose honk. That had to be our banner, that large, flapping bedsheet! The bright sun had drained it of both line and colour. There was no face to speak of, at that distance. A crown, thank heaven, was approaching, a glitter of upholstery tacks above two sparkling eyes of bright blue beads.

The morning's breeze, now a gale, turned the sheet into a sail that bent, forked, and folded back on itself. At a critical U-turn in the parade, Chuckchee and Lucy, bronze faces contorted and sweating, finally made their way back to base. The Lakeside Indian Day School children stood tall. The queen's likeness, visible at last, had arrived.

The long day, with its events and ribbons all around, was at end.

I dropped the children off at the school to the waiting parents in the soft evening light. They applauded and cheered as the children showed their ribbons. The townspeople had cheered them on, the children said, and adults beamed at them. The town ladies had pinned ribbons on them and praised them, they said. And hefty white boys had all but carried them in the three-legged race. Sophie Stevens won a red ribbon in the high jump; Tony, a red in the long jump. Leta won blue in the three-legged race, along with a muscular boy from El Cappo School. We had done our best in baseball but we lost to El Cappo, was said.

I willed myself to notice an infinite absence of white ribbons.

"You all did well," Sarah Stevens reminded us. Come Monday, in the bright electric light in the classroom, she said, we'd be able to see the queen on our wonderful school banner. "And don't forget that beautiful photograph of Queen Elizabeth and Prince Philip at the front of the room above the blackboard. And remember to sing 'God Save the Queen' with a strong voice." Especially now, too, she added, eyeing me, that little Lucy LaRue must surely win first prize for her scrapbook.

I would deal with Lucy next year, it pained me to think. Right now, I would pick myself up—and go ahead and polish and straighten the Royal photograph over my desk.

The Wedding Suit

LETA AND I DRIVE DOWNTOWN in Aunt Edith's old car. The feeling of sisters heading out into the big world, at the controls, lifts our mood to the heavens. We laugh, mouths wide open, no thought of modesty. The traffic light turns red and we wait, fingers tapping. We are filled with heady impatience, sure of ourselves.

Thin as *Vogue* models, our aunt Edith has said—we don't know what to make of this. Our bronze skin makes exotic international beauties of us. We have no idea what this means, either; so let the warmth of the sun caress our elegant arms!

We have come upon this morning as though straight from a beach. Except that working on a tan is a non-idea to teenage sisters who have grown up beside a slough, the sun a big purple onion pouring down its dizzying heat every July. Inside our aunt's car, we feel light; in fact, we are lightness itself—and to put a fine point upon it, buoyant.

To the left of our rusty, idling car sits the Army and Navy, one of Regina's department stores, a dull industrial-looking building. Through its dust-fogged plate glass we can see winter boots, overalls, flower-print dresses, cooking pots, and heavy-looking dishes. Naïve farm girls from the Cowessess Reserve, we wish to see and to sense around us something of our Aunt Edith's *Vogue* magazines, that fresh, crisp feeling from right off a *Vogue* page. We talk instead.

An uncle, we've been told, once owned the land the store stands on. Leta is certain—no, not a Native man but Lebanese, a dark-haired, handsome businessman called Frank, who married Aunt Lil and forced her to work hours and hours in his store. We had once seen a black and white photograph of her—a real beauty: short, dark shiny hair, flawless ivory skin, fine-cut features, and long limbs, like the Parisian models in perfectly fitted clothes that we pore over, teenage fingers pointing here and there among the pages, in Aunt Edith's basement suite.

Hands tight on the steering wheel, Leta delves into the past. Uncle Frank made money and died, she says. Aunt Lil made it big, after she got away. But, now, isn't there that story about the time he ditched her for another girl? Anyhow, she goes crazy, climbs into bed, and stays there? Lets herself waste away, did she? Pined for him, was it? Funny that women are driven insane by love, is my opinion. Plain sick, is Leta's. When we got our man—who knew where or when—there wouldn't be any of that. Better still, we'd do without men. Say it for luck. Say it again.

The car draws over the pavement. Sunshine begs we pick up speed. We'd step on it but for stalled traffic ahead. An accident. A couple of badly dented cars forces rusty farm trucks and implements to sit at odd angles in the road. "Love!" Leta snorts. "Remember Uncle Ernest? Mom's half-brother, the drunk who beat up Aunt Violet? Claimed he did it for love. She believed him, right? Or was it she suffered from love-sickness?" It's nothing to laugh at, we say, what with her broken heart.

Yet, there's no stopping this careless talk of aunts in love when, giddy as we are and locked in the pull of traffic, our wheels churn under us like roaring freedom. Still, the future couldn't help what happened, what pinched our eyes, and what stabbed our delirious hearts.

It began with love. Our mother's younger brother, Jack, fell in love with a girl called Priscilla, who had a child.

"She'll take advantage of him," our mother had told Winnie, a neighbour friend who lived across the creek. Worse, Jack didn't give two hoots about it, she said. It was hard to get him to open up, to show where he stood on things. Our mother wanted the real Jack, she said. She wanted to test his ideas, pry open his head, peek inside, and be able to finally say: *Here it is, Jack! Here's what's wrong! Here's where we've been hiding, you and I.* This could help them find a brother-sister bond. "We were kept apart in boarding school," our mother said, offering an excuse for Jack's empty-headedness, his flatness. "At boarding school, I'd watch him stumble along behind the big boys, a five-year-old, in a man's jacket down to his knees, an orphan, when you think of it."

Winnie had sighed. "Now, a girl wanting him. Imagine!"

Uncle Jack would not escape our notice now. The first time he stepped into the clearing, months ago, a stick man in sagging clothes, Leta and I could only stare. Paying no attention to us, he made his way into the house. We snuck along behind him, dodging and bobbing and, finally, peeking in through the window. He sat at the table in the big room, hand on his gaunt face, bony elbow on the corner of the table, foot pointing out the door.

Our mother had seemed to be trying to make sense of Jack's one-liners. We heard him say, "He killed his dad, I guess." But would he say who or how the killer did it? Like maybe a gun, an axe, a rope, poison, or even with his bare hands? No.

"Did they catch him?" our mother finally thought to ask.

"Could be," Jack said.

Leta and I sank to the ground under the window, dying for details.

But then only Winnie knew how to make a story leap up: be it about men fighting in town, or colliding with a train, or getting rushed to the hospital, or being hauled off to jail. With Winnie, it was about blood-splattered walls, glass flying, a policeman's weird amusements, groans, and wild screeches—her pictures and sounds haunted our dreams and followed our waking hours. Today, we heard Winnie say that Jack was a dead loss when it came to the news. Lack of news was what the soldiers complained about. The town's newspaper gave a good headline but less than half a story. "It's just one short hard twist, and done," Winnie said. "I wonder why Jack visits you, considering he has nothing to say or tell about."

"He wants to get to know me, a relation. Mind you, there's Priscilla, now."

Priscilla. Leta and I learned that, as a child, she had been placed by Social Welfare in a Christian home in Whitewood; she was five then. Priscilla's relatives, all drunkards, weren't allowed to visit her. But relatives had learned the child had been touched wrong. The foster father and fake uncles and male cousins would hold Priscilla on their laps, kneading her feet like dough. Men ran fingers along the insides of her panties. Leta and I squirmed at this. Our panties were homemade sugar bags. We'd be ashamed to have anybody catch a glimpse, let alone feel them. And why knead her foot? Leta demanded. She and I had hung around the women all the more now.

But Winnie hated the story. She rose like a hen disturbed off its eggs. "Why would the girl go and deny it?"

"Too young, I guess. It doesn't matter now, so she says."

Winnie scolded, "Imagine a foster mother putting the girl's hair in ringlets, then telling her she's the prettiest thing in church—with all that going on!"

"At least now she's grown up and in love," our mother said. "And Jack is making hay, going around on foot doing odd jobs. He's headed for the shock of his life, I say."

Because Jack proved less interesting, Leta and I were prepared to adore Priscilla. Jack would matter because of her.

Ahead in the street, traffic refuses to clear. "A truck full of turnips has jackknifed onto the road," Leta laughs. "Else a hog won't budge." Then she says, "We might have found out more about Jack and Priscilla. Think of grown-ups, though, hiding truth like some odd shivering thing." Leta says this in a way that makes it sound like she knows something. But, she said, she couldn't hope to say. And let's not forget," she says, trying to be wise, "memories of when you are eight and nine are sharp. And even as older girls now, we remember pretty damn near anything."

"Right?"

"Right!"

Take those months before the wedding. Jack had gotten enough money together for a trip to Regina to buy himself a wedding suit. On his return, he called on our mother. He stood in the kitchen doorway, a mysterious parcel under his arm wrapped in brown paper and tied with white parcel string. "It's my wedding suit! One to last! Gonna wear it on our tenth wedding anniversary too. Celebrate big!" His voice was strong.

Leta and I turned our faces up to him.

"Two big celebrations for Priscilla," he said. Our mother's gaze slanted down. She examined the suit, smoothing it out on the table. It was a black and white checked fabric that, when held at an angle, changed colour. "See? Soft white one way, and deep dove grey going into black, the other."

Our mother looked pleased. "Perfect," she said, "the cloth, and the stitching fine."

Jack's cheeks were bright. He knew his sister would like it, he said. She inspected it, inside and out, crooning over the tailoring, the supple worsted wool cut with such care, its double seams sewn whistle straight. She told Jack that, because of her love of sewing at boarding school, she could tell that the sleeve edges had been curved, basted, clipped short, pressed, and sewn flat by hand, before the final pressing. She held up the garment. "Quality," she said, "these black leather buttons, plaited and lovely."

"And Jack flinging his arms out like a rooster!" Leta snickers now when we remember.

We luxuriate in Aunt Edith's car, our thighs sun-warmed. An image of Jack's wedding suit hangs before us, especially now as we compare it to the shabbily dressed man at the traffic light. His face is contorted by a cloud of dust kicked up by a whirlwind, busy trashing the street. Men in pea caps and women in floral dresses push little children and the elderly ahead of them, hands over mouths and noses. Leta says that the man is not obeying that green means go. He's busy talking, arms making arcs.

Leta leans my way. "Roll down that window one damn minute," she says. The man's pea cap covers most of his forehead. "He's Native, one of us, how can you tell?" Leta says. His suit pants are wrinkled, torn at the knee, and topped by a yellowed white shirt. We ease ahead for a closer look. Dark eyes storm from their sockets. The man's face is filled with eerie excitement, yet strung with delight. He looks near to laughing, the world in his grasp. He takes a couple of steps our way. "Yeah!" he laughs, as if he has just heard something amusing. "Yeah, that's for sure!"

"The dope. Look at him." Leta says in undertones.

But then something in that voice, even in the midst of idling cars, drops disbelief like a metal net onto us. It cannot be.

"Wait! It is Jack!" Leta leans out my side.

But now, behind us, cars begin honking. The light is green. Leta pulls ahead. Our car lurches and coughs its way up the street.

"That was him?" we ask each other.

"Well ..." we say.

"You're certain, right?" Leta asks. But now, at this moment, let be there no mistake, even as we speak of things not yet firm in the brain ... our morning has faltered.

Leta tries distraction. "Remember those wedding preparations, Sophie?" she says, gunning the motor. "And how Priscilla's adopted mom came and took over? Roared into the yard, she did, in a blue car—remember the grunge to its shoulders? Yes, and you grabbed the dog by the ears when she breezed by, frizzy hair, chest like a board. We sat outside under the open kitchen window, remember?"

Laughing, we recall our own usual appearance: stringy hair, flour-bag dresses down past our knees, our legs skinny as sticks. "That woman though, she strong-armed Mom at tea and bannock, saying all planning belonged to a bride's mom, and the job was hers alone," I said.

"It's just as well," our mother had said about it to Winnie, making excuses for the woman's rude, pushy behaviour, "my nosebleeds have started up again."

Nosebleeds. We shake our head. Traffic has unravelled, but only by a single block. Something else was stuck in the street.

Leta wonders, "Didn't Mom say that Jack won't stand up for his rights? And didn't she tell Winnie he had agreed never to ask Priscilla about her past? About who fathered her child? Ah, she did! And Mom said it was wrong, because what would they tell the girl when she grew up? It's bound to be a mess, was what Winnie said."

Our mother had also said, "Think of Jack. Priscilla is one pretty girl. Those dimples at the corners of her mouth stop men in their tracks. Oh, I've seen her all right."

We have recalled that conversation exactly, we claim. Because on that day, Winnie sipped her tea and eyed Mom—not to forget how she brought a chocolate marble cake to prime the pump. And Mom says, "If Jack loves Priscilla he'll hang on. He has no choice." Then our mother had sighed. "They have no place to live, you know."

Winnie sat up tall. "Goodness! Where will they live? In Whitewood where she grew up? Poor Jack! Out here on the reserve, the way things are? Poor Priscilla! I had no idea, my dear Sarah!"

"They're going to live in our granary."

Winnie, seizing the moment, deftly cut a large piece of marble cake and handed it to our mother. "How on earth will she cook?" she asked.

Our mother held up the cake, studying its pattern of chocolate and cream colour. "No granary ever came with a stove, that's for sure," she said. "They'll have to figure it out, I guess."

Leta had pinched me and I pinched her back. The granary! Leta and I stared, wide-eyed. A bride in the new granary with its fresh smelling lumber and sagey scents coming in on breezes off the field! Earlier that spring, relatives from the Sakimay, Kahkewistahaw, and Ochapowace built it. The pounding hammers and ringing nails, screws, rivets, and washers filled the hills with echoes.

The granary stood in a stand of birch mixed with poplar, beside a golden wheat field edging the valley. In rain, a gold-pink lustre lit the building inside, its striated amber walls glowing. The fresh new smell reeled us in. Leta and I abandoned our old haunt, a sagging shed near the stable. We gave up playing among its tools and harness that hung from rusty spikes. We gave up sniffing at tins of axle grease, engine oil, carbolic salve, and sweat on the horse collars. We said goodbye to a bouncy pile of old tire inner tubes in the corner. In this new playhouse, the walls echoed our every move, while a lone spider strung a web across the rafters as though, like Leta and me, it was waiting for the bride and the groom.

"How's Len taking it?" Winnie had already begun spinning a story. "Giving up his new granary, I mean. And doesn't he dislike when people overstay their welcome?"

Our mother cleared her throat. "It's true. Right after the war, he settled us in the farthest corner of Cowessess. He wanted to keep me and the kids safe from gossip that rots reserve life. Think of the men who weren't called up to fight, and those who had to stay behind. Think about how they bragged about us love-starved wives and girlfriends, alone at home. And that wasn't the half of it. Anyway, Len is laying down the law. Says he'll insist the couple not gossip. That they earn their keep. And that Jack find work with honest people, like the Hutterites. And to step smart and see to it Priscilla does the same. In return for being fed, she's to help me."

"It's not too much to ask," Winnie said, shifting in her chair.

Now, driving away from the street corner finally, where we have seen a phantom Jack and his radiant smile, Leta expresses the misgiving that our father had not considered, Priscilla's little daughter. "Dad told Mom to tell Priscilla she'd better mind that kid of hers, or go hungry!"

"Right?"

"Right!"

But Leta and I are determined to hang on to the delight of the morning. And, because cars obey, Leta insists, she will be a taxi driver someday. So be it, we say. We turn down 11th Avenue to Woolworths. We mean to go in for a treat at the lunch counter, and to air things out before heading back to Aunt Edith's apartment. Having forgotten our errand until now, we hurry across the street to Tamblyn's Drug Store for Aunt Edith's medicines. Then we dash into Woolworths and sit at the end of the counter. Ladies in hats and pleated dresses, in belted skirts and white blouses, sit drinking tea and coffee. People appear to be miming conversation. Hissing spouts, heavy white cups clunking on thick saucers, and the shiny silverware clattering into bins drown out words spoken. The aromas of coffee, pies, and cakes wreathe our heads in scents of raisins and even licorice.

"That was Cousin Jack at the corner, wasn't it?" Leta says tentatively.

"If so, why in heck didn't he clean himself up?"

"Big dumb nut!" Leta exclaims, teenage laughter spouting.

Heads turn and ladies glare.

Leta stares back. I divert her temperament with a poke. "Remember Dad saying that Priscilla had better not wear a beaded buckskin vest over a satin dress from Simpsons? And didn't Mom say that the look was vulgar, or was it loud, she said?"

"Vulgar. She always used that word. Mom said Priscilla is a Whitewood girl now—and … no … it was loud." Leta wrinkles her brow. "Didn't Mom say, too, that Whitewood people shunned Indians but kept Priscilla just the same? But wait, I forget. Dad said something just as nuts. He says, 'Priscilla had better not talk about bad Indian medicine around the girls!'" We explode in a fit of laughter. "And Mom saying that bad medicines could make him doubt the army!" We snicker like weasels, that is, until a couple of town ladies stare meaningfully at our single Orange-Crush-with-two-straws drink. It begins to feel as if we had wandered into the town's church.

Trying to save our precious morning a little longer, we sit straight. Leta's final mischief, however, erupts in a long, loud sip of soda pop that shatters the sound barrier. It's no use. Weak with laughter, we tell each other to shut up—that is, before another word is said about Jack and all—which, at this moment, takes us closer to Aunt Edith's, and a revelation.

As we head back to our aunt's, we return to the day of Jack and Priscilla's wedding. "Didn't Mom say to Dad that Jack was very handsome at the wedding?"

"Yes, but she complained at how he kept rubbing his eyes. And that she didn't like the look of it. Although the suit swept her away."

That day the adults had gotten ready early to leave for the ceremony. Our mother inspected Jack from all angles. When the truck rolled up to the door, Jack hopped in the front beside Dad. Mom and Winnie, in broad-shouldered jackets over their print dresses and bright chiffon kerchiefs protecting curls and finger waves, leapt into the back, laughing like girls. Neither thought to wave.

"They're chewing gum, you know," Leta said.

We had been desperate to go. We had cried to be pitied in our wish to see the wedding party, especially Priscilla and the Whitewood bridesmaids in pink taffeta gowns we'd heard about. But it was not to be; we had no decent shoes and not a single good dress. "Everything's all patches," our mother sighed. She promised to bring us the details, though, and said there'd be photographs eventually. Still, we hung onto hope. In evening light our poor clothes wouldn't show, we said. "How can you?" our mother's voice rose steeply. "I told you once, already! Even the bride's relatives can't go. Her uncle and cousin, Franklin Assiniboine and Blake Smoker, have only plaid shirts. You're the lucky ones! Jack and Priscilla are going to live here with us in the end."

"Is Kokum going?" Leta pushed now, showing what was unfair. Kokum only ever dressed in black, head to foot. And those holes in her running shoes?

Our mother bit her lip. "Kokum will catch a ride later, after dark." So that was that.

But then our parents returned early that afternoon. They weren't going to the dance, after all. Our mother's nosebleed had started up at the ceremony. When she came in the door, she gave us girls a look that said *not a single word out of you.*

The rest was agony, waiting for any sight of the bride. At nightfall we went to the edge of the hill overlooking the valley, a few yards from the house. "They'll be dancing now," Leta said. We flattened a patch of grass, not yet damp with dew, and sat down. Fiddle music wafted up the hill. We imagined the Métis band playing in the depths of the valley, stars blinking overhead. Eyes watering, we struggled to pierce the dark for the exact spot the dance hall was, near to the pole light beaming steadily beside the Mission buildings. Cool air currents rose from the ground, winding into drifts of balmy air. We hugged our knees. The croaking of frogs mingled with bursts of laughter lifting off the ravine. We imagined an arm around our waist, a cheek against our face, like in our mother's *True Story* magazines.

Did we think Priscilla might share her secrets? Oh yes, we said. But now our father called. And so it was straight to bed, our feet like ice up past the ankle, our bums chilled.

The bride and groom arrived late. Hearing a motor, we girls crept to the window. Headlights bathed the granary door as the whine of a motor ground to a stop. A man leapt down from the back of the truck and began unloading a few boxes. Then a white cloud floated out of the truck's cab, followed by, possibly, Jack with a bundle in his arms. They disappeared into the granary. Soon the headlights turned away, sweeping across scrub brush that pitched fractured shadows onto the tall tree trunks. It grew quiet. No one came to the house. Crestfallen, Leta and I did our best to fall asleep.

At chores next morning, we kept a sharp eye out. It had rained in the night but the sky had cleared. Everything was bathed in brilliant sunlight. We whispered about Priscilla while we gathered eggs from the chicken coop and hauled firewood into the house. How did a bride behave? As for Jack, we expected a complete transformation.

At half past ten, the granary door opened. The couple emerged, squinting into the sunlight. Priscilla was in a sky-blue dress. Jack had on his old red plaid shirt, looking disappointingly the same. But he held the hand of a small blonde girl in white panties and an undershirt. A pair of white sandals covered little feet. Leta whispered, they're coming. The trio walked toward us, Priscilla's shiny coppery curls bouncing.

"Hello, there." It was a pretty voice. Jack introduced us. Overcome, Leta and I shook hands, even Jack's, our heads lowered.

"This is Pearlie," Jack beamed.

Pearlie turned away. Bold as anything, Leta crouched down and peered into the little face, but the girl hid in the folds of Priscilla's dress.

"She's shy," Priscilla said, laughing. Dimples darted in her cheeks.

Soon it seemed Priscilla and Jack had always lived in the granary. We liked their playfulness. They would sit on the steps in the sun, heads together, one black, the other gold. Whispering jokes, their laughter filled the whole yard. Our parents noticed and began to act young, too, hugging waists whenever Jack and Priscilla came to the house.

Priscilla made everything seem magical. Leta and I admired all the things she touched, even the dark blue, white-speckled enamel dipper she drank from, an ordinary utensil that had always hung on the lip of the rain barrel. Now the dipper seemed bathed in a lovely light each time we went to scoop up water for the kitchen reservoir, or for the stoneware jug on the washstand. And now, too, it was so much more fun to gather the eggs in the chicken coop among the fusty, muttering chickens, the heat from their feathery breasts vibrating on the tops of our hands. We'd steal glances at Priscilla, the crook of her arm filled with wood from the woodpile, her blue dress billowing as she walked by, humming, on her way to the granary.

But in time our parents cast disapproving glances all around. Leta and I worked harder, not knowing what to make of it. Add to that, Priscilla had yet to invite us to see her wedding dress. So we behaved.

By late summer, life grew strangely unkind. Our mother told our father how she had paid a visit to the granary that morning, without first giving Priscilla any warning. "It was a sight! Washbasin full of scum, dishes on the floor, clothes dumped everywhere, bed unmade!" Priscilla, she said, spent her time daydreaming and scanning the fields and road for Jack.

Our father had his own grievances. "Jack's a greenhorn with the implements," he said.

Later that summer a heat wave browned and curled the leaves of the trees and grass. Silence replaced laughter. Mealtimes now were filled with tension. Priscilla chose this time to try to make things better by telling silly stories about the happenings of our day. And if there was anything our father hated, it was a tall tale told by a liar.

At the dinner table one evening, Priscilla hushed Pearlie, who sat complaining on her lap. Jack tried to correct a suspected fault in himself, to absorb the trouble—if he knew but what. We girls, our joints tightening, stared at our plates. We passed the pepper and salt and sliced bread to stiff adult figures seated around the table. Slicing a beet on his plate, our father said, "It's a hell of a note how a rock, damn well bigger'n a headstone, wasn't called. Cracked my plough shear all to hell. Goddamn loss of money, is what."

Leta kicked me. Our mother looked out the corner of her eye at Priscilla. "The washing didn't get done today either; no time, I guess."

Our father slammed his fork down and glared at Leta and me. "You girls better look lively!"

It was then Priscilla tried making ordinary incidents seem funny.

One afternoon, she had taken us berry picking in the bushes above the valley. Pearlie napped in the granary, the dogs under the step in the shade. Our mother rested in the house.

We walked along the path, glad to have Priscilla to ourselves. In the roadside grass, grasshoppers clicked their switchblade appendages while invisible flies and bugs buzzed in the weeds and undergrowth. Hot and perspiring, we hurried to find shade. Leta spotted a pool of water at the foot of a stand of birches. We ran to dip our hands in and patted the damp coolness on our necks. Priscilla was picking chokecherries, but stopped to watch, laughing.

Leta whispered, "Dad said a baby in the granary is the proof!"

"What did he mean?"

Leta called out, "Priscilla! Sophie wants to know what it means—a baby in the granary is the proof!"

Priscilla stood still and stared, her face flushed. She came to us, bringing wafts of chokecherry and sweetgrass with her. She smiled into our faces. Hugging us to her waist, her breasts warming the top our heads, she said that no matter what, a baby is a baby.

And that was what happened that day.

But at the table that night, silence fell like dead weight again. And Priscilla, chirping like a sparrow, began. "We went berry picking today." Leta pinched me under the table. "Yes," Priscilla continued. Her dimples twinkled. "We should have stayed home in the shade. You could roast a gopher on the big hot stone we tried sitting on!"

Leta kicked me, *what stone?*

"The girls found a puddle in the bush and flopped in," Priscilla laughed.

Leta looked at me, *we did?*

"Ugh! Mud and leaves on their bellies, and the dogs jumping in, too, yipping and yapping."

We girls stared at our plate. The dogs had stayed by the granary, like we told them.

"The girls got up, wet mud head to foot, dresses sopping!"

The adults pretended now that the story was very funny. Jack shot a look of gratitude at Priscilla.

Still, things came to a head.

One morning our father pulled up to the house with the team and wagonload of peeled poles. He called down, "I'm going in to sell pickets to get new hame straps. Jack, too. An all-day trip."

For the first time in a long time, our father's face was clear. He even smiled at Leta and me when he said, "You girls behave."

Jack scrambled onto the wagon. His long-legged shadow rippled over the pickets. He grinned down at Priscilla and Pearlie, his face rinsed and shiny. Leta whispered that Jack smiled because he was imagining himself in his wedding suit in town in Sam Goodman's store. The dogs swarmed, barking up the road ahead of the horses. We ran alongside to open the gate, glad to see the wagon heading for the bend in the road and making that last turn.

We might have gone over to see what the crows were fussing about, but Priscilla was beckoning. We raced to the granary. She was breathing so hard that the buttons of her dress looked ready to pop. Her dimples leapt all the livelier. She cupped her hands under our chin. "Today," she said, "I have a secret. I need you to get me your mom's sewing basket, thread, needle, thimble, and scissors, all of it." Our mother had gone in for her mid-morning nap. Priscilla read our mind. "No need to waken her."

Intrigued, we snuck into the house past our mother's soft snores. Two steps closer to the bed and we were able to grab the red willow basket. Finger to her lips, Priscilla waited by the granary. She said that we'd have to do the chores on our own. But, she said, she would peel the potatoes later. Could she depend on us? Leta asked if we were allowed to clean up the granary, as well. Priscilla looked around, shrugged, and nodded.

Always the braver one, Leta threw in, "And can we see your wedding dress?"

Priscilla laughed, "Well, no. My Whitewood family has it. I could have sworn everyone on earth saw it at least once." She looked at our faces. "Oh my!" she said.

Leta, not to be left empty-handed, pounced. "What secret thing are you going to do?"

Priscilla pirouetted out into the yard, blue dress flaring, legs gleaming. "I'm making an outfit for Pearlie!" We had not heard that happy laugh in a long time.

"What's so great about that?" Leta asked. I knew what she was thinking. Our mother always cut down old clothes for us.

"What a thing to say!" Priscilla laughed. "You'll have to wait and see. But then ..." she spoke more to herself now, "it might turn out ... odd."

"Why couldn't we just ask Mom for the basket?" Leta could never just shut up.

Priscilla cocked her head. "I want to dress Pearlie nice—a surprise for Jack, and for your mom and dad, too. Your mom loves nice clothes. But now I have to get busy."

It sounded simple, but that afternoon changed everything.

Leta stands up to leave the lunch counter now. We make our escape, intent on protecting what is left of our fine day. In no time at all, we will turn the car around and head back to the Crescent Apartments on 14th Avenue with our purchase of green liniment, gauze, and adhesive tape for Aunt Edith's arthritic ankle. As we pull up, another dying-with-laughter moment begins. "Do you remember when Jack told

Mom about his plans for his tenth wedding anniversary?"

"You mean about inviting important people?"

"How did it all begin, again?"

"Jack comes in to see Mom and says, 'My sister, I need your help with a letter. I carry a heavy load.'"

Our laughter begins anew, what with Jack being so serious and Priscilla soaking in the tin tub behind the granary.

Leta, mimicking Jack, says, "'I want the best celebration ever, for Priscilla.' Yes, that's how he put it. Yes, and then he says he's going to invite the prime minister of Canada ten years ahead of time, him being so busy." Leta hits Jack's words and tone exactly.

Our laughter knows no bounds, out here on the sidewalk leading to Aunt Edith's apartment, despite our having spotted that shabby suit; besides, we had not called out a single hello to him. "On account of the honking," Leta reminds me.

But we can't speak of it yet. We are caught up in another fit of laughter—the bad kind that you should never do because of the sadness. And Leta agrees, "Bad, as when your best friend tells you that his mother got killed and you feel dying of laughter, peeing in your pants, to top it all. And Mom saying to Jack, 'Ee-a-how! The prime minister, yet! Don't you know he's the biggest white man in the country? Besides, we have no writing paper!'" Leta, mimicking just right, sets us roaring.

"How did Mom talk him out of it, again?"

"She says, 'As an Indian, you'll have to ask King George VI. That means you have to go through chief and council.'"

Laughter stitches our sides over Jack's reply: "I'll have to find a way around those gossips!"

We reach the main door to Aunt Edith's apartment building, but we cannot shake off our fit just yet, try as we might. We stagger up the stairs. Leta adds embellishments to Jack's troubles, intoning, "Dearest Prime Minister, I had a talk with our chief this day."

But then, catching hold of herself, Leta says, "Remember his wedding suit, and how he got that expensive tailor in the city to make it?"

Which leads us back to the day we took Mom's sewing basket out from under her nose and into Priscilla's world. Priscilla had taken hold of it like it was full of the rarest of bluebirds' eggs. She had cleared a spot on the granary floor where the light was bright.

"She sewed into the afternoon. And boy, did we work!" Leta says. "And Pearlie dead to the world, on the bed."

We had dumped onto the floor all the clothes and odds and ends out of cartons that lined the granary walls. We refolded and placed these in separate boxes: flared skirts, flowery dresses, blouses, sweaters, and pairs of stockings, with another box for baby bonnets, dresses, undershirts, and real panties. And there was that fall coat of Jack's, out at the elbow, along with a patched shirt, frayed pants, and socks in a small box.

Priscilla called us "fusspots." "You'll have enough of that when you get married!"

"When I get big, I'll have a house, but no husband!" Leta cried.

"I won't be a wife, neither, no sir," I added.

The sun had swung farther west and pitched a broad wedge of light onto the floor where Priscilla sewed, her head bowed. An invisible needle sent flying sparks into the air. By late afternoon the sun had browned the tips of grass lining the path connecting the woodpile, the garden, chicken coop, house, granary, and barn. "A real scorcher," Priscilla said, wiping her nose.

Finally she rose to her feet. She eyed the boxes, snug against the walls. "You girls are tidy, for such little sparrows," she said. But her voice was flat. She scooped up her sewing.

Priscilla went to waken Pearlie. "Come. Stand up. Right here. On the bed." She stripped Pearlie of her little dress. We waited, curious. Pearlie, trying to stand on wobbly legs, rubbed sleep from her eyes.

She appeared tinier than ever. Priscilla said not to look yet. So Leta and I, whispering, waited for a moment, imagining a blue satin dress, smocked, maybe, with lace trim and tassels and a gold cord belt, like those curtains in the window in town. Hands shaking, Priscilla began fussing with a little checkered skirt the size of a man's handkerchief. She placed a cap of the same fabric on the little curly head. She flipped a matching jacket over tiny shoulders. She now lifted Pearlie carefully off the bed and put shiny black shoes on her feet. Finally she stood her out in the sun. Leta and I stared. Pearlie, in an outfit of black and white checks, looked like a live doll.

Priscilla's eyes filled with happy tears.

But now, Leta, startled, looked up the road. Dad's wagon had clanked sharply, a short distance away beyond the bend.

"What, already!" Priscilla hollered. She pushed Pearlie into the granary and told her to wait there.

The three of us practically stumbled into the house. Priscilla popped potatoes into the pot, skins and all. "We'll boil and slice and fry them," she said. She flipped up the lid of the reservoir to check the water level for the men's wash-up, and eyed the woodbox. "Good enough," she said. Her hands shook as she laid the table.

"Jack will be surprised!" she said, but she sounded uncertain. She tapped a tablespoon of lard into the frying pan. "We'll fry eggs, too."

The wagon rattled and clanked to a stop outside the door. Mom emerged from the bedroom, combing her hair. We girls went out. Oddly, the dogs had stayed under the steps.

Our father wore a grim face. It was plain to see that less than a quarter of the pickets had been sold. Jack's half-smile was for Priscilla.

She grabbed him by the arm. "You gotta come and see!"

Jack peered into her face.

"Come!" Priscilla pulled him along.

"I'll put the team away later," Jack called over his shoulder to Dad, who, with a shrug, disappeared into the house.

Leta and I ran to the granary, hoping to catch a glimpse of Jack's moment of surprise.

"Close your eyes." Priscilla's laughter rang like little bells. She led Jack, his eyes shut, to the steps and sat him down. "Promise not to open 'til I say!"

He promised. Priscilla beckoned Pearlie to come outside and stand in the sun. Pearlie did as she was told. "Steady now, Jack." Priscilla had grown calm and still. "Ready?"

"Ready."

"Open your eyes!"

Jack blinked. He looked at Pearlie. His eyes moved from her head to her toes and back up again. A mix of feelings, mostly confusion, broke out in his face. Priscilla giggled.

"My suit?" he asked. He shaded his eyes. "You cut my suit?"

Priscilla's dimples were steady. She nodded.

But then our father's voice rang out, "You girls come inside!"

Jack and Priscilla did not come in for supper.

At dawn the next day, Leta and I awoke to deep stillness. We slid out of bed and crept into the chilly air. Goosebumps flashed across Leta's arms and jumped the gap to mine. From the field beyond the bushes, the sharp cawing of a crow cut across the treetops. The first flat glare of dawn held now, bringing with it the dread of summer's end. Something about the granary made it seem caught in a dream; as if, being shut, it held a secret. Knees trembling, we tore open the door.

They had slipped away. The granary was filled with blankness. Not a bed, spoon, or shoe lay in sight. Only our mother's red willow sewing basket stood in the middle of the floor. Priscilla's blue dress, forgotten, hung on the line outside.

In a not-so-distant summer of independence, Leta and I will recall everything with a sense of uneasy accomplishment. We had made it to the city, found odd jobs the last year of high school, and drove our aunt to distraction. Had we forgotten our manners? Did we really think short skirts on girls were gracious? Did it matter to us? Oh yes! Of course not! Sitting in our aunt's tiny living room, on a shabby burgundy sofa and worn velvet wing chair, we tell her of a sighting. "It was him!" we insist.

It had been Jack all right, a charmed, hovering presence—gesturing, conversing, a blend of dignity, neglect, and joyfulness in his over-bright eyes—for no other than Priscilla, right? We tell our aunt that he shone as if bound by a bright, undying love for his dear and darling Priscilla. We tell our aunt how wonderful little Pearlie had appeared, out in the sun that last day long ago. Jack's eyes had opened very wide when he saw, we say. Priscilla's laughter had rung out in the air, a tinkling of a town girl spiralling.

But no, we won't tell our dear, fragile old auntie everything just yet. Instead, we murmur an unbearable truth to ourselves. Priscilla was nowhere near that street corner this morning. She was not with Jack at all. He was alone, mad, and trapped in another time.

Tempting Mercy

WHEN THE SOLDIERS RETURNED to the reserve after the war, Mercy hoped she might get help finally. Mom was laid up with crippling arthritis, and Mercy and Dad had to cart her around. They cooked, washed, cleaned, weeded the garden—everything. Dad teased her, "Get married, Mercy. Nineteen is still young."

Good advice, but to her eye, ex-soldiers were cocky. Most drank and turned mean. None held her attention. Before Dad died of heart trouble that winter, he'd said, "Climb, Mercy." Climb, but don't leave Mom, was probably what he meant. In any case she decided then and there to go after a band councillor position, young or not, female or not: *just me, myself, and I—Merceline Hawk, otherwise known as Mercy.*

During the war she was so lonely she had set her sights on Trent Stone, of all people. This was before he went overseas to fight in World War Two. He would look at her in that way then, but never once wrote to her. Not one word. And then after the war, he returned home with an English girl called Hattie Newgate. Mercy was so stunned, she all but fell over.

One thing she knew: Hattie Newgate and her? —their paths

would cross. Everybody had their uses. And Mercy had hope. And a plan. A plan, as it turned out, that, in the main, depended on a fellow campaigner with loose lips, a captive illegal alien who was an English girl, and a new Indian agent, all stuck on the reserve.

The big opportunity seemed to drop from the sky. Mr. Passmore, the Indian agent living on the reserve, was retiring. Although Mercy had been helping out at the agency house the whole week already, his wife had asked her to come in to help with packing for that coming Monday. "I'll need you for the whole day, Mercy," she'd said. The extra day was more than fine with Mercy. Working inside the agency house made her feel closer to a power that ruled life.

Mercy liked the agent's wife. Mrs. Passmore let her in on things, although not all of it for Mercy's ears, really, she knew—more because she happened to be in the room. "The new Indian agent, a certain Mr. Wiggins, is coming from Ottawa. He'll arrive here at noon, Monday," Mrs. Passmore said, adding, "as though he couldn't find a better time! I need you to help out with a few things, like mind the table. I have so much on the go, like getting at those trunks in the attic shipped to Ontario by three, Monday, when the truck comes."

A new Indian agent! What a dance of feelings gripped Mercy!

It was Friday and she was in the basement, in the reception part of the office, sweeping floors and wiping down walls and furniture. Mrs. Passmore, obviously, had packed away most office things already. The room looked cold and bare. Even the picture of the three basset hounds had been taken down. It was what Cowessess people saw first thing when they came in, two males and a bitch, in coats of red and white patches. As a little girl, hanging onto Dad's hand, she would enter this space and stand there, wishing for that watercolour, even in its dull gunmetal frame. But it was gone now. It gave her heart a lurch.

Around ten o'clock that morning, as she wiped down Mr. Passmore's orange-toned oak desk, an odd rustling drifted in through a small, brown-painted window above her head. The window, its dusty screen full of bugs, gave her enough light to work by; but just now it had also let in a man's voice. The voice of Sonny Rabbitskin. He got around, that one, his vocal chords forever tight with gossip and sneakiness. By the sound of things, he and his pal were sitting on a bench installed years ago by the former Indian agent. The wrought iron and wood-slatted bench had been set in a leafy hedge next to the house, where Sonny was now seated. He was talking about Hattie Newgate, of all people, the English girl who lived with Trent Stone, Mercy's old flame.

What Sonny was saying came as a shock. "I fell for Hattie," he said.

He had to think he was out of harm's way to have said it. Fell for her! Mercy grabbed up a pencil from a wooden tray on the Indian agent's desk and whipped a blank permit form off the shelf behind her. She fell into the agency chair and wrote down everything he was saying. Sonny's words, silvery fish in a stream, slipped down into her net.

Each word told more about Hattie Newgate. "I want her but not because she's white, like people say. Not 'cause I feel sorry for her. And it's not like she picked Trent Stone over me, like he claims. No, I love Hattie. I quit being friends with Trent. When he gets tight, he has no room for nobody, not even Hattie. Hangs on to her just to prove he can. Me, I have nothing to prove. She's something, that girl. People say, imagine, a white girl latching onto our Trent, him and his hooked nose, and bringing her here from way hell and gone, London."

Mercy was flabbergasted. Dad had warned her about the gossiping Sonny. "For all his handsome ways, Mercy, he's five years your senior. Yet, where is he today? A gossip that uses rumour to gain people's trust as much as to hurt them down the road. Stay clear."

Dad never liked that Sonny was an army reject, and that he didn't get the nod at the last band election. And now here he sat, spouting off about Trent Stone, of all people. Mercy's yellow pencil was heating up, and about to get hotter.

Sonny continued, "Hattie told me her brother and cousin in England took turns on her after her mother died when she was thirteen. She ran away. Got a job as a domestic. Had little sleep and was hungry a lot. Then out of the blue comes this soldier on his way back to Canada. Asks her to come with him. She has no money. She steals clothes, cash, and papers off her roommates."

A thought lit Mercy's mind: Sonny had kept this information to himself? It wasn't like him. And now here he was spilling the beans, unknowingly to his competitor, Mercy, in this year's coming band elections. To have kept his mouth shut would have been smart. Had he been alive, Dad might have said that Mercy had no right to listen in. But eavesdropping came easy to her. She liked figuring out people's heads. Besides, knowledge was power. Dad used to say so, himself. "Evidence is real power" was her new motto.

And, sure enough, Sonny piled on more. "Hattie and her soldier step off the boat at Pier 21 in Halifax. She figures it's a short train trip to Winnipeg, where they're gonna live. But at the last minute, he owns up he's married. Has a wife and kids in Toronto. Gives her cash for meals for three days. Won't look at her when she begs. She knew, finally, to keep going. Yup, made it to Winnipeg. That's when she hooked up with my old buddy, there—that Trent, there. Jeez, I have no use for that guy."

Did she hear right? He said what about Trent? Mercy was all ears. Still, what came next made her jump to her feet. "Trent told me the first time he laid eyes on Hattie, she was one helluva tear-soaked bunny in an old grey sweater and blue hat, down at the train station there, in Winnipeg. Said he saw she was scared. Knew she was alone. He takes pity on her. She tells him everything, like about how people back in the old country helped her steal and fix up a passport. So now Trent knows she'll glom onto him. She glommed on, all right."

Mercy felt it happen. A cold thrill in the gut. Lady Luck had just turned on Sonny and walked right on over to her. What's more, she had new tools! Just you wait, Sonny! Three things blazed good and bright: Hattie, the London girl, had wicked secrets; Trent Stone was in on it, or had to be; and lovelorn Sonny had discarded an important ally in Trent. Goodbye to Trent and it was the end of Sonny's chances of getting the Indian Agent's nod to run as a candidate. Trent had Hattie's legal troubles, a list in his back pocket actually, one Mercy could pull out each time the new Indian agent began making his decisions. This was one big hammer. And if she worked it right, she could swing it hard. And knew to keep her mouth shut.

And so there she was back at the agency house, Monday morning, shaking the rain off her jacket in the hallway as she glanced around. Mrs. Passmore had been busy all weekend, she told her. "His papers have gone on ahead, his old correspondence, reports, and minutes, anything with government letterhead. I bound the whole works up with parcel string and twine and locked it all in a big wooden trunk. Gone, thank goodness! And look, Mercy, I packed my bone china and embroidered linens. And, oh, you'll have to work around the spring and winter clothes—those big boxes in the upstairs hallway, darn him."

She had also taken the time to box up a few things for Mercy's mother, a soft yellow sweater, chocolate fudge, Jergens hand lotion, and a large woolen shawl. "We make a good team, Mercy," she said, looking her up and down. "You're taller than me, and I'm wider than you." They laughed like pals.

Done with sweeping the upstairs hall, Mercy put the broom and dustpan back in the musty little hallway closet and fingered the note in her pocket. At that moment Mr. Passmore called up the basement steps to his wife, "I've asked Sonny Rabbitskin to come when he can today. No time last week. And by the way, Hattie Newgate is dropping in to meet with me around three, right after Wiggins."

Mrs. Passmore called down that she was too busy to take notice of such trivial matters right now, thank you. She had at least two huge trunks to sort and pack for their removal at three, when the truck came.

"For all the help you are," she added. It was plain Mr. Passmore wasn't about to reply. He slammed the basement door behind him on his way out.

In the kitchen, while Mrs. Passmore and Mercy prepared the noon meal for the Ottawa guest, she let Mercy in on her thought. "I suppose I'll just have to show the more gracious side of me," she said. "Don't ask why. The young Mr. Wiggins will be stepping over that doorsill soon, into this house—my home these twenty years!" Crossing back and forth between kitchen and dining room, she stopped to pick up and then bang down things, as she and Mercy set the table. "While not shutting the door in his face, exactly, my manner will nonetheless convey a touch of frost, like that window at freeze-up." She nodded at the kitchen window, its sill lined with potted herbs and geraniums. She let two heavy stoneware dinner plates drop on the table. She ran fingers through greying reddish-blonde hair and sighed. "Mind, I must receive his handshake in kind." Clang went the cutlery. She dished hot food into bowls and slid them in the oven to keep warm. "And I'll tell you this much, I'll climb right back up the attic stairs, leaving the men to worldly affairs. After which, Mercy, I'm afraid the serving is up to you."

Mercy had her own plan for handling the guest and table: say nothing. And stay in the dining room as much as possible. Listen for band management clues. Learn how the new Indian agent planned to run things. Find out what he needed in the way of help. See what kind of person he was. She was practically wringing her hands by the time there was a shuffling and scraping of shoes at the front door.

Peeking out, the kitchen door ajar, she saw a youngish man enter the dining room. He wore gold-rimmed spectacles and his blond hair was swept back. He and the Indian agent laughed their way in. It was booming laughter from both; mainly for the sound of it, she knew. Telling thumps came from the attic now, too. Soon it would be her turn.

Not knowing exactly when to enter, she waited, stomach rippling.

To ease her nerves, she forced her mind on what she saw around her. She had never seen agency life in all its power, at least not from the inside, complete with agents. This was the private dining room, with its wall of multi-planed windows looking upon a wide green yard, bounded by tall green caragana hedges. Out the other window, a dark red wooden balustrade hugged wooden steps that led down to a paved walk up to the gate. Stomach fluttering, Mercy tried settling her nerves by pretending she, too, was a regular visitor to the agency. Like a mining engineer in khaki pants and plaid shirt. When that didn't work, she tried a land surveyor in a hard hat, and then a government consultant from town in a navy suit and a red, white, and blue striped tie. No, pretending didn't work. Only powerful people, not Mercy Hawk from Cowessess, ever lifted the brass knocker on the front door. Reserve people, on their way to the basement, entered through a scuffed, oxblood side door, its flat iron latch and patched screen a sight.

Mr. Passmore cleared his throat. It was time.

A plate of sliced bread and a pitcher of ice water in shaking hands, she squared her shoulders and entered the dining room. Mr. Wiggins nodded briefly in her direction. But Mr. Passmore uttered something so startling that the handle of the water jug slipped in Mercy's fingers. He said, "That bloke is filling his pal in about an English girl who lives Indian style with his ex-friend."

Mr. Passmore sighed, as if suddenly bone tired. "You, too, will understand their lives more than they ever will."

"How so?" Mr. Wiggins seemed to be trying to help the conversation along. But his gaze stuck to the radiator just above the baseboard, from where, likely, Sonny's voice had drifted in. The two agents paid no attention to her. Mercy poured the water, ice chunks clinking into their tumblers, and almost dropped the pitcher again. Sonny's voice flowed from the radiator. His words rang very clear. "I'm gonna cut Trent off. And I don't give a damn how. Hattie's mine."

Her face gave nothing away. She was good at this.

Mr. Passmore, spreading a dab of orange-yellow butter on a slice of bread, laid his knife down. "I pay attention to all forms of news," he explained. He rose to kick the radiator flap shut with the point of his Oxford shoe, thus stifling Sonny, and sat down. Mercy set the bowls of potatoes, vegetables, and meat on the table and removed their steamy glass covers.

Mr. Wiggins, looking warm in a wilted navy suit, was unruffled. A younger man of medium build, when he had walked in, his traveller's confidence propelled him like it did the usual visitor passing through— *don't know, don't care.* He had a boyish face, his unblemished skin adding to the brightness in his glance. His spectacles were clear as polished mirrors. Mercy tried to tell herself that when he looked at his new life around him, he saw the difference he intended to make. But she wasn't fooled for long. The smile he wore appeared more and more like a careful smile, a smile carved in code. In fact, he might have already shut down the better part of his brain. Still, she sensed room in the things he said. A person with give, Dad might have supposed.

She was impatient for the two agents to shift gears, step on the gas, and speed up their thoughts on making reserve improvements. Repairs, alone, were needed, and now. And the reserve was to elect a new band council this fall. The thought of an election set Mercy's head ablaze. Women had no say. Yet, women needed a fresh well dug, like the health official had warned this spring. Mercy had tasted and smelled what he meant. Other problems came with the outbreak of leafy spurge that gave cows' milk a bad taste. Kids cried and mothers couldn't help.

Now, Mercy hoped Mr. Passmore knew to speak on her behalf, as an agency worker. The new agent could let her go if he wanted, even as early as this coming Friday. Agency jobs were scarce and often disappeared overnight, wartime or not. People with paying jobs, Dad would say, had gotten into the habit of tattling on one another, and then using rumour as a weapon to get rid of the competition.

In or out, for now, Mercy was content to be a fly on the wall, patiently waiting for Hattie Newgate.

Mr. Passmore, in the company of an incoming agent, adopted at first a breezy manner, like he was moving a barn and on-lookers applauded. "I always say man's like a bee," he intoned. "Buzzes loudest when a wing's off. A man talks most then." There was a fat note in his voice, and growing fatter. "All you have to do is fill in the blanks. An Indian agent's bread and butter, in fact."

She listened all the harder. She knew to watch both face and gesture for clues, like the raw pride blooming in Mr. Passmore's cheeks. He was headed for boasting, Mercy could tell. She would just have to pick her way through it. Mr. Passmore began by saying that, ultimately, success lay in human management, so much so that he often had to stop and wonder at his skill. Oh, he had felt grandeur in his bones, he said. "And yes, I've heard the clash of cymbals, and mystical bugles out across the low and level plains." He was definitely trying on something, and it sounded like a fit. "And finally," he added, "here we are, emperor and ambassador!"

"Or tutor with tutee," said Mr. Wiggins.

Mr. Passmore scraped his chair good and loud across the floorboards, and then, holding himself in check, tilted at the gravy.

As the agents sorted the passing around of food between them, Mercy tried to see beyond a wall that Mr. Wiggins suddenly threw around himself. She wished to see into the depths of eyes that changed, like watercolours, from hazel to green and gold and back again. It seemed his gaze also held a beam of light that, by turns, brightened and dimmed, or warmed and cooled as it moved between Yes, Maybe, and No.

Mercy knew enough to look busy. She slid over to the chiffonier and reached around inside, hoping to find things to sort and pack. In doing so, she accidentally scraped her shoe against the wooden floor.

"Yes, indeed," Mr. Passmore said, apparently readying himself to settle into a review of his work. He looked sideways at Mercy as she tugged at what lay out of sight on the shelf. "Blasted piece of furniture, eh, Mercy?" he asked. She nodded, heart thumping.

He turned to his guest, whose fork busily chased peas across his plate. "There it stands, Mr. Wiggins, bulky with inheritance, what it all boils down to in the end—a musty chiffonier against these faded walls." The yellow floral wallpaper did look dull and worn. But it was on account of the afternoon light not come around yet; the half-light had drained colour from the littler cabbages. But Mr. Passmore wasn't thinking about wallpaper. "It has always only ever been a dim and fading light," he said, "when you come to think about it."

Mr. Passmore gathered himself up, as if only now recalling that his task was to prepare the new man. "One thing," he said, his face shining with pleasure, tool kit at hand. "Take the situation out there— our Sonny Rabbitskin." Mr. Passmore tilted his head toward the hedge outside. "What have we got? A love triangle? Something of no utility, you say? Oh, the stage might look small, the actors wanting, and the action measly ... but. You see, thing is, Mr. Wiggins, relationships are the real currency here. Some would argue the only currency. So it is not ours to ponder that our boy hankers for a girl called Miss Hattie Newgate. And by the way, that attraction isn't mutual. There's utility in it, if you know how to look at it."

Eyeing his fellow agent, Mr. Passmore picked up his knife and cut a piece of meat. However, Mr. Wiggins, leaning back in his chair, made no reply; his slightly raised chin might even have suggested that he had finished with the topic.

"Give up?" Mr. Passmore, pressing, was impatient with the long silence.

Mr. Wiggins might only have been waiting to speak his mind, although he had, in fact, drummed his fingers on the table top. When he finally spoke, his voice carried a contrary note. "Hearsay stunts development. Wouldn't you say?"

Mr. Passmore nursed an answer. He leaned back, squinted at the ceiling, and said something quite senseless, to Mercy's ears. "A city accustomed to freedom is easier to rule through its original citizenry, says Machiavelli. But you have to isolate the quarry first, say I."

Mr. Passmore sounded like an expert, apparently even to his own ears. The manner he had adopted was not unlike the one Mercy had heard his wife knock down just last week. "You're good at counterfeit," she'd said. "You'd think you were an Elgin marble sprung to life, but for lack of shining sword." Mr. Passmore, turning red, had given a short tinny laugh.

The new agent had an answer. "How can eavesdropping add a single ounce of good? Aren't listening devices and hearsay hallmarks of the dictator? Isn't surveillance his only choice? I'd question its applicability to an Indian agent's work in Canada." His mouth held the U-shape of a dry crust of bread. "Knowing history, and I admit, my best subject, I think Machiavelli was a bit of a cynic."

Her back to the table, Mercy hastily scribbled a list of words according to the sounds they made, their safekeeping on notepaper awaiting time later for finding their true spelling and meaning.

But now Mr. Passmore refuted Mr. Wiggins's claim. He said, "Machiavelli was a strategist, a damn sight better than a cynic. An historian hoping to run an Indian affairs agency would do well to get to know him." Mercy wrote *strata-jist*. She fretted. Just what did she know about this Make-a-Valley guy? She knew "dictator." She knew "hearing device." As for "cynic," she would ask around. Mercy could see that Mr. Wiggins realized he had come face to face with a man unused to stepping aside.

"Ever since my university days," Mr. Wiggins began, like a cheeky kid to his big brother, "I simply haven't equated natural cunning with man-made strategy."

A scowling Mr. Passmore, who liked to boast to his wife that he was a reader and not just some snot-nosed university kid, twisted the crust off his slice of bread and popped it into his mouth, whole.

Mr. Wiggins, feeling for the straightness of his tie, continued to say exactly what he felt like saying. Mercy felt like shouting, *that's telling him!* Nobody she knew of ever talked back to the Indian agent. But now Mr. Wiggins went only so far. "I read Jack London's *Call of the Wild* as a boy and, again, as a man," he said. "I gained respect for the wolf pack. But man is more than the wolf. And domination is the lowest form of human impulse. Machiavelli knew this. Though, I have to agree, he played to it."

Mercy told herself not to worry when they talked like that. It was just talk. She knew the tone: ex-soldiers playing cards Saturday night for a two-dollar pot. She need only get past the big words. But even she wasn't prepared for Mr. Passmore's bark. "Oh, he said a lot of things!" Mercy feared he might start swearing and march out; however, clearing his air passageway, he remarked, "I feel like I'm talking to an Indian."

Mr. Wiggins's right hand jumped in his chair, as if to catch a fly ball. His face flushed deep red. Mr. Passmore had taken command. "The mind is apt to stray off course," he was saying, "way off Columbus's path. I ask you, can an Indian agent afford to ignore the abyss, the white man's burden, the weight of the albatross?"

Mercy stopped digging in the chiffonier. She looked to see if Mr. Wiggins had made friends with the words "white man's burden." Forget the albatross. Mr. Passmore was taking in that boyish nose across the table from him, the gold wire-rim glasses, the girlish hair swept back. As for Mr. Wiggins, his face remained unreadable, even to Mercy.

Strangely, something in Mr. Passmore's demeanour gave way. It seemed he realized that he had run unexpectedly into a man in possession of "the manner"—the manner that stalled, that withheld a key that turned on its own axis. Mr. Wiggins, it was plain, had decided to exercise an ability to present a face as blank as an agency permit—

no love lost on the flip side. A couple of times already he had laughed in a way that pitched honest delight into a lead box and slammed the lid shut.

Mr. Passmore, on the other hand, had already come back to Earth. "May I draw your attention to our Indian outside," he said.

This was not a question. He went on. "Clean. Though I have to say he does have a traditional side—believes in a creator, in generosity, giving your last shirt, that sort of thing. Remnants of primitive religion, you might say. Aside from that, he has utility."

Utility. Mercy noted this word again, a clue that could mean Mr. Passmore planned to give Sonny an agency job. Or worse, recommend him for band councillor! People claimed the Indian agent had power over band elections. Only men with bendable wills ever got in, was said. Mercy did not want to believe it. All the same, bendable or not, Sonny had nothing on her—before he could cry uncle, she'd spring. She had the means, and she meant to use them.

Mercy pretended to be as busy as a bee. She stuck her hand deep into the chiffonier's lowest shelf and felt around. She pulled out three baskets heaped with an assortment of small-framed photos. She made a show of taking up each one and of inspecting its protective glass and frame. And then, too, of dusting off each one with a flourish. She also made a real show of smoothing out each piece of felt separator with the flat of her hand. Afterward, she stood the framed photos vertically, side by side, in the basket.

But then she caught sight of a tiny movement at the table. The air in the room quivered. It seemed Mr. Wiggins had inclined his head toward her, that she had missed the raised eyebrow. It was Mr. Passmore who had, in fact, perceived something. He waved his teacup at her without turning her way. She leaped up to pour. Then she resumed her work on the second basket of photos, leaving the other nearby uncovered as evidence.

Mr. Passmore studied Mr. Wiggins's face. He said, "When you

start here, it's easy to think that people have the required skills. Well, they don't. Observation is a finely tuned art for an official. Other than the gossip mills out here, nothing sophisticated plays into it all. It's all just interpersonal." He sighed and checked the clock on the chiffonier.

Mercy knew he had three o'clock in mind—and Hattie Newgate.

"Well now," he said, leaning back and smiling. He placed his knife and fork square alongside his plate, like a doctor readying instruments. "There's this other fella you want to consider, by the name of Trent Stone, living with Miss Newgate, as I've said." He allowed a hard swallow of tea. "Trent Stone is a worry. But for all his bull-headed ways, you'd best be aware that he has the psychology down pat—pure instinct, you understand. Mark my words. There'll come a time, useful or not, when you'll have to cut him down. But until then ..."

Mercy's shoe slipped in a loud creeeek! Mr. Passmore turned, master to his basset hound. "Makin' progress down there, Mercy?"

"Yes." Her voice sounded soft, even to her.

"What's that you say?"

"Yes," Mercy spoke a bit louder, trying to hold her volume clear of any notion of a hound dog wagging its tail, or, worse, an overgrown St. Bernard not wagging.

Mr. Passmore, shrugging, looked at Mr. Wiggins as though they shared a burden.

Mercy's heart beat loudly in her ears. Did he just say Trent Stone was useful? To whom? What could Mr. Passmore mean? This was a concern. Cutting down Trent Stone, she understood. But useful? Probably only to her, if she played it smart.

Mr. Passmore pushed on with his lesson. "Putting it mildly, Trent Stone places controls on the English girl. People like the Elders here have tried talking sense to him, tried telling him to stop. The old people gave warning that Hattie's not from here; warned him about retaliation from the outside, from across the ocean, if you can believe it. Suspicion is never far to seek." He shook his head.

That last remark galled Mercy. People had reason to suspect. Anything ever spoken aloud was fuel for talk, and never safe with Mr. Passmore. And why did he repeat the Elders' advice like it was just some kind of salve for a dog's quill-studded nose? It seemed that Mr. Passmore lacked real feeling—like grief for betraying old people who were not in the room. Besides, laws did reach across the ocean. Dad used to say so, mainly when people from the reserve got into trouble and were jailed, which was often.

The old Indian agent rolled on. "Trent Stone doesn't let Hattie see people. He answers the door to visitors, tells them Hattie's sick, or that she's trying to start a fight, or, worse, that she doesn't wish to speak to Indians. I suspect a few believe him, might even take pains to."

Mr. Wiggins seemed to be struggling to line up his thoughts. "There's always the gossip's nose for bad smells," he said. "Why repeat that for which no evidence exists?"

"Whatever the case," Mr. Passmore said, growing impatient, "she's one of us."

Whatever the case. Mercy felt evidence enough burning a hole in her pocket, her notebook and pencil on fire with the truth. What's more, she had learned a couple of things about Mr. Wiggins, and a whole lot more about Trent and Hattie.

It seemed Mr. Wiggins stood for things. The way Mercy saw it, it was most likely that, in a game of tag or kick the can, he'd play fair. And, maybe, anyone could play.

She picked up a photograph lying face down beside the basket. Colourless faces stared out of a deep stillness: ladies in black dresses; sad, tired children in black lace-up boots; men in moustaches or full beards dressed in puff-sleeved white shirts and black suspenders. But what was this? A fair, curly-haired young man with nice features, eyes crinkled in a joke he has just told. She had seen white eyelashes like that before, that wide toothy grin. She nearly jumped out of her skin. It was Mr. Passmore. He looked happy, his broad shoulders back, long fingers on narrow hips, eyebrows lit …

"What you got there, Mercy?"

"I'm trying to find where they fit."

"Where what fits?"

"The pictures, Mr. Passmore."

"Well, see you don't take all day!"

Mercy hurried her trembling hands even as she stole quick glances at Mr. Passmore's eyebrows, rogue hairs sprung every which way. His build was bulky now. The picture and he didn't quite go together. A shiver ran through her.

The aged walnut railroad clock on the chiffonier ticked on. It was a quarter past two. But Mr. Passmore was stuck on Hattie Newgate. He talked about her while Mr. Wiggins, a king-size grasshopper stroking its antennae, seemed to be listening and unmoved.

"Point is," Mr. Passmore advanced, "Trent Stone works on the basis of domination. People say he goes so far as to manage Hattie's conversations, answers for her and interferes with her business, that sort of thing." Mr. Passmore shook his head, his fork chasing a small sweet pickled onion on his plate. "Elders say he interferes with Miss Newgate's efforts to learn even the skills of survival: how to hunt, make quilts, cut patterns for clothes, that sort of thing. He has put a stop to her learning Cree, too. But again, I assume you understand how forced dependency comes into play."

Mr. Wiggins, making no reply, sat tall in his chair. He opened his mouth to speak, but Mr. Passmore, fixed on his picture of things, droned on. "I spoke to Miss Newgate a month or so after she first arrived. She comes into my office, tense as a ruffled finch, upset about the toddlers she's seen. She insisted I come and see the scabby-faced babies for myself. Tells me of eyes glued shut with pus after sleep, of scalps scratched raw, and grandmothers picking lice. 'I'm telling you,' she says to me, thinking I had never seen it. I set her straight. I told her to stop giving people wild ideas. Well, she flounces out the office and climbs onto the wagon—Trent Stone waiting for her, of course. If I didn't know better, Wiggins, I'd say she'll be trying to see you the day my office opens ... your office."

The agents shuffled their feet. There came a scraping of chairs at the table. Here we go! sang Mercy's mind; they have arrived at the buffalo jump, the band election. Who would get the nod, Mercy wondered, feeling a bit sick, Trent and his reputation? This much she knew: he and she were approaching an undeclared election war.

But instead of talking about the election, Mr. Passmore turned back to talk of Hattie Newgate. "Consider this," Mr. Passmore was saying, "Hattie needs work. She's got skills. She reads and writes, and is trainable, I would suspect. You ought to divine the waters now, Wiggins. She'll add the juice, if anyone can." He lifted his utensils and cut the length of his boiled carrot. "Work all relationships to advantage, or they'll work you over. Give me an Indian agent sitting in his office writing policy and I'll show you a reserve full of ex-soldiers on their way to bright ideas, like paved roads and electrification, same as towns and farmers around here. Perhaps even a high school on the reserve. Explain that to Ottawa. No, sir, I'd watch it. Give full mind to what brought you here. And it's not new policy, either."

Mercy gritted her teeth, willing her mind to stop worrying about Hattie Newgate's sudden pile-up of skills—for now.

It seemed Mr. Wiggins had taken charge, even if Monday had yet to arrive. "Policy is instrumentation," he said, as though taking the bull by the horns. "Policy turns wisdom into action. That's how man achieves what society values. So, like it or not, history bears out that policy is the salt to roast beef."

Mr. Passmore, reddening, did not shut the discussion down, which he was good at doing. Mercy thought answers would surely begin to flow, such as, did either of the agents have something in mind for her? Or were they stuck on the idea the English girl was their only choice? Mercy simply had to continue working at the agency, at least until the fall. This would help her sort out people, win them over as supporters, come Election Day. She needed Mr. Passmore's recommendation in the worst way.

But the outgoing agent's temper was on full boil. Face smouldering, chest heaving, he clearly wished to make a point. "Accountants tend to dive into a program, with no ear for reality. I suspect you'll miss Ottawa. Out here there'll be no policy or professor to guide you. Take it from me, the moment I arrived I had to buckle down. To this day, I can handle ex-soldiers made hostile by hard luck with their stories of hunger, disease, and drunken assaults." But now Mr. Passmore realized he had strayed from "the manner." He tried to come around, to appear untouched and in command. "I mean, I can look them in the eye, and tell them no. I can, and do, select band council members despite cries for proper elections—whatever the devil that could mean out here. It's not a bunch of bright boys we need. It's fellas like Trent Stone, like Sonny Rabbitskin, and even a woman, for certain aspects of management."

There! Blink and it might be gone—a fastball pitched over home base—a woman for band council! Mercy's heart leapt in her chest. She had a baseball bat. What's more, she would swing it.

"Mercy!" It was the high-pitched voice of Mrs. Passmore calling down the stairs from the attic. "Mercy, tell Mr. Passmore to come up here at once!"

Mr. Passmore and Mercy involuntarily locked eyes. They knew the tone. His wife had used it this morning when speaking of his "indifference to every manner of thing." He had been of no help, she complained, even with regard to deciding whether or not she pack his souvenirs, like that useless gold-tipped horn from Spain. The horn was a worthless trinket, she'd said. But it was his horn, damn it, he had replied.

"Coming!" Mr. Passmore hollered up the attic stairs.

Getting out of his chair, he stopped for a moment to gaze out the window and up the gravel road with its awkward elbow bend. The wind had gone out of his sails. He turned to Mr. Wiggins and murmured, "Ottawa can be tight-fisted. But do the right things, the right way, and you'll reap the benefits. Once you marry and have children, you'll appreciate it all the more. The thing to keep in mind is permanence. It isn't dead philosophers who steer this ship. It's essential that you select a new band council right away. I daresay you'll know to mind appearances, with the soldiers being back and all. A first principle, this."

There was a loud thump in the attic. Mr. Passmore disappeared up the stairs.

Mercy felt a kind of will tighten in her gut. She opened a conversation with Mr. Wiggins, who had remained seated at the table. "Would you like more tea, Mr. Wiggins?"

The new agent spoke as though he were adding numbers in his head. "Yes. A bit of water, too, please. Mercy, is it?"

"Yes, Mercy. Merceline Hawk."

"Well, now, Merceline Hawk, do you live on Cowessess?" The even tone made her think that he might well be reading columns from an accounting book in his head, like the grocer in town when being asked to extend credit.

"Yes, I work here." It was all or nothing now. "Do you need a cleaning lady, Mr. Wiggins? I can clean." Her voice sounded like she had leapt onto a stool and might fall.

But Mr. Wiggins appeared more in tune with his own thoughts than with hers. "Me, a cleaning lady? Not likely. I manage pretty well on my own. So far, anyway."

Mercy wasn't sure she had heard right. Was she being dismissed? She was about to rattle off the many kinds of things she could do, and did do. And that her mom depended on her.

But Mr. Passmore was heard yelling from the attic out into the yard. "Sonny, give me a hand up here with this trunk. The movers are coming right about now. Just walk in."

Mercy saw that, of course, Sonny needed no second invitation. He didn't knock. He swung up the stairs, his baggy overalls climbing steps two at a time.

Mercy began clearing the dishes. It came to her that the faster she worked, the more the new agent might see quickness of mind and hand. Mr. Wiggins, however, was much too deep in thought to notice how deftly she handled things. Still, she stacked and carried plates and saucers and cutlery into the kitchen like the wind, and whipped back into the dining room, ready for orders. But Mr. Wiggins remained in his chair, his clean hands smoothing the tablecloth down the edges of the table where he sat, obviously weighing something.

In the background, Sonny and Mr. Passmore clumped down the stairs. The heavy trunk thudded against each tread of the stair. Mercy dusted the last bits of crumbs off the table. The men entered the dining room.

Water, Sonny dared to mouth at her. She filled a tumbler and handed it to him. He grinned like a goofball. *Don't think you're so smart,* her mind warned him. She wished to hear the agents, who were saying something about an inventory and the need to place orders.

But now, in the doorway, Mrs. Passmore stood with Hattie Newgate.

"I found her coming up the walk," Mrs. Passmore said, as though the girl wasn't there, "and I have brought her to you."

The old and new Indian agents moved in unison and stood side by side. Hattie Newgate stepped forward. She looked like a rabbit let loose in too big a garden. Her voice was soft. "I came early. I wasn't sure I could make it. So I snuck out." She covered her mouth with her hand, a nervous giggle escaping anyway.

"Mercy, see to it everyone gets tea," Mrs. Passmore said.

Silence reigned. A fly droned against the window like a tiny airplane. And yet, as Mercy poured a stream of hot tea into the cup taken from off the top of the chiffonier for Hattie Newgate, she noticed what was unmistakable: Mr. Wiggins and she were lost in the charm of a strong, mutual gaze.

Cold water flowed through Mercy's veins. It was as if Hattie Newgate had said something and Mr. Wiggins had caught her meaning. Two sets of eyes swarmed and overflowed in orbits of bliss that held the cry *home at last!*

The front door burst open and Trent Stone walked in. Shoulders squared, hands on his belt, he had guessed quite rightly how steady power in the hands of an inexperienced Indian agent might now be fishtailing, however momentarily. Trent wasted no time. "Hattie, get in the wagon," he said.

The young Mr. Wiggins stepped forward, and, like a preacher twice blessed from above, said, "She's with me. And that'll be the end of it."

Mr. Passmore's wife turned swiftly away and hurried a trembling Hattie up the attic stairs. Mr. Passmore said to Trent, "This is highly irregular," and then followed his wife and Hattie.

But Mr. Wiggins was already making his move. He turned to Trent. "I'd like to talk to you, Mr. Stone," he said, "about your willingness to sit on band council. I hear you are a dead ringer for the job."

Mercy fingered her bat and gave a final sift to words that now fell together in a picture of power. A new band council flashed before her eyes: two males and a female who knew the ropes—and much, much more.

Acknowledgements

THANKS TO THE SASKATCHEWAN Arts Board for the grant that enabled research of my childhood home, Cowessess Reserve. A very special thanks to Dianne Warren and Joanne Gerber for their assistance. Thanks to the Saskatchewan Archives Board for making available valuable oral records of Indigenous voices in its collection "Toward a New Past". I am indebted to George H. Barr (1878-1960), King's Counsel for Saskatchewan (appointed 1917), whose fonds provide rare insight into local governance and constitutional issues specific to 'Indians'.

Thanks to my brother, Donald Ross Stevenson (d.2017), for facilitating actual visits to childhood haunts and for setting up meetings with oral historians from Cowessess First Nation and its neighboring reserves Sakimay, Kahkewistahaw, and Ochapowace. A special thanks to Joseph Taypotat, Darlene Taypotat, and Rosalie Kinistino for kindly inviting me into their homes. Their shared recollections added depth to my work. Thanks to Ronald Redwood and to Gill Kay, veterans, for providing valuable insights into the war years.

Many thanks to Tom Stevenson, Winnipeg, for his generosity and kindness in sharing local history with me in the form of maps, stories, and photos of home and family.

Much gratitude to Dr. Peter Midgley (UAP) and his readers who provided guidance in the mid-stages of this work. I am grateful also for his generous sharing with me, inspiring books of poetry and stories that prove the importance of the unique voice - especially his published poetry "perhaps I should know/miskien moet ek": Mackie Lecture and Reading Series No. 8, Kalamalka Press, Vernon BC, 2010 and the narrative works of South African writers Zoë Wicom and Agnes Sam.

Sincere thanks to the Regina Public Library Board (especially its rare collection in the, then, living Prairie History Room); and to the North Vancouver District Public Library staff at Parkgate for maintaining many critical links to Canada's story.

A big thank you to the Institute for the Study of Women, Mount Saint Vincent University, Halifax, Nova Scotia, for publishing my first story "Pin Cherry Morning" Atlantis, Volume 30.1, 2005, A Women's Studies Journal/ Revue D'études sur les femmes.

Major thanks to Jesse Archibald-Barber and Karen Clark (U of R) for their kind encouragement of my work and for including my short story in the anthology kisiskâciwan: Indigenous voices from where the river flows swiftly (University of Regina Press 2018). In addition, Karen Clark's having shared a list of local publishers led me to Radiant Press and to Debra Bell, publisher, whose clear vison for Adam's Tree ensured a true ally at the helm.

My deep gratitude to editor, Patricia Sanders, whose sensitive editing of Adam's Tree has added strength and vigour to this work; and to Susan Birley, copy editor, for whom detail defines and refines. A very special thanks to author and writer, Dianne Warren, for her encouragement and inspiring works. A warm and special thanks to Peter, my husband, for his constancy and his fine ear for stories.

Many thanks to Gabrielle and Dan Ollinger for their loan of the watercolour by my mother Delma Stevenson (nee Wasacase) that now graces the cover of Adam's Tree. Thanks to Morris Zima, Vancouver Island, for his digital reproduction of the original.

GLORIA MEHLMANN grew up on the Cowessess First Nation in Saskatchewan before leaving to pursue a career as a public school teacher from 1962-1983. Her diverse vocations include serving as a public library trustee and as the Director of Aboriginal Education. She has been recognized with many awards for her contributions to educational, aboriginal, and civic initiatives, culminating in the Saskatchewan Centennial Medal in 2005. She is the author of *Gifted to Learn*, a memoir, published in 2008. She is also a recipient of an SLTA honorary Lifetime Membership in 2004. Gloria now lives in Nanoose Bay, BC.